Darcia Hell

MW00941395

Copyright © 2010 Darcia Helle

ISBN: 1453630732
EAN 13: 978-1453630730

Darcia@quietfurybooks.com
www.QuietFuryBooks.com

The Cutting Edge is set in a real town in
Southeastern Massachusetts. The salon and
the plot within this book are fictional.
Many of the conversations and incidents are based
on the author's experiences working as a stylist in
a small-town salon. However, all of the names and
identifying details have been changed to protect
the innocent and hide the guilty.

Other Novels by Darcia Helle:

Enemies and Playmates
Hit List
No Justice (A Michael Sykora Novel)
Beyond Salvation (A Michael Sykora Novel)
Miami Snow

For Bob Helle: a brilliant editor and even better friend.
I am forever indebted.

I'm sending this book out with a huge thank you to the women I worked with and all the clients who made our salon such a crazy and memorable place.

Murder in the murderer is no such ruinous thought
as poets and romancers will have it; it does not unsettle him,
or fright him from his ordinary notice of trifles;
it is an act quite easy to be contemplated.

~ Ralph Waldo Emerson

The Cutting Edge

The Cutting Edge

1

My name is Lilly Skye Destiny Summers. My parents thought it was a great idea to give me three names with the initials LSD to go with my last name. For years they called me LSD Summers. They lived in a commune and did way too much acid.

Most people call me Skye. Except my father's parents, who always call me Lilly, and even that name is said with some disdain. They're partial to my father's sister's kids. My cousins' names are Victoria Marie and Benjamin James. Benjamin is a gay surgeon living his life in the closet and Victoria is a P.T.A. mom with a Princeton degree in bullshit and an addiction to painkillers. My grandparents are in their late eighties and live in a fancy housing complex for old people. My grandfather wears Depends and drool constantly dribbles from the corners of his mouth. He still puts on a tie before going down to dinner every night. The whole thing is rather comical.

I'm 37, married to an electrician who could have made huge money as a porn star. I've kept my maiden name for reasons other than my love of LSD Summers. My husband's name is Scott Skyler. Had I changed my name, I would have been called Skye Skyler. Skye Summers is bad but Skye Skyler is ridiculous.

I work as a hairstylist in a salon called The Cutting Edge. When I started my career 17 years ago, I had visions of my unfettered creativity transforming ordinary women into sexy tramps or glowing goddesses. I was terribly naïve. Now I spend my days trying to explain to the round-faced Oreo-addict that, no matter what I do to her hair, she will not leave looking like Angelina Jolie. Try and pull that off tactfully.

At the moment I am contemplating murder. Today is Friday and I have been on my feet since 8 a.m. The clock above the desk tells me it is now 2:10. I have not eaten lunch. Have not even peed all day. The woman in my chair is speaking nonstop and I am thinking about killing her.

I smile and nod while Marla prattles on incessantly about her existence. She watches my reflection in the mirror – or, more likely, her own. She is talking about Amy, her 5-year-old "princess". According to Marla, Amy is gifted beyond measure. I'm told that everyone she comes in contact with comments on the child's extraordinary charm and intelligence.

Amy recently stuck a wad of chewing gum in a classmate's hair. This is not something Marla would ever tell me. I know this because I had to cut the wad out of the other child's beautiful blonde curls. That child's mother is also a regular client and not a fan of Marla or Amy.

I gave Amy her first haircut when she was 3. She bit me twice. Last week, Amy kicked me while I tried to cut her bangs. Amy is indeed a princess.

Marla turns the topic to her son, Justin, age 8. Apparently he should be declared a child prodigy because he has read an entire Dr. Seuss book to his sister.

I continue to smile, snip the requested one-quarter inch from Marla's bangs. Yes, precisely one-quarter of an inch. And one-eighth of an inch off the back. Am I supposed to hold a measuring tape to her hair? Does she?

My jaw aches from the tension of my phony smile. I catch a glimpse of my reflection and marvel at how relaxed I appear. No one would know that I am currently harboring fantasies of cutting off Marla's perfect little ears that hold the perfect pearl studs that her perfect husband presented to her on their Alaskan cruise last month.

Marla is saying, "When I watch Amy and Justin interact with other children, I realize the tremendous advantage my children have with me being home, rather than selfishly pursuing a career."

I smile, fantasize about cutting Marla's tongue off with my surgically sharpened $500 shears.

I don't have children, which Marla has made clear she feels is a tragedy of epic proportions. The real tragedy is that people like Marla are allowed to procreate.

I have three dogs. Neal is a terrier mix, Cassady is a Chihuahua, and Jack is a chocolate lab mixed with something of questionable descent. They are named after Neal Cassady and Jack Kerouac, two famous writers of the Beat Generation.

My parents were thrilled that I named my dogs after figures that were so central to life in the sixties. Of course, having been raised by flower children and given the name Lilly Skye Destiny Summers, you'd have to expect some of the sixties subculture to rub off on me.

My three dogs are rescues and tend to be spoiled brats with bad manners. At the moment, they are probably lounging on my couch, watching Jerry Springer and raiding the snack cabinet. Okay, in reality they are probably sprawled out in their respective beds, sleeping blissfully. Either way, I wish I could join them.

My mind has wandered and I missed the last minute or so of Marla's monologue. She doesn't seem to notice. I continue to smile and nod.

I glance at Renee, my coworker and good friend for the past decade. Being surrounded by mirrors makes it impossible to roll our eyes or gesture obscenely. Renee's client is talking with her entire body, her hands moving rapidly and her head bouncing like one of those stupid Bobblehead toys. Do people not realize how hard it is to work on a moving target?

Renee and I often toss around the idea of quitting The Cutting Edge and going to work at a funeral parlor. Our clients would then have to sit still. And they wouldn't speak, so we wouldn't have to pretend to care what they say. I don't tell Renee that I constantly fantasize about turning my live clients into cadavers.

I move on to the blow-dry stage of Marla's hairstyle. Unfortunately, the noise does not deter her from speaking. "Amy has her first jazz recital next month," she says. "We'll need you to do her hair early that morning. I'm thinking that she should wear it up, maybe with tendrils around her face…"

Tendrils. Why do mothers want their young daughters to look like the fashion models in Vogue? What is wrong with looking like the children they are? I keep my smile in place and tell Marla that of course we can do that.

My next client walks in the door. She is booked for a highlight and has her newborn son with her. He is already fussing. I can now understand how people suddenly snap and commit mass murder.

~

Saturday morning, barely 7:30, and here I am unlocking the door to The Cutting Edge. My 8 a.m. client watches from her car like a newly released inmate on a combination of crack and Prozac. Eyes wide, lips parted, waiting to lunge out her door and pounce on me. Ten years retired and the woman's main entertainment seems to come from crawling up my ass.

I have maybe five minutes to get the coffee dripping, flip on the curling irons, get the air conditioner started on venting the stale air from the building, and all the other assorted tasks that come with opening the business each morning. Then Lillian will be on my heels and I'll have no reprieve for about nine hours.

My coworkers will arrive soon but not before Lillian waddles her way inside. A few times I've tried leaving the lights off, thinking maybe she'd realize the salon doesn't actually open until 8, which is why I write that time on her appointment card each week. I've since come to believe that she doesn't feel business hours or appointment times apply to her.

Muttering to myself, I shuffle into the back room, switch on the lights, and scream. Then I laugh. Not because it's funny. Well, okay, it is sort of funny.

Roxie, our newest stylist, is straddled over a young male, presumably her boyfriend. This male is kicked back in one of our waxing chairs. His pants are around his ankles and her skirt is hiked up to her waist. Roxie scrambles off the guy and I notice that my entrance has done nothing to diminish his excitement.

"Pull your damn pants up," Roxie mutters.

The guy obeys. Roxie looks at me, her face flushed with either embarrassment or sexual stimulation. She says, "Oh my god…"

"Lillian will be walking in any second," I tell her. "You'd better pull yourself together."

"I..." Roxie stammers. She can't meet my eyes. "I didn't realize the time. I thought… We were alone and…"

"I've always wanted to do it in one of those chairs, too," I say.

Roxie laughs. She is all of 20 years old, has a pierced eyebrow and bright pink streaks in her hair. I feel old standing beside her.

"You won't say anything to Lorraine?" she asks.

"No," I assure her. "I won't. But she'd probably laugh too."

Lorraine is the owner. She isn't around much anymore, being semi-retired and sick of people. I can't say that I blame her.

Roxie steps into the bathroom to put herself back together. And, hopefully, to wash her hands. Her partner slips out the back door, looking like a 5-year-old who'd just been ripped out of his sandbox.

The front door pops open and Lillian calls, "Good morning, Skye! I don't smell coffee, yet. You're moving slow today."

I bite my lip to keep from spewing obscenities her way. We are directly across the street from a coffee shop. Lillian has probably been in that parking lot since the crack of dawn. Yet it never occurs to her that we run a hair salon, not a coffee shop, and maybe she should drag her fat ass across the street and get her own damn coffee.

⋏

I manage to make it through an entire Saturday without stabbing someone's jugular vein. I must admit that I considered it more often than not. Maiming or killing my clients has become a fantasy I indulge in with disturbing frequency. This should probably concern me. It doesn't.

Scott and I have plans tonight. We're going to a party at a friend's house. The occasion is another friend's birthday. No party hats. Just a lot of booze and food. I'm in charge of chips and dip, which means I have to stop at the grocery store on my way home. I guess I should learn to plan ahead.

I hate the grocery store. And I'm running late. The combination doesn't help my already sour mood.

My 1 p.m. client had been 20 minutes late. Her boyfriend had spent the previous night at her apartment. They'd woken up late and he had taken her out for a big breakfast. Time had gotten away from them. How nice for her.

Their sappy little love story had thrown off my schedule for the remainder of the afternoon. Now I'm irritated and late and I have to stop at the dreaded grocery store.

Naturally the place is crowded. Is there ever a time when a grocery store isn't swarming with people who consider the trip to be a major family outing? I see a parking spot open up near the front of the lot. Finally something is working in my favor.

I have my directional on and I'm about to turn into the spot when a bitch in a Volvo swings around from the opposite lane and zips in front of me. She almost takes off my bumper. I want to take off her head.

She gives me a smug smile. I stay where I am. I'm thinking of running her over.

Okay, so common sense kicks in and I realize that running the bitch over in broad daylight in a crowded parking lot probably isn't the best idea. I step on the gas and park at the end of the lot.

As I'm getting out of my car, I see the bitch walking away from her pristine silver Volvo. Her hair is bottle-blonde, her clothes high-end flash. I can imagine the type of nightmare client she is and I feel instant pity for her stylist.

I'm walking by her sparkling Volvo and I notice the cover for the gas cap is open. I have a thought and it's not a nice one. But it's better than the one about running her over.

I shake my head, tell myself no. I'm all grown up now. I'm an adult, I tell myself. *So what*, myself says back. I ignore that childish self.

I step into the grocery store and nudge my way through the sea of people. I get the chips and two kinds of dip. I'm about ready to leave. Then I see the Volvo bitch. She's flashing her diamond-covered fingers at an employee, demanding the poor kid search their stockroom for a specific flavor of salad dressing that she must have tonight. I want to hit her over the head with a bottle of *Newman's Own*.

I pass the aisle but can't escape her shrill voice. That's when my childish self wins over and I grab a canister of sugar off a shelf. I stand in the *20 Items Or Less* lane. Hadn't it used to be *10 Items Or Less*? I count the stuff in the cart of the person in front of me. She has twenty-one items. I think about kicking her in the ass.

I have a clear memory of being in the grocery store with my father. I was 8. We had stopped to get marshmallows and Rice Krispies. We were going to make Rice Krispies Treats and watch Disney movies all night.

We were standing in line at the checkout. The store wasn't all that busy but there weren't many checkouts open. I remember we were fourth in line. I couldn't wait to get our night started.

A woman strode toward us, then cut in front of us in line as if we weren't there. She simply stepped in the space my father had courteously left between us and the old guy in front of us. The guy had a strong smell of whiskey and sweat, which might have been why my father had left that space.

I was livid. My 8-year-old mind couldn't comprehend that an adult would behave so unfairly. I tugged on my father's sleeve and said, "That lady just cut us! That's not fair!"

My father looked down at me and smiled that carefree smile of his. He said, "And that just means you'll get to stay up a little later tonight!"

At the time, I thought that was a great deal. Now I think it's total bullshit.

After five minutes that felt like 30, I pay for my items and hurry out to the parking lot. People are scattered about, loading groceries in their cars, walking back and forth, chasing unruly toddlers. No one looks my way.

I approach the Volvo. A quick glance tells me I am alone in the immediate area. I slip the sugar from my bag and casually dump most of it into the bitch's gas tank. Two minutes later I am in my car, heading home, and laughing like a giddy child.

2

Four days have passed since I poured the sugar in that woman's gas tank. I kept waiting to feel remorse. I didn't. Not even a twinge of guilt. Instead I fantasized about killing her.

Today is Wednesday. It's 2 p.m. and I'm at work. Andrea has the week off and Renee won't be back until 3. Roxie and I are working alone and the phone will not stop ringing. We desperately need a receptionist.

I have just finished shampooing Tyler's hair. He settles into my chair while I answer the phone yet again. Another client wants to make small talk. I want to tell her to get to the point already. I'm busy. I finally schedule her appointment and move back to Tyler. The next few calls are Roxie's problem.

As I start Tyler's haircut, he tells me that he recently got out of the hospital. "Want to see?" he asks.

Before I can reply, he shoves the plastic cape off his lap, unfastens his pants, yanks the zipper down, hooks his thumbs into the waistband of his blue plaid boxers, and tugs them away from his skin. I'm standing behind and also above him. I'm staring straight down at his flaccid penis and scrunched up testicles. I say, "What am I supposed to be looking at?"

"My appendix scar," Tyler says.

"Oh." I'm not sure if he even has an appendix scar. Confront me with a strange penis or a scar, I'm going to notice the penis way before the scar.

Roxie had been at the other end of the salon mixing a color. She must have noticed Tyler's pants pulled open, because she wanders slowly over and asks, "Is everything okay?"

"Sure," I say. "Everything's fine. Nothing to see here."

Tyler flushes. Roxie gives me a funny smile and walks away. I don't think I meant the words to come out the way they did. But, honestly, an appendix scar?

Tyler is a skinny, arrogant brat fresh out of high school. I don't know whether he truly meant to show me only his scar or if he intended to rock my world by displaying his manhood. I'm married to a closet porn star. It takes more than a flaccid penis to rock my world.

Tyler is unusually silent throughout the haircut. He walks out without leaving me a tip. I guess that's what I get for disrespecting the guy's penis.

I expect the rest of the day to go smoothly. After all, it's hard to top a flaccid penis and scrunched up testicles. My next few clients are among my favorites. I actually begin to enjoy my job once again. That is, until Ariel walks in the door.

She was 5 when I started doing her hair. A sweet young girl; quiet, well-behaved. The kind of child who almost made me want to have kids of my own. I did her hair through her miserable teen years, when evil gremlins took over her body and she suddenly became a pompous little bitch.

Evidently the gremlins took up permanent residence. She's now 20, attends a fancy private college in Boston, dates a law student at Harvard, and acts like her ass spits out rose petals. I hadn't seen her in a while and hoped that she'd flown off to Paris to live among the more deserving human beings. But, no, she's back, Coach purse displayed prominently on my counter.

I'm fixing the sloppy haircut she'd gotten in one of those ridiculously expensive upscale Boston salons. She's telling me about her experience, glowing as if she'd encountered Jesus Christ himself.

"My parents gave me the gift certificate for my birthday," Ariel tells me. "The best gift I've ever received! The stylist, his name is Vincent, is simply amazing!"

I have that fake smile frozen on my face. Vincent? Please!

"The salon is huge and absolutely stunning," Ariel says. "All Vincent does is cut. I'm sure you've heard of him. His reputation is stellar."

I shake my head no. I haven't heard of him. But Ariel doesn't notice. Nor does she pause to hear my answer, if in fact I'd bothered to offer one.

"He did my entire cut while sitting on a stool! Isn't that amazing?"

Amazing? No. Her hair looks as if someone had sat on a stool and grabbed chunks to cut. If I sat on a stool, she'd consider me lazy. Vincent? He's the king of elite.

"Vincent said I should absolutely always use this particular shampoo. Rejuvenate Plus. Have you heard of it? I know you don't carry it here. It's one of those very exclusive lines. I bought two bottles, as well as the conditioner to go with it. Cost me a small fortune but it's worth it!"

I want to slap her. No, I want to cut off her tongue and make her swallow it. Then I want to shave her head.

Does she think I live in a cave? Because I work in a small town salon, I am not privy to products that the "elite" use?

This bitch wouldn't even pay eight bucks for a bottle of leave-in conditioner I told her would make a huge difference in her hair. Yet, she's buying $25 bottles of shampoo because some phony who calls himself Vincent and sits on his ass all day claims she needs it?

I do not trust myself to speak. That doesn't matter, since Ariel has not paused long enough to allow space for my words.

She continues to gush over Vincent and his "staff". He has his own shampoo girl and his own assistant. Kind of like owning slaves. The idea holds vast appeal for Ariel.

She sputters endlessly. I fantasize about my scissors slipping and slicing into her jugular vein. I truly want to kill her.

This should worry me, this sudden obsession with murder. The only worry I have is how to get away with it.

It's Friday night and I should be happy. I'm out with Scott, my porn star husband. We're having a nice dinner at one of my favorite spots. He looks good enough to eat and should be on the dessert menu.

Instead of focusing on this, I am thinking about work. I have one more day to get through this week. Then I'll have two entire days away from clients and my facial muscles can finally relax from the constant phony smile and clenched jaw. I don't know how much longer I can do my job. I'm going to end up in one of those awful places where they strap you to the chair and no one bothers to wipe the drool from your chin.

I would like to quit. I would like to do something else or, even better, nothing at all. I would like to give my brain time to heal and perhaps I will begin to like people again.

I cannot afford to quit. No other job is going to pay me enough from the start. Scott and I have bills, like everyone else. Our mortgage company won't care if I have a breakdown. They want their money.

A big part of our financial stress comes from Elyse, Scott's daughter. She is the product of a drunken one-nighter 19 years ago. Scott had been 20 then. Young, stupid, and careless. Condoms weren't on the forefront of his and his partner's drunken minds.

Elyse is a snitty little bitch. Scott and I got married 16years ago. Elyse was 2 then. She stayed with us every other weekend. She had tantrums when we told her no for any reason. She'd scream and spit. She did this until she was 5.

By the time she was 5, she knew how to use a phone. She would call her mother, crying hysterically, and say I had beaten her. I should have, though I never did.

Lawyer's fees buried us. I was judged innocent of the charges but no one reimbursed the many thousands we'd spent. Then the child support continued to grow. Diane, Elyse's vindictive mother, had us in court at least once a year.

Now Elyse is 18 and in her first year of college. We're paying for half of her tuition. If I had a kid of my own, I wouldn't be paying the tuition. Or at least I'd have a choice. I'd be able to say, no, sorry, we can't afford it. Why is that choice taken away when the parents aren't together?

This irritates me. Apparently I scowl, because Scott asks, "What's wrong?"

I look into the green pools that are his eyes and I smile. "Nothing," I say. "It's just been a rough week."

He leans forward and drops his voice to a low growl. "How about we go home and you let me strip you naked. I promise I will work very hard at making you stop thinking."

Fifteen minutes later we are home. Seventeen minutes later I am no longer thinking.

ɾ

I'm muddling through another Saturday. So far I haven't felt the uncontrollable urge to kill anyone.

Liz is in my chair. She's in her late forties, attractive, with long dark hair. I can picture her at a biker rally, kicking the men's asses on the track. Liz lives her life on the edge. And she likes to tell me about it. In detail.

Her husband's best friend fell into some hard times about a month ago. Liz didn't go into detail about those hard times, which is unusual for her. I imagine it has something to do with the guy spending all his money on alcohol and not enough on his mortgage. At any rate, Larry, the best friend, moved in with them three weeks ago. Six weeks before that, Liz and Larry started having sex.

Apparently Dan, Liz's husband, is pretty stupid. Or he's happy to have someone else attending to his wife for a change.

"I know the room must have smelled like sex," Liz is saying. "I managed to get the bed half-assed put together before Dan came up the stairs. Next thing I know, he and Larry are parked in front of the TV, having a beer together. I couldn't look at Larry! I still had his smell on me and I know he still had mine on him. And, incredibly, the scene made me so hot that I wanted to take him again right there!"

Liz makes me laugh. She's like a rebellious teenager. I wonder, though, if she realizes that half the salon can hear what she's saying. And people talk. People thrive on gossip. How long before her affair is headline news in the town's gossip chain?

I'm thinking she might want to get caught. Then Dan might leave her and she wouldn't have to make the choice.

That's about as far as my psychoanalysis goes today. I'm not paid enough to delve deep into the psyches of my clients.

I glance at the clock. Nearly 2. Only a couple more hours to go. I might get through this day without any bloody thoughts. Those thoughts are beginning to concern me a little. I mean, it's not like the average woman goes around visualizing herself committing gory murders.

Liz is telling me about her favorite lube when Chris walks in the door. I feel my nervous system shudder. Chris is not even my client and I want to kill him.

Renee leads him to the sinks. I hope she drowns him there.

Chris is of Italian descent. He's got deep golden skin, like a perpetual Caribbean tan, dark brown eyes, and a rock-solid body. He's a boxer at a local gym. He holds some kind of amateur title and thinks that buys him the right to be an arrogant prick.

I've just finished blow-drying Liz's hair when he sits in Renee's chair. Renee hands him the hand mirror before she starts cutting. He holds it up and scrutinizes her every move. Seriously, the guy's ego is so big that there is no room left for a personality.

His head is shaved to about a quarter-inch. The haircut is far from rocket science. Yet, he sits there with his hand mirror like he is the inspector general of stylists.

Renee is wearing her fake smile and pretending her stomach isn't twisting into knots. She shows amazing restraint. I want to shave the guy's head bald, erase his eyebrows. I want to take a straight edge to his neck. And he isn't even my client.

So much for not wanting to murder anyone today.

3

I know I've become obsessed with murder. I should probably consider a retreat in the mountains or something. Maybe a monastery, where the only people around are monks and they don't speak. I need people to stop speaking because that's when I think about cutting out their tongues.

My mother is sitting across the table from me. It's Saturday night and Scott and I are hanging out at my parents' home. Scott and my father are in the garage, building an elaborate birdhouse. My mother and I are in the kitchen, drinking nonalcoholic coconut smoothies. Let the party begin.

My mother's name is Celia. She teaches yoga classes and volunteers at an animal rescue. She's wearing dangly peace-sign earrings and a white Gypsy Goddess dress. She pushes aside her coconut smoothie and grasps my hand. "What's wrong?" she asks.

"Nothing," I say.

"There's no need for lies here. If you'd rather not talk about it, simply say so. You know that honesty is easier on the spirit."

I sigh without meaning to. My mother has never moved on from the communes. "Rough week," I say.

"Work?"

"What else?"

"What is it about your job that's disturbing you?"

I hide my expression behind my coconut smoothie. I was raised by peace-loving hippies. I held my first protest sign before I was 2. I am not supposed to think about murder. Gory murder, at that. How do I go about telling my war-protesting mother that I am constantly fantasizing about watching my clients bleed?

I'm rescued from the conversation when Scott and my dad wander in. My dad's name is Theodore. His parents wanted him to be a lawyer, so they gave him a name they thought commanded respect. Everyone except his parents calls him Teddy and he never even came close to law school. My dad is a carpenter and volunteers his time with *Habitat for Humanity*.

My dad is holding a two-story birdhouse with double perches outside the doors and a thatched roof. It's stained a reddish color and matching splotches cover his t-shirt. My dad only uses environmentally friendly products. The stuff is probably edible.

"What do you think?" my dad asks.

My mother claps her hands together. "Perfection," she says.

"It's beautiful," I tell my father. "And huge. You should have had Scott wire some lighting in there."

My father's eyes twinkle. He's about to latch on to the idea when my mother takes the birdhouse from him. "She's joking, Teddy."

"Who is this one for?" I ask.

"One of the foster mothers from the rescue," my mother says. "She also rescues finches."

The "foster mothers" are the women who keep the dogs during their transition from homeless to permanent home. Many are in need of intense medical care. Some have been abused and require a lot of time and love. My parents currently have eight dogs in their home. Two live there. The other six are guests.

One of the guests is a black Great Dane named Zena that is currently nestling up against Scott. She is big enough to ride and thinks she is a lap dog. He strokes her head as he looks at me.

"No," I say.

"No, what?" my mother asks.

"Scott wants to take Zena home."

Scott grins at me. "She loves me."

"She wouldn't fit in our house."

"I could build her a doghouse," my father volunteers.

"And you think she's going to stay outside?" I ask. "Chances are better that I'd be sleeping in the doghouse and she'd be sprawled across my side of the bed."

"That's doubtful," Scott says. "Zena's sweet but I'm not looking to replace you."

Zena's tail bangs into one of the dozens of plants my mother has sprawled around the house. The pot tumbles sideways and dirt spills onto the floor. My mother shakes her head and says, "Now Zena, look what you've done."

The words are far from an admonishment. She pats Zena on the head and scoots her away from the dirt. My father gives Zena a treat while my mother sweeps the dirt. The seven other dogs hear the treat bag rustling and come running in. We are surrounded by wagging tails and greenery. Scott catches my eye and winks. Life feels pretty perfect at that moment.

*

Monday comes and I am home alone. I usually spend my Mondays doing errands and catching up on all the housework I avoid during the week. So far today, all I have managed to do is get out of bed. I am still in my pajamas. I'm cranky.

Scott and I argued off and on all day yesterday. That's not normal for us. And though I have yet to admit it to him, it was my fault. The last few months, I have been constantly on edge. People drive me nuts all day at work. I want nothing to do with people on my time off. Scott is social. We used to be social together. Now I'm a cranky loner obsessed with murdering my clients.

Scott wants me to quit my job. He says that we'll work out the financial stuff. He just wants me to be happy.

Lots of people are unhappy with their jobs. But they don't go around fantasizing about murder. I don't tell Scott that. He doesn't know his wife is bordering on homicidal. The point is, I should be able to deal with my misery. I should be able to ignore the fact that a large percentage of my clients are self-absorbed parasites. Renee calls them energy vampires. They feed on our energy instead of our blood.

I'm considering going into dog grooming. Trimming and fluffing a dog's hair is a lot less complicated than designing the perfect look for a human. And the worst a dog will do is bite.

I make chamomile tea and sit at my computer. The chamomile is supposed to relax me. I'd probably have to eat an entire field of plants to get that benefit. One cup of tea isn't likely to help, though I'm holding out hope.

My dogs are holding out hope as well. They are currently crowded around me like an intervention team. Neal is licking my toes and Jack is trying to get in my lap. Jack is the lab mix. He's too big for my lap, though he doesn't agree. He figures if the other two can do it, he should have the same privilege.

Cassady, my little Chihuahua, is sitting by my chair. Her eyes, however, are focused on the half-eaten bagel I left on the plate. Cassady's concern for me will always be second to her obsession with food.

I give Jack a gentle nudge as he tries to clamber onto my lap. He looks at me, dejected, and curls up on the floor beside me. I swear he is pouting. Neal continues to lick my toes. I'm not sure what the fascination is there. He loves toes. Everyone's toes. Cassady's eyes dart back and forth between me and the bagel. I tell her no, that she's on a diet. She continues to stare at the bagel.

I turn back to my computer. My homepage is Google and a headline immediately grabs my attention. *Does Massachusetts Have A Serial Killer?* I click the link and the story pops up on my screen. I read the article twice. Something about it fascinates me. A morbid fascination, no doubt.

Two women murdered, maybe three, by the same killer. He calls himself *The Mass Avenger*, which the reporter speculates to be a sick play on words. Mass is what all of us from New England call the state I live in. No one says Massachusetts. We all say, "I'm from Mass." Then there's the definition of mass as in a whole lot. Does this guy plan on killing a whole lot of women? And all in Massachusetts?

The police remain silent. No official will confirm the existence of a Mass Avenger running wild throughout the state. What is more telling is that no one is denying it, either.

I do a search for further details but find nothing. I want to know how he is killing them. My blood thirst seems to be growing. Maybe I'm trying to live vicariously through this demented serial killer who might or might not exist.

I wonder what type of women he's killing. Does he have a type? Size? Shape? Age?

Is he close by? Is it possible that he'll kill one of my clients? Immediately I think of Patricia, my9 a.m. appointment tomorrow and one of the most uptight, irritating, self-righteous people to walk the earth. I picture this faceless serial killer wrapping his hands around her chicken neck. A minute passes and I realize that I am smiling way too much. I close the page and grab my tea. I'm going to need a side order of Prozac to go with my chamomile.

*

When Scott comes home Monday night, I am waiting in a black thong, matching demi bra, and strappy heels that scream slut. Our make-up sex starts there in the kitchen and finishes in our bedroom. We roll through the living room somewhere along the way. Make-up sex can be as exhausting as it is exhilarating.

We shower, eat Chinese take-out, then have sex again. Not the frenzied make-up sex like the first time. This is the slow, touch me all over kind. Now Scott is sleeping beside me. I'm pretty sure he is actually unconscious.

I'm thinking about my day tomorrow. One of my most dreaded clients is coming in at 10. Jenny is one of those people whose mere presence can bring down the mood of an entire roomful of people. You could suck on a tube of laughing gas, take one look at her face, and break down into tears. Just the thought of dealing with her tomorrow makes me physically ill.

I'm fantasizing about killing her.

Jenny has beautiful wavy brown hair scattered with gray. She comes in once a month for a color, cut, and blow dry. She insists that I color her hair jet black, so that every wrinkle on her face stands out. While I cut, she sticks her fingers in her hair and complains about the wave. A few times I almost cut her fingertips off. She doesn't seem to think that's her problem.

After the cut, I have to blow dry her waves into board-stiff submission. No hint of wave is allowed to survive. She wants it jet black, stiff, straight, flat, and stuck to her head. And she finds this flattering.

Jenny speaks in a whine, no matter what the topic. Nothing makes her happy. Her kids don't visit enough, her husband doesn't give her enough attention. She walks like an old lady with hemorrhoids and bunions. She is 57 and healthy.

I would like Jenny to die. And I would like that to happen in my chair. I know this is a problem. Fantasies like this aren't healthy. They're beginning to consume me. I should see a psychiatrist. Maybe there's a medication that will fix me. A magic "No Kill" pill.

I've almost convinced myself to search the yellow pages for a psychiatrist. Then I realize that I can't very well tell anyone, even a psychiatrist, that I want to kill my clients. He or she would have to report that to the police. I don't think the doctor-patient privilege extends to murderous intent.

I'm stuck on the fantasy of Jenny and murder. Chances are, I couldn't actually kill anyone. Sure, I think about it almost constantly now. But thinking about something and doing it are two different things.

I close my eyes and imagine myself sticking the blade of my surgically-sharpened shears into the side of Jenny's neck. Straight into her jugular vein. Blood spurts out, covering me. Her eyes open wide. She stares at me, pleading silently, begging for help. The life seeps out of her. She dies knowing that I have killed her. She dies with her eyes fixed on mine.

I make the scene in my mind as vivid as possible. I see the blood. I can almost smell it. I see the fear in her eyes. This should upset me. Hell, this should horrify me. I find myself aroused.

I open my eyes and blink at the darkness. I fidget. This isn't right. I can't be aroused by murder!

Again I close my eyes. I replay the scene, slowing it down. I feel the blood covering me. Jenny's blood. She dies with my scissors sticking out of her neck.

I open my eyes and look over at Scott. I am wildly aroused. This is sick. Twisted. What is wrong with me?

Scott is on his back, naked. I slide the sheet down. Two minutes later he is awake and I am on top of him. I tell him that I had an erotic dream. I don't tell him what it was about.

4

I have lost my patience for stupid human behavior. By some miracle, I survived the first two days of my work week. Today is Thursday. My work day began at 11 this morning. I will be here until at least 9 tonight. It is now 3 and, the way things are going, I may be in prison by 4.

Ellen, one of my regular clients, has stopped in on her way by. This is just one of the many curses that come from working in the center of a small town. She wants to schedule an appointment to have her hair colored. This should not be the ordeal it is turning into.

"I've looked at the hair color in Wal-Mart," Ellen tells me. "And I picked out the shade I wanted."

"That's good," I say. "But the picture on the box is not necessarily what it will look like on your hair. I'll show you some swatches when you come in."

"Can you tell me what to buy?"

"We have color here," I say. "You don't need to buy anything."

"Oh," she says. "I was thinking you could tell me which product to buy. Then I can do it myself at home a lot cheaper."

I look at her. She has a manicure and massage every four weeks. She has a Gucci purse slung over her shoulder and an iPhone in her hand. Two-carat diamonds wink at me from each earlobe. Lack of money does not appear to be an issue in Ellen's life.

I'm standing here wasting my time, falling behind schedule while my paying client sits in my chair frowning. Ellen wants me to spend a half-hour on a free consult, so that I can tell her what color to buy at Wal-Mart. Then she can spend the extra 30 bucks on a tube of lipstick.

"I'm sorry," I say. "I'm not familiar with Wal-Mart's products. We don't use them."

"Well that's okay," Ellen says. "I can go to Sally's Beauty Supply."

Sally's is the stylists' nightmare. They sell beauty supply products, many of which used to be available only to stylists. Now the average client is able to buy the things we use. They are also able to price them. And argue with us about what we later charge to use those products on their hair.

I shake my head. I'm sure the rage is going to bubble out the top of my head any minute now. I say, "I'm sorry but I have to get back to work. If you plan to color your hair at home, you're better off buying something a shade lighter than what you want it to look like."

Ellen frowns. "If I buy a color at Sally's, will you put it on for me?"

"We have plenty of products here. You don't need to bring anything in."

"Well, I mean, will you do it cheaper? The color doesn't cost that much, after all."

I grit my teeth. Renee walks by me. She purses her lips together, doing her best to keep from laughing. Some friend.

I want to ask Ellen if she barters with her dentist this way. Or her doctor, electrician, plumber. Does she offer to go to Home Depot and buy the pipes the plumber needs, then expect him to charge her a lot less because she's providing her own supplies? Does she not realize that she is paying me for my experience, for the service I provide?

I calm myself by visualizing a crack in Ellen's scalp. The crack slowly opens and her brains fall out in a gooey heap.

I back up a step, distancing myself from this annoying waste of my time. I keep my smile in place. She is, after all, a client. And this is a small town. I can't very well call her a stupid bitch and expect to still have clients the next day.

"I'm sorry," I say. "We aren't able to use any products provided by clients. We're responsible for anything that happens with the chemicals, so we only use what we buy directly from our suppliers."

"Oh."

Ellen stands there looking at me as if I've spoken Hebrew. I say, "Why don't you think about it. If you decide you want to come in for a color, give me a call."

I escape back to my paying client. She makes a point of looking at her watch. Does she think I was off having martinis with a bunch of friends?

♫

I am barely in the door of The Cutting Edge when the phone rings. It is 8:20 Friday morning. Because of a late client, I had been stuck at work until almost 10 the previous evening. I should have brought a sleeping bag, camped out in the back room.

I answer the phone because I happen to be standing a foot away when it rings. Renee is in the back making coffee. Roxie is already working on a client. She hasn't been able to look at me without blushing since that incident with her boyfriend in the waxing chair.

I have the phone to my ear and Ellen is rattling on in a high-pitched sort of wail. Ellen is my client who walked in for advice the previous day. I'm picking out words here and there but the frantic pace of her speech is hard to follow. From what I gather, she went with the Wal-Mart color and isn't happy with the results.

"You need to fix it," Ellen says. "It's horrible! I can't go through the weekend this way."

"I have no appointments open today," I say.

"Oh, please, can't you squeeze me in somewhere? I have to attend an important business function tomorrow. I simply can't go this way. My hair is almost black!"

Why is it suddenly my problem that Ellen screwed up her own hair? She chose to take the cheap route because she didn't want to pay for my knowledge. Now I'm supposed to somehow fit her into my already overbooked schedule? Such is the nature of the business.

I stifle a sigh as I look at my day's client list. "If you can be here around 1," I say, "I'll work you in. But you'll have to wait in between my other clients."

"That's fine,' Ellen says. "How much is this going to cost?"

I want to laugh. Wasn't bartering what got her into this mess to begin with? I quote her a price double that of our normal fee for a hair color and I smile when I hear her gasp.

"Why so much?" Ellen asks.

"Because correcting a bad color is twice as much work," I tell her. "Before I can lighten it, I first have to pull some of that color out of your hair. The process is time-consuming and requires more products."

"Oh."

I wait for the argument. Maybe she'll ask me what she can buy at Wal-Mart to fix her mistake. To my surprise, all Ellen says is, "Thank you. I'll see you at 1."

I hate to do corrective color, particularly when I'm not the one who screwed it up. Running away and joining the circus sounds like a good idea right about now. Or poison. Now that thought makes me smile! Could I put poison in a color bottle? Is there something that would absorb into Ellen's skin and make her miserably sick? Give her huge red itchy welts that eventually ooze toxic waste? Something that would slowly kill her?

Renee steps close and says, "You're thinking something evil."

I smile at my friend. "Yes I was," I say. But I don't tell her that I was thinking about inflicting a slow horrible death on a client.

*

The Mass Avenger follows the dental hygienist to her cubicle. She motions to the chair and smiles at him with seductive lips. "Have a seat," she says. "Get comfortable."

Her name is Sara. She's younger than he is but not too young to understand her power. She wraps the paper napkin bib around him and her fingers linger on his shoulders. He knows what she is doing. Teasing him. She is no different from the others.

Sara's lips are painted a rich plum. Her eyelashes flutter as she speaks and her soft brown eyes gaze into his. He sees the longing there. He feels the vibrations coming off her silky skin.

What would she do if he pulled her down onto his lap? Like the others, she would probably scramble away, tell him he misunderstood, threaten to call the police. This is all a game to them. The seduction gives them power and control. Confront them and they crumble, no longer bravely tossing their sexuality in your face.

The Mass Avenger had not always understood that. He'd given them the power and the control over him. He'd been awed by their provocative ways. Alone, in his own mind, he'd even admit to having been inhibited, a little afraid to pursue them.

Kathy had been the first to truly open his eyes to their game. She'd been a waitress at the diner he frequented. She remembered his name, what his favorite foods were. She'd smile at him and that sparkle in her eyes would be for him alone. She'd hand him a menu and her fingers would lightly graze his. She'd draw smiley faces on his bill. Then one day she touched his hair, told him she was envious of his thick waves.

He'd always been quiet around women. He hadn't been allowed to date in his youth, which put him at a disadvantage. But, on the bright side, he'd had a lot of time to watch and learn. After a few months, he'd been sure that Kathy wanted him as much as he wanted her.

On a cloudless Friday, he'd gotten up all his nerve and gone to the diner to see her. He chose mid afternoon, when the place was least likely to be crowded. He sat at his usual table and she greeted him with a smile and a cup of coffee just the way he liked it. He'd stammered over his words, desperate to take her home and feel her hands on his naked skin.

He would never forget her reaction; could never erase that image from his mind. The smile in her eyes had turned to pity. She'd given him an excuse about a boyfriend she'd been dating for months. He didn't understand and told her so. She'd flirted with him. Why would she do that?

She'd taken a step back. He could feel her laughing at him, though the smile never touched her lips. He'd gotten the wrong impression, she told him. She was nice to all the customers.

And there it was, said aloud for the first time. He was nothing more than any other man in that diner. She flirted equally, led them all on in the same way. She loved the power she held over him. But she would never love him.

He'd brooded over Kathy for weeks. He'd sit in his car at the far end of the lot and watch her work. He'd followed her home, to the apartment she shared with her boyfriend. By the third week, he'd known what he had to do.

"Is that uncomfortable?" Sara the hygienist asks.

The Mass Avenger blinks away the memory. Sara holds that horrible little pick between her long, slender fingers. She'd had her hands in his mouth. Could anything be more intimate than that?

"No," he tells her. "That feels fine."

She flashes him a smile. "Good. I want you to be relaxed."

He smiles at that. Sara is like the others, teasing men into submission. She thinks she has the power. But she doesn't. Not anymore.

5

Wednesday afternoon I am winding perm rods into Clara's hair while she tells me about her latest bowel movement. Clara is 84 and partially deaf; therefore, she tends to speak at a volume more conducive to a concert hall than a small salon. Consequently, everyone inside The Cutting Edge - and probably a few people outside - is now privy to the intimacies of Clara's bathroom habits.

Naturally, I had not asked Clara for this information. According to salon protocol, I had not even asked Clara how she is. We absolutely never ask Clara that question because she will tell us. In detail. Evidently, Clara is on to us because she now offers the information without prompting.

I'm thankful that I have not had time for lunch. The detail Clara provides about this "mishap" has too many adjectives and nouns that I would never have thought to associate with a bathroom experience.

Renee is working beside me and her client's eyes are shooting daggers at me through the mirror. Does she think that I somehow instigated this conversation? I would like nothing better than to stuff a towel in Clara's mouth to shut her up.

When Clara breaks for air, I say, "I hear your granddaughter is having a big sweet 16 party."

Clara rolls her eyes. "That child is spoiled rotten. They hired a DJ to play all that obnoxious noise the kids call music. The kids don't dance, so what do they need a DJ for? And never mind the three-tiered birthday cake or the fancy caterer they hired just to serve pizza! Supposed to be their specialty, 15 kinds of pizza. That stuff gives me horrible gas. And sometimes that cheese goes right through me."

And here we are, right back to Clara's bathroom habits. I wind her three-inch strands of gray hair around the perm rods as quickly as possible. Finally, I get the solution applied and bring her usual cup of coffee. I feel like I should offer her some Imodium to go with it.

The day tumbles along at a bumpy crawl. At 3:15, I usher Clara out the door and into the arms of her daughter Madeline. They are arguing before they reach the sidewalk.

My 3:30 client has not arrived. I rush to the bathroom to pee and inadvertently recall Clara's bathroom woes while in there. I splash cold water on my face. That doesn't help. I imagine Clara dying of flatulence – farting so much that she deflates and collapses to the ground in a wisp of stinky air. That makes me laugh.

I am still chuckling as I step out of the bathroom. A client of Roxie's is waiting outside the door. She gives me a funny look but my grin only widens as I walk past. Half the town already thinks I'm crazy. What's one more person?

My next client is the town crier. Nothing happens in Whitman, Mass, without her knowledge. The population hovers around 8,000 and Joy probably knows every resident's name and address. Her entire family has inhabited this little town for four generations. Only one family member managed to escape and that's because he is in a prison in Plymouth.

While I am cutting Joy's hair, she says, "Did you hear about Eddie Templeton?"

Eddie, his wife Sue, and their three children all come to the salon. I shake my head. "What about Eddie?"

"He's been cheating on Sue! Some woman from Boston."

Joy says this as if being from Boston explains everything. Those city people simply can't be trusted.

"That's too bad," I say.

I'm careful with my words. The salon is crowded and many of our clients are connected. Family, friends, neighbors. The last thing I need is to be accused of spreading gossip.

Joy shares a few more tidbits about her neighbors' teenage children. I walk that tightrope between showing interest in what my client says and remaining politically correct in my reactions.

As I'm blow-drying Joy's hair, she says, "What do you think about this serial killer we have running around?"

"Serial killer?" Margaret repeats with astonishment.

Margaret is sitting in Renee's chair. She's about my age and her normal state borders on hysterical. As an example, today's forecast is a slight chance of rain. She is dressed in bright red galoshes like you'd see on a 2-year-old. She carried in a matching red raincoat made of some sort of rubbery vinyl and a compact little umbrella ready to sprout open at the first drop of rain. She probably also has one of those awful plastic rain hats in her purse.

Joy's face lights up. At last she is able to stun someone with her knowledge of current events. "Yes," she says. "We have a serial killer loose!"

"I didn't hear anything about a serial killer," Margaret says.

"It's all very hush-hush," Joy replies. "The police are using the excuse that they don't want to scare the public. That's hogwash! They don't want us to know there is a psycho running around that they aren't able to catch."

"A psycho?"

Margaret has gone completely pale. Renee gives me a look, eyebrows raised. Do I muzzle Joy or do we risk having to dial 911 when Margaret drops to the floor?

"He calls himself The Mass Avenger," Joy says.

I inwardly groan. "I read about him," I say. "The police refused to verify the story."

Joy gets that smug Gossip Queen look. "Yes, but they also didn't deny it. That in itself is telling, wouldn't you agree?"

"How many people has he killed?" Margaret asks.

"Three. All young women!"

Renee puts her blow dryer on high and holds it close to Margaret's ear. Margaret is visibly trembling. "These women were from nearby?" she nearly shouts.

"All in southern Mass," Joy hollers back. "I believe one was in Middleboro."

"That's horrible!"

"I know!"

The conversation goes on like that. Renee and I can do nothing to curb the hysteria bubbling from Margaret. Joy seems to feed off it.

She becomes more animated with each shudder that ripples from Margaret's core.

Al, a long-time client who resembles Santa, leans into the conversation. "You ladies looking for protection?" he asks with a twinkle. "I can be bought real cheap!"

I'm thankful for his attempt to break up the drama. Joy responds with a surprising blush. Her eyelashes even flutter. She's about to take the bait when Margaret asks, "How is he killing them?"

"He's cutting them to pieces!"

I am astounded by Joy's response, particularly by the delighted way in which it is delivered. "I don't think –"

My words are cut off by Margaret's wail. Renee anticipates Margaret fainting and says, "I'll get you a cold cloth."

By the time I get Joy out the door, Renee is on the phone asking Margaret's husband to come pick her up because she is unable to drive.

Thankfully, the rest of the afternoon passes incident-free. Five o'clock comes and suddenly the females clear out at a frightening speed. Renee and I work alone on Wednesday nights and, for some unknown reason, this has turned into an unadvertised men's night at The Cutting Edge. By 6, the place has so much testosterone flowing that I'm afraid I might start sprouting a beard.

For the most part, men are particularly easy clients, as well as great tippers. I probably have one difficult male for every twenty difficult females. That's not to say that my male clients don't irritate me. They just irritate me less and it's generally unrelated to their hair.

Bill is one of those irritating males. He strolls in 15 minutes late, as he always does. Bill doesn't like to wait for anyone or anything, ever. Being late ensures that I will be waiting for him. Apparently, the fact that he keeps me waiting and consequently makes me late for my next client is not an issue that concerns him.

Bill grabs a *Star* magazine and plops down in my chair. He buries his nose in the celebrity gossip while I cut. *Star* seems to be a guilty pleasure for many of our male clients. I wonder if they sit in the bar with their buddies and discuss the latest headlines.

"Did you see what Jennifer Aniston was wearing?"

"Oprah is fat again! She goes up and down more often than a yo-yo!"

The thought makes me laugh. Bill looks up from the magazine and catches my eye in the mirror. Clearly, he has said nothing funny and wants to know what I find amusing. I cover for my thoughts by pointing to a photo on the open page in his lap. I say, "I can't believe she wore that outfit out in public."

Bill snickers, then proceeds to rattle on about the supermodel in the photo. I don't know who she is; didn't even know that she is a supermodel. Bill, however, knows her life story. He would be a great host on the TV show *E!* or *Inside Edition*.

At 8:20, a man eases his way inside like he is stepping out onto a minefield. Due to Bill's tardiness, I am slightly behind schedule and still have two more appointments to go. Renee is ahead of schedule and is waiting for her last client. She approaches the man who has now managed to sidle his way up to the desk. "Hi," she says. "Can I help you?"

I watch the man's reflection in the mirror. I don't think I've ever seen him before, though I'm not sure. Average height, average weight; light brown hair. Probably in his mid-twenties. Nothing distinctive about him, aside from the fact that he looks completely uncomfortable in his own skin.

"Could I get a haircut?" he asks.

"I'm sorry," Renee says, "we're all booked up for the night."

He shifts his weight and darts a glance my way. He has big brown eyes and a shy smile.

Renee asks, "Would you like to make an appointment for another time?"

He looks back at her. "Sure. Saturday, maybe?"

He tells her his name is Kyle. Renee makes him an appointment with me for Saturday afternoon. As he's leaving, I say, "See you Saturday, Kyle!"

He tosses me another shy smile as he scurries out the door. Renee gives me that raised eyebrow grin that tells me she's inwardly laughing about saddling me with this new guy who looks like he might shatter if the wind makes too much noise.

I finish cutting Alan's hair. He's been dozing in my chair for the past 10 minutes. I had considered shaving a design on the back of his head but I figured someone would point it out to him and I didn't want to piss off a 6-foot-5-inch construction worker with a bad temper.

Alan leaves and Ed sits in my chair. He's here every four weeks and is among my easiest clients. With some luck, Renee and I will have the shop cleaned and locked before 9:30. A quick shower and I can be naked in my bed before 10. Scott has promised me a massage that I've been eagerly anticipating since 7 a.m. There's nothing like my husband's experienced hands to make me forget that I hate what I do for a living.

6

On Fridays, my workday normally starts at 9 a.m. I am at the salon late on Thursdays and rarely get home before 9:30 p.m. I like to have some space between the time I leave and the time I arrive, so maybe I won't feel like I am chained to the building. This particular Friday allows me no such luxury. The day is insanely busy and, for me, begins at 8 a.m.

By 8:05, Kathy is in my chair speaking at lightning speed. Her speech is laced with so much profanity that I wonder if it's possible for her to converse without swearing. She is loud and crass, full of caffeine and maybe a shot or two of whiskey. I am bleary-eyed and prefer silence in the morning. We are not a good match.

Kathy is talking about Tommy, her teenage son, who was a "little bastard" yesterday and isn't going to make it to his 15th birthday if he doesn't "knock off the shit". The shop is quiet and the only other client is a minister from a local Protestant church who is sitting in Roxie's chair. Kathy attends the Catholic Church and evidently is not worried about offending the leader of a rival religion.

"What did Tommy do?" I ask.

Kathy huffs as if the mere recollection of her son's misdeed causes her physical discomfort. Then, her voice a loud cackle, she tells me, "He snuck a girl into his room after Andy and I went to bed."

I don't know what to say to this. The fact that there is a minister sitting about 20 feet away keeps me from voicing the first three thoughts I have. I settle on, "Oh."

"Do you believe that shit?" Kathy asks. "We only caught him because Ashley heard voices and she still likes to tattle on her brother. The little bastard claimed they were only going to play video games. Talk about a freakin' lame excuse! What the hell was he thinking?"

"I'm pretty sure teenagers don't think," I say.

Kathy snorts a laugh. "Ain't that the damn truth!"

Roxie has been trying to occupy the minister with idle conversation. His eyes keep darting our way. I don't want to encourage Kathy to continue on this topic but I also don't want to be rude. I figure the minister has heard worse and I let her rattle on.

Kathy proceeds to tell me that she had to call the girl's parents. "These damn teenage girls are forward as hell," she says. "The little bitch didn't look the least bit embarrassed. Her father came to pick her up and she just strolled right past him like a freakin' princess. How the hell am I supposed to keep my kid out of trouble when these teenage bimbos are making it so damn easy for the boys?"

I don't know how to reply to that. My experience with teenage boys is limited to my own backseat escapades. I say, "I doubt Tommy will be pulling a stunt like that again."

Kathy shakes her head and moves to another topic. She is chaperoning a ski trip for the Girl Scouts in December. She will be in charge of her daughter, as well as five other 12-year-old girls. Kathy's best friend, Lena, is also chaperoning. "We're going to get freakin' trashed," Kathy says. "Lena and I are stuffing our overnight bags with brandy and vodka nips. No husbands for three entire days! The girls will be exhausted at night, so we'll tuck their asses in bed and have ourselves a good time!"

And Kathy wonders why her son is difficult to handle.

When Kathy finally steps out the door, I have a raging headache. My next three clients are children between the ages of 3 and 7. After that, I have a man from a local halfway house who writes me poetry and always has fragments of his last meal lodged in his beard. By 10:30, I am ready for a padded cell.

I manage to regain some sense of calm and I am no longer gritting my teeth when my 1 p.m. client walks in the door. His name is George. He is 56 and already comfortably retired. He is married and his two children are out on their own, doing fine in life. He and his wife are both healthy. But, to look at George, you would think he is suffering from terminal cancer, his dog just died, his children have schizophrenia and are living on the streets, and his house burned down the day after the insurance was canceled.

You would assume all this simply by looking at the man. To hear him speak would verify your opinion and you'd be inclined to add a few more things to the list, such as his wife is having an affair with his son's best friend.

None of these things are true.

I'm not sure if George has ever experienced a truly happy day. However, I am sure that George's unhappiness is internal and has absolutely nothing to do with his circumstances in life.

One thing about George is that he is not stingy. He always shares his misery.

His hair has to look the exact same way every day. The part must be in the exact same spot. He comes in every three weeks so that his hair never appears any longer or any shorter. He fusses more than a woman on her wedding day. I have been cutting his hair for five years and he still feels the need to direct me as if I am a novice student.

I want to jam my scissors into George's neck. I want to paint a bloody smile over the ever-present frown. I want George to die so that both his misery and my own will finally end.

"I've been thinking about going a little shorter," George says.

George has made this declaration the last four times he's been in for a haircut. I suppress a groan. I want to jam my scissors in his ear. I somehow refrain from the violent acts I've been considering and I muster a smile. "It would look good shorter," I say.

"You think so?"

We've had this same conversation on four separate occasions. I could have made a recording of my replies and simply played it back for him. George wears the sides of his hair at precisely the halfway point on his ears. He has been considering cutting his sides up over his ears. Life-changing stuff.

"I've told you it would look good," I say.

"What if I don't like it?"

"It will grow."

"But it will take a long time."

"A few weeks," I say. "It will be covering your ears again in no time."

"I don't know…"

"Then wait until you're sure."

George has his fingers in his hair. The way he is primping, you would think he has a starring role in an upcoming blockbuster film. "I don't know," he says again.

I glance at the clock. I don't have all day to hold his hand and coddle him over this epic decision. "If you aren't ready, then you probably won't like it," I say. "You should wait."

"I've been wearing my hair this way for a long time. It's tough to change."

"Yes, change can be hard sometimes."

"But I won't know unless I do it, right?"

"Right."

"I could hate it."

We go around like this for a few more minutes. Finally, George makes a momentous decision. "Cut it a little shorter," he says. "Not over the ears, though! Maybe halfway between where it is now and the top of my ears."

I try to look impressed with his bravery. What he is asking amounts to about a quarter-inch. "That sounds great," I say.

"You think it'll be okay?"

Can he honestly be this neurotic about a quarter-inch of hair? The man needs Prozac. Better yet, I need Prozac. Maybe then I won't be visualizing my scissors snipping off George's earlobes. What would he do then, without his earlobes? How would he judge whether his hair is the appropriate length?

This amuses me. I can actually see myself cutting away his earlobes and I have to blink several times to clear my vision.

George scrutinizes my cutting while he complains about leaves. They are changing color and will soon be falling from the trees. That means raking. And raking is work that requires physical movement. George believes he should no longer have to do anything even remotely considered work. He is retired, after all.

"Don't bother raking them," I say. "The leaves will eventually turn to mulch."

"They blow all over the place."

"True. But they look pretty on the ground. They hide the dead brown grass."

"We get them stuck to our shoes and track them inside. Damn things get everywhere."

"Then I guess you need to rake them."

"Problem is, the neighbor's leaves blow in my yard," George says. "They have more trees but I end up with all the damn leaves. I shouldn't have to rake their leaves."

"Yeah, nature has a way of being unfair."

"I should use one of those leaf blowers and blow them all back to the neighbor's yard."

"There's an idea."

"Are you sure that's not too short?" George asks.

He has turned his head to the side and is studying the quarter-inch difference. I have to stop cutting. "I like it," I say.

"Can I still brush it down?"

"Sure. Or you can brush it back. Whatever you want."

"I don't think I'll like it brushed back.

"Then brush it down."

"Can you brush it back, so I can see if I like it?"

We go on like this. What should have been a 15-minute haircut takes me 45. My teeth are gnashing together by the time I finish. I grab my blow dryer and flick it on while George is taking a breath. I'm hoping he has worn himself out by now.

I visualize George's hair blowing away with the leaves. What would George do if he lost his hair? Would he wear a wig? Get hair plugs? Have a nervous breakdown?

He studies my blow-dry technique through the mirror. I want to conk him in the head, then shave him bald while he is unconscious.

Once George's hair is dry, I spend another five minutes watching him play with it. He takes the brush from me and brushes the sides back, then down, then back, then down again. "I don't know..." he mutters.

I am seriously off schedule. My next client has been waiting. Fortunately, she looks amused rather than irritated. George can be quite amusing when you don't have to deal with him directly.

All sorts of bloody fantasies are rolling through my mind by the time I get George out of my chair. Is this how serial killers start out? That thought is a little unsettling. I should probably get some help.

7

My alarm startles me out of a sex dream at 6 on Saturday morning. Scott groans beside me while I fumble for the off switch. He rolls over and returns to a dreamy bliss. I stumble out of bed and battle the lingering arousal that makes me want to bury myself under the covers with my husband.

I lurch down the hall like a drunk, my eyes half-closed and a litany of curses rolling through my head. I love Saturdays because they are my last workday of the week. I hate Saturdays because they start too early and they last too long.

I shower, dress, and apply enough makeup to help me pass for professional. When I step out of the bathroom, I find Jack dancing by the back door. He will stand there waiting all day if no one notices. He won't bark. He won't come get me. The silly mutt just stays by the door, his large chocolate body quivering with the need to pee.

I open the door and Jack charges outside. Cassady and Neal are curled up in their little beds, which are lined up beneath the window in my bedroom. I try to coax them up but they want nothing to do with me or the outdoors. Neal cracks an eye open and I swear he is calling me a crazy bitch. I pull Cassady's little blanket over her and leave the lucky dogs to sleep.

Jack is waiting by the back door, ever the patient gentleman. I wonder how long he would stand out there before he would think to bark. I open the door and he trots inside, his tail wagging so hard that his entire back end is swaying. I give his furry head a kiss and he licks off part of my makeup. Then he's off and running. He leaps onto my bed and snuggles beside Scott. I envy my dogs.

At 6:45, I am out the door. I own a red MINI Cooper. It looks small but actually has plenty of room for my dogs, which is why I bought it. Scott drives a sleek black Pontiac Solstice. He is taking all three dogs to the vet today, so I get to drive his car. I know it's my imagination but I think I look sexier when I'm driving the Solstice.

I needed to leave earlier this morning because I have to stop at my parents' house to pick up a birdhouse my dad made for one of my clients. I had planned on getting it last night but my dad needed more time to complete his custom paint job. The birdhouse is for indoor finches and my dad is painting the birds' names on the side with some sort of fancy calligraphy.

I manage to sleep-drive the 15 minutes to my parents' house. I'm halfway up the walk when my dad pulls the door open. "Good morning, Skye-baby!"

My dad is one of those people who is always happy. And always wide awake. I grumble a good morning as he envelops me in a crushing hug.

The house smells like French toast. I rarely eat before 10 a.m. but the smell has my taste buds begging for satisfaction.

"Want some breakfast?" my dad asks.

"I don't have time," I say.

My dad frowns. "Not even five minutes for one quick piece of my famous French toast?"

I can't help but smile, despite my aversion to mornings and Saturdays and the job I am heading to. My parents are vegans, which means they do not eat, drink, or wear anything even remotely connected to an animal. This means that there are no eggs in my dad's French toast batter. Yet, despite this anomaly, his French toast would be the envy of chefs everywhere. My dad does something magical when he cooks.

"Maybe five minutes," I say.

My dad's face lights up. "Then let's not waste any time!"

We are seated in the kitchen when my mom wanders in. She is wrapped in an organic cotton robe and has her feet tucked in to hemp slippers. Four dogs trail behind her. The other four had already invaded the kitchen and are drooling by my feet.

My dad hands my mom a steaming mug of green tea. My mom grins at him and settles into the chair beside me. She isn't much of a morning person, either.

I am almost finished with my French toast when my mom says, "Benjamin is moving out of the city. He bought a condo in Beverly."

This surprises me. Benjamin, my gay surgeon cousin, has lived in a fancy Boston loft for the past 10 years. "Did he get tired of city life?"

My dad is grinning like a child. "I think he's hoping Beverly will be too far for Liz and Al to travel."

Liz, Elizabeth to most people, is my dad's sister. Al, whose full name is Alan and hates to be called Al, is her husband. They are Benjamin's parents and a shining example of what happens when two screwed-up people get together and mix their genetics.

"He plans on having a roommate in the condo," my mom says.

"Todd," my father says through a smirk.

"His boyfriend?"

My dad roars with laughter. "His best friend, according to Liz. Benjamin and Todd remain single simply because they haven't found the right women yet."

I roll my eyes at this. "She and Alan have got to know that he's gay."

"Alan would rather die than admit to having a gay son," my mom says.

"And my sister is a moron," says my dad.

"Yeah, there's that," I say with a chuckle. "But isn't it about time that Benjamin came out of the closet? Geesh, he's 40 years old!"

My dad's eyebrows dance on his forehead. "Ben has been hiding in that dark closet with the door locked tight for so long that he wouldn't know how to find his way out."

"He should just tell them," I say. "Won't he have to explain why he and Todd are sharing a bedroom? I mean, seriously, Liz and Alan cannot be that stupid."

"Todd will probably maintain the façade of having his own room," my mother says. "I doubt Liz and Alan will visit that often, anyway. They expect everyone to come to them. We live three blocks away and I can count on one hand how many times they've been in our house."

"Would you want them coming over here?" my father asks.

My mother chuckles. "It's not high on my list of wishes, wants, and desires."

I shake my head at the absurdity of my father's family. Their wackiness makes me feel sane by comparison. "I need to go," I say. "Work awaits."

My dad retrieves the birdhouse. His creation is a masterpiece and I tell him so. He grins at me and engulfs me in another of his bear hugs. I wish I could stay there, in my parents' crazy little world. No matter how old I get, they always make me feel like a child; safe and loved and protected.

♫

My day goes downhill after the French toast. My morning is a blitz of complainers. The weather sucks, their finances suck, their jobs suck. One lady goes on and on about how exhausted she is from her workweek, as if I have no clue. Her job requires her to sit at a desk for six-hour days, four days a week. I stand on my feet for 10-hour days and my workweek has not ended. She tells me that I am fortunate to do something creative that isn't like work. I gag on the reply I have to swallow back.

I have just finished perming Alison's hair. This is a redo that I'm not getting paid for on a client that I don't like. A month ago, she had requested a "body wave". I had spent 10 minutes painstakingly explaining that a body wave on thick, shoulder-length hair would not last. She had claimed to be fine with that. She did *not* want curl.

Three weeks later, she was complaining that she'd wasted her money.

Alison now has curl, which doesn't seem to be making her any happier than the lack thereof. "Why does my hair look so short now?" she asks.

"Because the curl shrinks your length," I reply.

"You didn't tell me that."

I also didn't tell the lady at the grocery store that my eggs would break if she tossed the 5-pound bag of potatoes on top. Some things would seem to be common knowledge. I do my best to keep the nasty edge from my voice as I reply. "You look really good with curl."

She fingers one of the spiral curls as she studies herself in the mirror. "I'm not sure I like it."

"Your hair was very straight. You probably need a little time to adjust."

"Can you blow it out for me?"

If my life were a sitcom, this would be the part where I tell her to get her fat ass out of my chair and everyone in the salon applauds. Instead, I hear my teeth gnash as I clench my jaw. "Don't you want to leave the curl, give yourself time to see if you like it?"

"I have a date tonight. And he likes my hair long."

"Your hair is still long," I say, touching the thick mass that extends to her shoulders.

She shakes her head, her eyes now glassy with the threat of tears. "I don't think I like the curls."

I bite back a curse as I fumble through my drawer for a large round brush. By the time I finish pulling out the curl, I am sure that my arm has been disconnected from my shoulder.

Alison is happier with her hair now that it is blown out. It's full and fluffy and, according to her, long again. I can't imagine her spending a half-hour with a giant round brush every day, which means I will probably be receiving a frantic call from her next week, asking me to straighten the perm. I have spent two hours on her hair and she doesn't even bother to tip me. I'm thinking that a kick in the ass would be a nice parting gift.

I have five minutes before my next client is due to arrive, so I run out back to pee. I haven't had time all day and my bladder is about ready to burst. The bathroom door is closed. I stand there, shifting my weight from one leg to the other, feeling much like Jack waiting by my back door. I suddenly have immense sympathy for my dog.

The door finally pops open and a woman in a tailored suit emerges. She's wearing pearls and high heels and her makeup is perfection. I think her name is Jacqueline, though I'm not sure. I do know that her speech is always peppered with large words that are pulled from the depths of some ancient dictionary. She is the ultimate feminine professional, all proper speech and good manners wrapped up in a designer suit. I feel like a high school thug beside her.

I excuse myself and slip past her in a hurry. I close the bathroom door behind me and I'm about to sit on the toilet seat when I leap back in disgust. A puddle of yellow pee awaits me. The prim and proper Jacqueline has peed on our toilet seat. Does she do this at home, then send the servant in to clean the mess?

I hastily grab the sponge and the Soft Scrub from under the sink. Even after cleaning the seat, the thought of sitting where she has peed creeps me out. I line the seat with toilet paper and pee as fast as I can.

Kyle is waiting when I come out. He's the new client who walked in on Wednesday night. He looks, if possible, even more uncomfortable today. That is probably due to the dozen squawking women, one subdued teen boy, and the fact that I was missing in action.

I lead Kyle to the sink. His eyes flit away from mine as I drape the cape around him. I lean the chair back and start wetting his hair. Kyle seems surprised by my touch. Maybe his last stylist had a setup like the car wash, just sit your client on a conveyor belt and off they go.

Three minutes later, I have Kyle seated in my chair in front of the mirror. His eyes dart around the room, seeking a safe landing zone. He doesn't appear to be comfortable looking at me through the mirror. Or maybe it's himself he's not comfortable looking at.

Kyle is a good-looking guy by most people's standards. His features are boyish, like his face hasn't realized that he's grown into a man. He has long, dark eyelashes that frame what would be nice eyes if they stopped bouncing around the room. He's average-sized, thin.

Kyle's brown hair has a slight curl. I run my hand through his hair. He startles, like I have sent an electric current through his skull. His extreme shyness must make life difficult for him. I feel like I am in charge of his torture at his inquest.

"How do you want your hair cut?" I ask.

Kyle briefly meets my eyes. "Just trim it, I guess," he says softly.

I shoot for some small talk while I cut. After a slow start, I land on the topic of art. This loosens him right up. He smiles and relaxes. I tell him about the class I took at the community college over the summer. "I love to paint, though I'm not very good at it," I say. "The class was for learning techniques with oil paints. The clothes I wore are now a creative masterpiece of paint splotches. I didn't manage to learn much but I had fun."

"I paint," Kyle tells me. "And draw. I love working with charcoal."

With a little prompting, Kyle proceeds to tell me about his art projects. By the time I finish Kyle's haircut, he has all but forgotten his shyness.

Kyle leaves me with a generous tip and a shy smile. My next client, another male fairly new to the salon, is waiting for me. His name is Jason and he is quiet in an uncomfortable way. He is in his mid-twenties and would be handsome except his features have too many sharp lines.

I get Jason settled at the sink and wrap the plastic cape around him. He stares up at me the entire time I am washing his hair. Finally, I "accidentally" drip water in his eyes so he'll close the damn things.

I get Jason to my chair and he stares at me through the mirror. He has nice eyes but I don't want them drilling into me like he's trying to uncover the secrets I keep. "How do you want your hair cut?" I ask.

His eyes never leave mine. "Above the ears. Leave just a little length in back."

Jason has thick, wavy hair. The cut requires very little conscious effort, which is a great way to end a Saturday. Now if I could only blindfold the guy. I make small talk as I cut, hoping to distract Jason's potent stare.

"What do you do for work?" I ask.

Jason gives me a look of annoyance. "That always seems to be a woman's first concern."

He reacts as if I have asked how much money he has in the bank. I ignore his sarcasm, which is not an easy feat for me. I plaster on my fake smile. "Actually, I was only making conversation."

He gives a little shrug. "I work at a sewer treatment plant."

"I've read they have quite the complex setup."

Jason doesn't respond. He just continues with his unsettling glare. I would like to jam the tip of my scissors into his eyeballs. Pierce them like a shish kabob. Seriously, the guy doesn't even blink.

Jason's gaze flickers in the mirror. He appears to be studying my hands. "You're not married?" he asks.

"I am married," I reply. "You?"

"You're not wearing a wedding ring."

"I don't wear it to work. The chemicals get underneath and irritate my skin."

"That doesn't bother your husband?"

What, am I supposed to be branded? "No, he'd rather my skin didn't peel off."

Jason's piercing stare narrows. I know that my tone was sarcastic but I couldn't help myself. This guy is getting on my nerves. I take a long, slow breath and fix the fake smile back on my face. I picture myself cutting Jason's eyeballs out and making him eat them.

I am in desperate need of a vacation.

A screechy toddler runs past me. Andrea's last client. The young girl has a lollipop, minus the stick, stuck in her long, baby-fine red hair. The mother is pleading with the toddler to sit in Andrea's chair. Andrea is standing by her chair, mouth slightly parted, looking defeated. The mother finally scoops up the child and plants her in Andrea's chair. The toddler immediately begins to wail.

Jason's gaze continues to bore into me. His expression seems to be blaming me for the unruly child. He says, "Do you have kids?"

"No," I reply. "You?'

He flicks a glance at the toddler, now squirming and slapping at her mother. "I don't see the point," he says.

The point? In having children in general or in extending his personal genetic line? Maybe he is smart enough to know that his genes grew corrupt somewhere along the way. I want to ask but there is simply no polite way to do so.

The toddler spends the next 10 minutes vacillating between angry screams and tearful wails. Jason scowls at the mother. Thankfully, the grating noise takes center stage and my conversation with Jason stutters to a halt. Good thing, too, as I was enjoying a vivid image of cutting his tongue out and beating him with the bloody end.

8

The Mass Avenger follows Sara the hygienist to church. She goes by herself. Her boyfriend stays at home, most likely sleeping off a hangover.

He has seen them together, Sara and her boyfriend. They frequent a local bar, where they drink a lot and hang on each other. She dresses in skimpy clothing and wiggles her ass in his face.

Now, dressed for church with her parents, she looks almost angelic. She hides the trashy whore from her parents and God.

She acts so innocent while she cleans his teeth. Like she doesn't know her powers. Like she would never use sex to get what she wants.

Whore.

The Mass Avenger parks in the back of the church lot and watches Sara go inside. She's beautiful. Moves with a fluid grace. She's wearing form-fitting tan pants. The material shimmers as she walks. A chocolate brown sweater hugs her breasts. Her hair is the color of melted caramel and is pulled back in a ponytail. Neat and reserved. For church. But God knows the truth.

The parking lot clears of people. Everyone is inside, listening to the priest. Hoping that he can wash their sins away.

The Mass Avenger waits for Sara to cleanse her soul. He thinks about her hands in his mouth, how her fingers lightly brushed his lips while she cleaned his teeth. Her body had been so close. She'd leaned into him, knowing her powers, using them shamelessly.

He feels his erection build and angrily shakes the thoughts away. That power. Whore. He will show Sara who has the true power.

The sun beats into the car. He shifts his weight, checks his watch. Ten more minutes.

He is beginning to sweat. He runs a hand through his newly cut hair. That makes him smile and, for a moment, he is distracted with thoughts of his stylist. Skye. Her hands on his head, massaging his scalp. She has powers. Dangerous powers. He would like to know what it feels like to possess her. No, that wasn't being honest. He would like her to possess him. All of him. Just melt into her and allow her powers to consume him.

He is now hard and aching with desire. He reaches into his pants and pinches his testicles. Hard. The way his mother taught him.

The pain is a welcome release. His erection deflates. His testicles throb. He focuses on the church and the people now emerging.

A few moments later, Sara crosses the parking lot. She stops beside a white Lincoln and leans into the older woman beside her. Kisses her cheek. Then hugs the older man. Sara's parents. Smiling and proud of their whore daughter.

Sara's parents disappear into their shiny Lincoln and Sara makes her way to her own car. A green Toyota. She slips inside and soon joins the trail of cars exiting the lot.

The Mass Avenger follows, though not too closely. He knows where Sara is going.

Five minutes later, Sara pulls into the parking lot of The Cookie Jar. She stops at the bakery every Sunday after church, to pick up coffee and pastries for herself and the no-good boyfriend waiting at their apartment. She hurries inside the building, oblivious to him. Her mind is focused on getting back home, using her body to hypnotize her boyfriend. Laughing at the men she leaves drooling in her wake.

The Mass Avenger parks a few spaces from Sara's car. He gets out and moves quickly to the rear of the Toyota. A glance around tells him he is alone. He squats beside the front right tire and takes the plastic cap off the valve stem. He uses the valve stem remover and there is a sudden whoosh of air. He's smiling as he scurries back around to his van. When he spots Sara coming around the building, he strolls casually in her direction.

Sara is balancing two coffees and a small bag with pastries. She sees him and her pace slows. He looks up, pretends to be startled. "Oh, hey," he says. "Sara, right? You're the hygienist at Dr. Paulson's   office?"

Sara hesitates, then comes closer. "Yeah," she says.

She says his name. He likes the way it sounds coming from her lips.

He nods. "Funny meeting you here! I was just going in to grab a coffee, noticed someone's not going to be very happy to come out and find a flat."

Sara looks down at her tire. "Oh, crap!"

"This is your car?"

"Yes. It was fine a few minutes ago!"

"You have a spare?"

Sara shrugs. "I guess. But I don't know the first thing about changing tires." She sighs, bats her long lashes. "That will teach me to listen to my father. He's always telling me that I should learn how to do things like this for myself."

The Mass Avenger smiles. He knows Sara would never change her own tire. Why bother, when some sucker is always willing to do it for her?

Sara balances her coffees on her trunk. "I'll call my boyfriend," she says. "He'll come fix it."

"I don't mind doing it for you."

Sara rummages in her purse for her phone. She looks up, fixes her large eyes on him. They are the color of black coffee. Her eyelashes flutter. She says, "No, really, I couldn't ask you to do that."

"It's not a problem."

Sara's plump lips curl into a grin. She believes she has won. Her power has controlled him. She'll know the truth soon enough.

⌁

Sundays are my favorite day. It is the one day of the week that Scott and I have off together. And it's one of only two days that I am not forced to smile and pretend I give a shit what people are saying.

We have come to the park with Jack, Neal, and Cassady. Scott tosses the Frisbee for Jack, who takes great pleasure in showing off to his smaller brother and sister. Neal tries his best to get in on the game. His little body leaps into the air, though he barely manages to reach Jack's knees. Cassady considers the whole idea of physical activity to be foolish. She stretches out beside me on the grass, content to have her tummy rubbed while the sun warms her face.

Scott gives the Frisbee one last toss, then joins me on the grass. Both Jack and Neal give him a look, dejected, pleading with their big dog eyes for him to play some more. He laughs at them. "No more," he says. "Go do dog things together."

Defeated, the two dogs plop down beside us. I open a bottle of water and pour some in their bowl. All three of them fight for position. Jack laps greedily. His long tongue splashes water droplets at the other two. They shove closer. Cassady gets under Jack and her little head disappears into the bowl.

Scott slips his arms around me and leans in for a kiss. "The dogs are watching," I say.

"Aren't they always?" he asks.

I laugh at this. "Yes, sadly. It's a good thing they can't talk."

Scott's kiss sends a tingle down my spine. Sixteen years together and he can still work magic with a simple kiss. I slip my hand inside his jacket. He works out and his stomach is hard and flat. Those guys in the Bowflex infomercials have nothing on my husband.

Neal has wormed his way between us. He offers to wash my face with his tongue. I politely refuse and push his face away from mine.

"He wants in on the action," Scott says.

I am about to respond when I spot a woman pushing a toddler on a swing across the park. My stomach twists into a knot. "We have to go," I say.

"Why?" Scott gives me a look, then rolls his eyes and sighs. "Which client is it this time?"

"Her name is Diana. She's over there pushing her kid on the swing." I tilt my head in the general direction, though I don't turn my face that way. I don't want her to see me. I certainly don't want her to know I've seen her.

Scott squints at the swings. "She won't see us. Hell, I can barely see her."

"She's crazy."

"Crazy?"

"Yes, crazy. Like she wants to be my best friend or something. Confides all her secrets. And she whines! Seriously, the woman cannot speak without whining. If I have to listen to even two minutes of her whining today, I swear I will lose it. You'll be visiting me in a padded cell."

Scott chuckles. "Aren't you exaggerating just a little bit?"

I feel myself pouting. "No."

He kisses me, then begins gathering our things. "Sorry guys," he says to the dogs. "We have to protect your mother's sanity."

"It's not funny," I grumble.

"Maybe we should find a nice park in Rhode Island. You can't possibly have clients who live there."

I scoop Cassady up and head off toward the car. I keep my head down, just in case Diana is watching. We settle the dogs in the car and Scott kisses my neck. "We'll just have to think of something to occupy us at home," he murmurs.

That makes me smile and a little less grumpy. I might be forced to live in seclusion in order to avoid my clients but at least I have Scott and my three dopey dogs to keep me sane.

*

The Mass Avenger drives a 7-year-old white cargo van. One of millions on the road. He is indistinguishable from the rest.

He pulls his van into his driveway, up close to the side door of the garage. His garage is old but sturdy. It's not attached to his house, which is a two-story farmhouse 300 feet away. The house and garage were once owned by his mother. She doesn't own anything anymore because she's dead.

He'd removed the one window in the garage, replacing it with cement blocks. The space is dark. The Mass Avenger steps from his van and fumbles with his keys. He unlocks the deadbolts, then finds the light switch on the wall. He moves back to the van and slides open the side door.

Sara blinks up at him. Her eyes are wide with fear, red-rimmed, wet with tears. She shakes her head frantically. She would probably plead if she could. Promise him the world if he will let her go. But her mouth is covered with heavy duct tape and no sound escapes.

The Mass Avenger smiles down at his prey. "Not so powerful anymore, are you?" he says.

He leaves her in the van and walks into the garage. The area is large. More like a barn or workshop. And always spotless. The smell of bleach tickles his nose. He should air the place out soon.

He takes a pre-cut sheet of plastic from the top shelf. His van rocks gently. Sara is struggling. He hums to himself as he spreads the plastic over the cement floor. He spreads a blanket over the plastic. Green and blue plaid. He bought it special for today.

He goes back to his van and peers inside. She blinks up at him. He checks her wrists and ankles. Still bound tight. Her wrists are chafed from struggling.

"I'm going to lift you out," the Mass Avenger says. "If you fight me, I will kill you. Do you understand?"

Sara nods. Instant acquiescence. How quickly they surrender their power.

He slides his arms beneath her and lifts her from the van. He's stronger than he looks. He goes to the gym, keeps weights in his basement, keeps himself in shape. Prepared.

He takes Sara inside and lays her on the blanket. Then takes the Gerber Gator II hunting knife from his pocket. Shows it to her. "You'll do exactly as I say. Understand?"

Terror forces her eyes wide. She nods.

The Mass Avenger chuckles, touches himself. He is already hard. The power is his. He will take what he wants, let her believe she has a chance of surviving. Then he will show her what true power is.

9

Ellen sits in my chair, while I apply lightener and wrap chunks of her hair in tin foil. She is a seventh-grade teacher. Twenty-four, tall, slim, and oozing sexuality, I'm sure she is the star of her male students' fantasies. Probably a few female students, as well.

"Did you hear that we have a psycho serial killer on the loose?" Ellen says.

"The Mass Avenger!" Cheryl chimes in. "The creep even named himself.

Cheryl is in Renee's chair beside me. Her face lights up with this new topic. We're all from a small town about an hour south of Boston. We have two gas stations, four liquor stores, and a half-dozen bars. No grocery store and certainly nothing that would attract visitors. We don't get much excitement here. A serial killer in the area provides endless hours of conversation.

"Did you hear they found another victim?" Ellen asks.

Renee pushes her thick blonde hair from her eyes. We've had this conversation already. I know she's tired of repeating herself. "Sara Rawlings," she says.

"Was that her name?" Cheryl asks. "I heard they found another girl but I didn't catch the details."

"She lived in Hanson," Renee says.

"Yeah, that freaked me out," Ellen says. "A little too close for comfort."

Hanson is the next town over. Another small-town atmosphere, though larger and more rural than Whitman. Cheryl shakes her head, which makes it difficult for Renee to wind the perm rods in her hair. I feel the frustration oozing from Renee's pores.

"She used to live next door to my husband's parents," Renee says. "Her parents still do."

"Oh my God!" Cheryl squeals. "You knew her?"

The perm rod escapes from Cheryl's hair. Renee scowls and tries again, gripping Cheryl's hair a little tighter. "Not really. She lived there with her parents. She was young, you know? Recently moved in with her boyfriend. We said hello a few times in passing."

Ellen keeps turning her head, trying to look at Renee. I'm working with a high-lift color and don't have a lot of time to chase her head around. I give in and spin her chair so that she can look directly at Renee and Cheryl.

"Are you talking about that serial killer?" Judy calls to us.

Judy is sitting about 20 feet away, in Roxie's chair. She has a pretty face but is horribly overweight. She actually has to wiggle her ass back and forth in order to sit in our chairs. One of these days, the chair is going to refuse to release her when she attempts to stand.

"Yes," Cheryl calls back. "Isn't it horrible?"

"Did you know that Renee knew her?" Ellen asks.

"No way!" Judy replies. "Oh Renee, I'm so sorry. Were you friends?"

Renee looks at me, a silent plea for help. Cheryl's head is on a pivot, spinning back and forth to look from Judy to Ellen. Renee chases her hair with the perm rods. We need to attach vice grips to the chairs to keep our clients' heads still.

The day continues on this way. Everyone wants to talk about The Mass Avenger. Finally the day settles into early evening and the crowd thins out. Renee and I are left alone with our Wednesday evening male clientele. The men aren't so interested in discussing the serial killer, though one appears to be fascinated with Renee's boobs.

We get through the night with our sanity intact. I realize that I had very few murderous fantasies today. All the talk about the serial killer must have offset my desire to make my clients bleed.

Renee and I clean up and leave the salon together at just after 9:30. We both love the night and have never given any thought to hanging around the dark parking lot and venting the day's tension. Tonight, however, we are each a little more cautious. The town is quiet, the streets empty. I can't help but think about The Mass Avenger.

No lingering this evening. We say our good nights and climb into our cars. Tonight I even lock my car door.

ᴧ

I am sitting on the floor in my parents' living room. My mother has lit the candles, made from chemical-free soy, that are scattered around all the available flat surfaces. Moya Brennan is playing on the stereo, which means my mother is in one of her mellow, reflective moods.

Four of my parents' dogs are sprawled out around me. My dad and Scott have taken the other four for a walk. Zena, the black Great Dane, is with them. I have a feeling she might soon be coming home with us.

It's Friday night and I am one day away from surviving another workweek. A wedding party will be taking up most of my Saturday morning. The bride, six bridesmaids, the bride's mother and grandmother, and two little girls who are flower girls will be invading the salon at 8 a.m. The bride and one bridesmaid are regular clients of mine. The bride's mother and grandmother are Andrea's clients. The two little girls have never had haircuts and the other four bridesmaids have never been in the salon. It will be total chaos.

"What's on your mind?" my mother asks.

I realize I am frowning. "Thinking about my day tomorrow," I say.

My mother stretches out on the floor beside Taffy, a scruffy Shi-Tzu with a fussy temperament. She scratches the dog's belly while she studies me. "Do you remember when you loved your job?" she asks.

"Barely."

"What changed?"

I shrug. "I guess I'm just burned out."

"People don't normally get burned out from doing something they love."

"I don't love it anymore. Which is why I'm burned out."

"And therein lies the problem."

"What?" My mother frustrates me at times. This is one of those times.

"You don't love your job anymore," my mother says.

"I know."

"You need to find that part of you that loved what you do. It's still in there somewhere. Reconnect with that person you were."

I give her a look. She knows the expression well. I've probably had that same expression since I was a toddler and I wear it each time she starts to babble her esoteric bullshit.

"Are you unhappy?" my mother asks.

"No."

"Not even with work?"

"Well, that's different."

"How so?"

"Can we change the subject?"

My mother sighs. Taffy licks her hand. She sits up and kisses my cheek. "I don't like to see you unhappy."

"I'm fine, mom."

Scott and my father are led inside by four tired dogs. The dogs head straight for their water bowls. Zena keeps turning her head, checking to see where Scott is. They have bonded. It's only a matter of time before we bring her home.

My dad is wearing a white organic cotton sweatshirt that says *Chemical Free* in big black letters. People probably think he's an ex-addict. He also wears his ever-present smile. The world never seems to irritate him. I wish I had inherited that trait.

Scott sits on the couch. Zena immediately trots over and climbs up beside him. She nestles her head in his lap. The rest of her body stretches across the couch.

My dad lands in the rocker by the window. He looks at me and says, "Scott tells me that Renee knew that young woman from Hanson."

My mother's eyes widen. "You mean the one who was murdered by that serial killer?"

I scowl at Scott. "She lived next door to Renee's husband's parents. They weren't friends or anything."

"I've never known anyone who was murdered," my father says.

My mother shoots my father a look. "Be careful what kind of energy you send out into the universe, Teddy."

"I didn't say I wanted someone I know to get murdered."

"Do they think this girl knew the killer?" my mother asks. "Renee might know this man and not even realize it."

Scott scratches Zena's ear. He looks a little guilty, though I'm not sure if this is because he's responsible for this conversation or because he plans to bring Zena home with us tonight. He says, "I heard on the news earlier that the police believe the victims are random. They can't find any connection."

"That will make the guy harder to find," my dad says.

"It's very unnerving," my mother says.

My father is looking at me in that way that tells me he thinks I'm still the little girl he needs to protect. He says, "I don't like you working alone at night."

"I don't work alone," I tell him. "Renee works with me."

"Yes, just the two of you. And you leave alone at night."

"We leave together."

"Make sure you always wait for each other."

"We do."

"You should carry Mace," my mother says.

"I bought her some last year," Scott says.

"Maybe I should meet you there at night," my father says. "I could walk the two of you to your cars."

"That's crazy, dad. We're fine."

"I offered already," Scott says.

"Does your car have a panic alarm?" my mother asks.

"Mom, really. I'm fine."

"I'm sure that's what that poor Hanson girl said, too."

I lay back and hold a throw pillow over my face. "Can we please change the subject?" I say through the pillow.

Shiloh, the three-legged German Shepherd nudges me. My parents adopted him two years ago. He'd been hit by a car and his owners didn't want to get stuck with the vet bill. They'd left him at an animal hospital where a friend of my mother's works. Told my mother's friend to have the vet put the dog down. The friend called my mother. A few days and a few thousand dollars later, Shiloh had a new home.

I lift the pillow and Shiloh nudges me again. It's hard to stay irritated when a three-legged dog is smiling at you.

10

Another weekend has slipped by and I am back at work. It's noon on Tuesday and I am fantasizing about murder. I have counted the clients I have to get through before Saturday ends. Some people mark off the days of the week. I mark off people. I have 51 left. I don't think I'm going to make it without killing one of them.

Becky has just left. She was my 10 a.m. client, in for a color and cut. Becky is a diabetic. She had skipped breakfast and didn't bother to bring a snack or drink with her.

Diabetes is not new to Becky. She certainly should have foreseen the outcome of her stupidity. At 10:30, she was sitting with color on her head and suddenly tells me she thinks she might pass out. Her words were slurred and she sounded drunk. I ran across to the donut shop and got her an orange juice. Then a cool, wet towel.

While I played doctor for Becky, Cathy, my 10:30 haircut, sat waiting for me. Cathy pointedly checked her watch three times in 10 minutes. She had places to be. Let Becky pass out with a head full of color.

I managed to get things under control without anyone dying or having a tantrum, although I did consider squirting color in Cathy's narrow, judgmental eyes. I used what should have been my lunch break, from 11:30 to 11:55, to play catch-up. Now I'm back on schedule and my noon client is walking in the door. Her plastic smile makes me want to barf. I am doomed.

Joan is having a perm, cut, blow dry, and half her face waxed. She could have been the bearded woman in a circus freak show. I've suggested that she get her hormone levels checked. Her testosterone must be off the charts. She tells me it's just a consequence of "the change". I'd rather have my period than a beard.

I get Joan's perm wound. As I'm drizzling the solution onto each rod, Joan says, "I am starving!"

Roxie catches my eye. She lifts an eyebrow and smirks. She's had an easy day with easy clients and she's finding immense joy in my misery.

"I'm a little hungry, too," I say.

"I should have brought a sandwich with me."

"We have a tin of cookies out back, if you want one with your coffee."

"Would you mind running over to that sub shop around the corner for me?"

I am momentarily stunned into silence. I make an odd kind of strangled noise while I search for a polite way to answer. Get her a sandwich? Like I'm an errand girl?

"I'm sorry," I finally manage. "I have another client due any minute."

"Maybe just a donut from across the street? I'll buy you one as well."

I want to punch her. I want to shove an entire box of donuts down her throat and watch her choke on them. "I have no time," I say. "I have no breaks today."

"Oh."

"But we have menus in the desk drawer. A few of the places deliver, if you want to call."

"Well, no…"

My next client comes in. Kayla is 5-years-old and is being dragged in by her frazzled mother. The mother looks at me and says, "She's in a mood today."

I stifle a groan and work on my fake smile. "I'll be with you in one minute," I say.

Turning back to Joan, I say, "Help yourself to the coffee. You can have a seat in the back room for now."

She looks at me as if she wants to protest. What is she going to do? Demand I act as her waitress?

Kayla shrieks as her mother attempts to pull off her jacket. Joan decides she has no leverage and is probably better off in the back room. She gets up with a huff.

The rest of the day goes on this way; a steady stream of irritations. My thoughts drift to our local serial killer, The Mass Avenger, and I think maybe I can relate. I'm not that far from a mass killing spree myself.

≈

It is 8:30 on a Thursday morning and I am dressed and ready to walk out the door. My dogs are not happy. I work late tonight and don't have to be at work until noon. They know this. We are supposed to lay around on Thursday mornings. They get lots of attention, sometimes even a walk. This morning they got rushed out the door with a demand to pee.

Cassady is rebelling. She stands on the back deck and stares at me for five minutes, flat out refusing to obey the pee command. I have to pick her up and carry her out to the grass. She finally does her thing, though I'm sure it is more to satisfy her bladder than to please me.

My parents have the day off and I promised to go with them to visit my father's parents. They had asked me in a moment of weakness, after feeding me the most amazing homemade fudge. Not a fair tradeoff; fudge for a couple of hours with my grandparents. I got cheated.

My grandparents live in assisted-living housing in Plymouth. They have a nice one-bedroom apartment, in which they attempted to fit all their belongings from their four-bedroom home. My grandmother collects Hummels and fancy china teacups, which are now crammed on every available surface. My grandfather collects *Life* magazines from the beginning of time. Stacks of them are decaying in rows beneath the living room windows. You can't get to them without climbing over aging furniture hidden beneath green floral throw covers.

I leave my dogs with apologies and treats, then head to my parents' house. I follow them in own car, since I have to go straight to work afterward. Talk about a torturous day.

My grandmother opens the door and embraces me in a cloud of Jean Nate. She is wearing a pale blue dress, a pearl necklace, and matching pearl earrings. She has her feet crammed into matching blue heels and her nylons are wrinkled at the ankles. Her lips are painted red, her eyelids pale blue, and her cheeks are dotted with too much blush.

Olivia, my grandmother, gives my mother the same stiff hug I received. Then she gets hold of my dad and crushes him against her sagging and rather immense boobs.

"Come in," Olivia says, as she ushers us inside. "It's been so long. We don't get to see you often enough."

Less than two minutes together and she's already laying on the guilt. I squeeze around the furniture and perch on the edge of the uncomfortable couch. "You look great, Grandma," I say.

Olivia prefers to be called "Grandmother" or "Meme". I refuse to use either. She fixes her milky brown eyes on me. "You look tired, Lilly."

I bite my lip. I hate that she calls me Lilly. I've never been called Lilly by anyone else. I think she does it to get back at me, because I won't call her Meme. "I am a little tired," I say. "I worked late last night."

"You're still designing hair?" Olivia asks.

She says "designing hair" with an air of disdain. "Yes," I say on a sigh.

"Where's Dad?" my father asks. He has managed to maneuver around the furniture and join me on the couch.

My grandmother flushes and her blush glows brighter. She waves down the hall. "He's having stomach issues. He'll be with us momentarily."

"He's okay?"

"Oh, yes. He insisted on fried eggs this morning. The man can be as stubborn as a mule."

My mother is standing behind my grandmother. She makes silly faces at me. I chuckle and look away. My mother says, "Have you made coffee, Olivia?"

"Not yet, dear. I wanted to wait, to be sure you would come."

We have never not shown up, yet my grandmother uses that line every chance she gets. My mother smiles and says, "I'll make it, then."

"Thank you, dear." Olivia eases into her rocking chair. She looks at my father and says, "Theodore, you've lost weight." The words are like an accusation. My dad has never been overweight. And he is not now underweight. He shakes his head. "I haven't," he replies. "Probably just the baggy sweatshirt." "Well, yes, that could be," Olivia says. She frowns and studies the sweatshirt with dismay.

The toilet flushes and my grandfather ambles down the hall. He is wearing a crisp white dress shirt and a yellow striped tie that hangs crooked. A spot of drool leaks from the corner of his mouth.

We spend the next two hours listening to tales of the heroic Benjamin and selfless Victoria. To hear my grandmother speak, you would think that my cousins are superheroes. I finally escape, only to exchange one pit of hell for another. I find it unreasonable that the world expects me to get through the entire evening at work without killing someone.

11

The Mass Avenger spreads the newspaper on his kitchen table. He props his elbows on the table and leans forward. His mother would have slapped him for this. Elbows didn't belong on the kitchen table. Neither did newspapers. Only food and dishes. He is a barbarian. No manners.

Now and then, he still hears his mother's voice chastising him. She'd lull him into a calm, tuck him in at night, praise him for the A's on his report card. Let him believe that he measured up, that she loved him. Then she'd turn around and call him an idiot. Tell him that he would never amount to anything.

She'd held all the power. She could love him or ruin him at her will. If he cried, she would laugh and call him a sissy. Tell him that he would never be man enough to handle a woman.

In the end, he'd proven her wrong.

The Mass Avenger reads the article a second time. He beams with pride as he reads the details. The police have finally come clean. Sara Walsh had been The Mass Avenger's fourth victim. He chuckles at that. They'd missed one.

Much to the dismay of the citizens of Massachusetts, the police still have no leads on this savage serial killer. If only they knew. He is just like the rest of them. He blends in. Shops with them, works with them. Slices them to pieces.

I was raised a vegan. No one in my communal world ate meat. We didn't eat ice cream and I didn't know that junk food like Twinkies and Fruit Loops even existed. When I was 13, in a moment of true rebellion, a friend and I walked to a local diner and ordered cheeseburgers. I got halfway through mine and threw up on the table. I never ate meat again. Nor did I go back to that diner.

At age 12, I discovered ice cream at a friend's birthday party. It's been my guilty pleasure ever since. I also eat eggs and cheese and occasionally wear leather. I'm surprised that my parents haven't disowned me.

Today is Monday. I'm sitting on a bench with my longtime friend Kate. We're eating ridiculously large ice cream cones while we watch the cows graze in the field. The farm is one of the last of a dying breed. Family-owned, their ice cream is made daily and sold to a steady stream of customers. They also sell their own milk, cream, and butter. My house is five minutes away and it's incredibly difficult to live so close to such temptation.

Kate takes a lick of her double chocolate ice cream and gives a contented sigh. "Comfort food," she says. "I needed this."

My mocha ice cream is quickly disappearing. "Me, too," I say.

"Still hate your job?" Kate asks.

"Yes, but I think I hate people more."

"You wouldn't hate them so much if they didn't talk."

I laugh because she's right. Kate is a massage therapist. Her clients are more likely to moan than speak. Still, she has her days when people shred her nerves. She understands.

Kate also understands what it's like to grow up in an unconventional family. We bonded over that issue and we've been best friends ever since.

I spent my younger years sheltered from the larger world. I lived, played, and was schooled in a commune. We lived on a huge farm. Five homes, holding 12 families and a few assorted strays, stood in the center. We grew most of our own food and a couple of the women sewed most of our clothing. Long tie-dyed dresses and matching bandanas. At night, we would all sit around a campfire. Some people would play instruments. We'd all sing.

Life was pretty simple back then. Sometimes I long for that simplicity now.

When I was 10, our commune life began to fall apart. Two families chose to move out to San Francisco. Losing them made maintaining the farm much more difficult. Then one of the men was arrested for possession of marijuana and LSD. The adults went a little nuts, ripping plants out of the ground. At the time, I didn't know they were marijuana plants.

After that, social services paid us a couple of visits. Nothing came of it, though the adults were tense all the time. The mood changed. Soon afterward, my parents packed up and we moved to a regular neighborhood. I went to a regular school. Talk about culture shock.

Fitting in at junior high, when you'd spent your life with hippies on a commune, was no easy task. That's when I met Kate. We were misfits together.

Kate has three brothers and one sister. She'd thought of her family as normal. She fought with her sister, was teased by her brothers. Her father was a lawyer, made good money. Her mother stayed at home with the kids. In many ways, Kate's early childhood was also sheltered.

Shortly after Kate turned 10, her parents began to argue frequently. One day, Kate walked into her parents' bedroom and caught her father trying on her mother's frilly blouses. He grew his hair and experimented with her mother's curling iron. Before long, he was dabbling with makeup. Lipstick and blush. Pink nail polish.

Kate's mother pretended not to notice. Privately, Kate's parents fought. In front of the kids, they behaved as if all fathers painted their nails on Saturdays.

Months went by. Kate's father began wearing dresses around the house. One day, he did his makeup, his hair, put on a dress and heels, and went out. When he came back home that night, he asked Kate's mother to start calling him Rhonda instead of Ron.

Kate now has two mothers. Her parents still live together, still share a bed. Her father, Rhonda, dresses and speaks like a woman. He – she – is taking hormone therapy but has not had surgery. He is still anatomically male, though he lives life as a woman.

Kate understands how hard it can be to fit in.

We are almost done with our ice cream cones when Kate says, "What do you think of this serial killer that's on the loose?"

"The Mass Avenger," I say with a groan. "My dad wanted to escort me home from work at night."

"It's nice that he still wants to protect you."

"Yeah, I suppose."

"You have to admit, it's creepy to think that this guy could be anywhere near us."

"He could be one of your clients."

Kate laughs. "That wouldn't be a stretch. I have some odd ones."

"I can relate."

"Do you think you'd know?"

"If one of my clients was this serial killer?"

"Yeah," Kate says. "Do you think you'd be able to tell?"

I consider my male clients. Many are nice, normal guys. Some are complete jerks. A few tip the scale in favor of crazy. "I doubt it," I say. "You?"

Kate shakes her head. "One of my regulars was arrested last week for beating his wife. I never suspected."

"What would you have done if you'd known?"

Kate looks at me as if this question surprises her. "I don't know," she says. "I definitely would have refused him as a client."

Kate harbors no murderous fantasies. If I had a wife-beater as a client, I would probably want to stab him in the jugular. Or tie him to the chair and burn him with my steaming curling iron. Unhealthy thoughts. I keep them to myself. Not everything is meant to be shared.

*

Another Wednesday evening is here. Men's night. Being surrounded by men makes me think of the serial killer. What are the chances that he would come here for his haircut? Kate's question has me thinking. Would I know if I had a killer in my chair?

My 5 p.m. client is Billy, a 13-year-old boy. Patty, his aunt, is a regular client. She has made the appointment and brings him in. I've never met Billy or his parents. Patty has a hard edge and doesn't come off as the most nurturing person on earth. One look at Billy tells me that this is probably a family trait.

Billy has sandy blonde, unruly hair that looks as if someone has cut it with toenail clippers. He's thin and, though clean, somehow looks dirty. His face is mean, which is an odd thing to say about a 13-year-old.

I tell Billy to follow me down to the sink. He stands by the desk and folds his arms over his chest. "I don't want you to wash my hair," he tells me.

"It's part of the service," I say through a forced smile. "And it only takes a minute."

"No."

Billy scowls at me. I look to Patty for help. She shrugs. "Can't you just cut it dry?" she asks. "Spray it with water or something?"

I sigh. Easy to see who is in control here. Hair is much easier to cut wet. Hair that has dried, particularly unruly hair, is difficult. It doesn't sit right. It's more work. I look at Billy's scowl and don't bother with these arguments. I point to my chair. "Have a seat," I say.

"Cut it short," Patty says.

"No," Billy growls.

"Don't be such a little bastard," Patty tells him.

"I don't want it short."

"Your mother wants it short."

"Too bad for her."

Normally, in these situations, I listen to the paying adult. I glance at Billy. He narrows his eyes and glares at me. I turn back to Patty. She shrugs. "Do whatever," she says.

I have never been as uncomfortable with any client as I am with Billy. He has these razor-sharp brown eyes that I swear could bore holes through a person. Maybe if I can get the kid to talk about something he likes, he'll ease up on the death stare. "Do you play any sports at school?" I ask.

Billy rolls his eyes. "That's for losers."

"Okay. What do you like to do, then?"

"Shoot."

"Shoot?"

"Yeah," Billy says. "My father takes me out. I love shooting his gun. He's taking me hunting this winter."

Hunting. Yuck. Not a topic I do well. "Do you target shoot?" I ask.

"Yeah. My dad lets me shoot those targets that are shaped like people. I shoot them in the chest, right in the heart. Once I hit right between the eyes. That was the best."

I'm not sure how to respond to this. Patty is standing nearby, her hands stuffed in the pockets of her jeans, looking totally unfazed by the conversation. "You're a good shot, then," I say.

"I have a knife."

"A knife? Like a pocketknife?"

"A nice one. My dad gave it to me. It's really sharp."

"Okay. I'm not much into guns or knives."

"I'd like to stab you with it," Billy says. "Stick it in your stomach, twist it and watch your guts spill out."

I stop cutting and take a step back. Patty whacks Billy in the back of the head. "What's wrong with you?" she asks. "Knock it off. I'm going to tell your mother what you said."

"I don't care," Billy says.

He grins at me. I stop talking to him and finish the haircut as fast as I can. Patty hands me the money and mutters, "Sorry about that. He's a handful."

I just look at her, not sure how to respond. A handful? Billy is a killer in the making. His father should be taking him to a psychiatrist, not on a hunting trip.

I can't help but think of our local serial killer. Is this how he started out? Could Billy's father be The Mass Avenger?

By 8 p.m., I have stopped thinking about Billy and the serial killer. My legs ache, I'm tired, and my main thought is how many more haircuts I need to do before I can go home. Then Jason walks in the door.

I have my fake smile in place and stifle the groan that bubbles up. Jason is one of my newer clients. He comes in every three weeks to maintain the perfection that is his hair. The last time he'd been in my chair, he'd seriously irritated me with his comments about my lack of a wedding ring and his unblinking stare. This must be my night for crazies.

I wash Jason's hair while he stares up at me. I try to ignore him. I wonder if he's checking out my nose hairs but refrain from asking.

Once in my chair, Jason continues his stare through the mirror. Since he snapped at me the last time, when I asked what he did for work, I avoid personal conversation. We talk about the unusually warm October weather. A song he likes comes on the radio. Bruce Springsteen. He gives me the rundown on all Springsteen's albums, which are the best and which were poor efforts. I listen without offering my opinion. It's easier that way.

I'm happy to get Jason out of my chair. I want to sterilize myself when he leaves. The question Kate asked me earlier in the week floats back in my mind. Would I know if a client was a serial killer? Billy will almost definitely kill someone not far in his future. Maybe more than one person. Maybe he'll be a serial killer.

If a prerequisite for becoming a serial killer is creepiness, Jason scores at the top of the charts. He doesn't scare me but he sure is uncomfortable to be around. Not a suave killer like Ted Bundy. More like Jeffrey Dahmer.

I grimace as I realize that I am comparing my client to a cannibal serial killer. Now I'm on edge. Renee's client is telling her how to barbeque chicken to perfection and I feel like throwing up. I don't ask Jason about his favorite recipes.

12

My Saturday morning passes almost enjoyably, filled mostly with clients that I actually like. Then Dawn, my 12:30 client, walks in the door and just like that my day turns to shit. Dawn is neurotic. She's loud, opinionated, and requires constant attention. Dawn has probably always been this way but five years ago her life tipped upside down. Since then she continues to get crazier, while everyone in her life walks on eggshells.

Shortly after the attack on September 11, Dawn's son Brian enlisted in the Army. He couldn't wait to go to Iraq, to rip apart the country and people he thought responsible for our loss. Brian got his wish and was soon in the heart of the horror. He saw things no 18-year-old kid should see. Did things no one should be forced to do. He had yet to make sense of his hormones, much less make sense of the world.

Brian served 17 months in Iraq. He came home a different kid. He refused to leave the house. Refused to see his friends. Three weeks after arriving home, Brian shot himself in the head, in the middle of the day, while standing on the sidewalk outside an Army recruiting center.

Dawn turned Brian's bedroom into a shrine. All of his things are exactly the way he left them. She set up a shelf with his photos, his high school awards, his trophies. She lights candles there for him every night, talks to him as if he is in the room with her.

Her husband wants to move. They rent an apartment and he wants to buy a house. Dawn refuses. She won't leave Brian's room behind.

Dawn has another son, a couple of years older. He's on his own. Dawn rarely talks about him. She talks about Brian constantly. Family and strangers receive equal time with her Brian stories. She can't give up the ghost. Can't let him go.

We all feel sympathy for Dawn. I can't imagine experiencing that kind of tragedy. Yet, my tolerance can only be pushed so far. Dawn needs help and I am not a psychiatrist.

Dawn has a high-lift blonde color. The process takes about two hours. I wish I could stuff a towel in her mouth, keep her quiet for a while. Or dissolve a few Valium in her coffee. The last thing she needs is the caffeine she's sucking down at an astonishing rate.

I am about halfway through getting the color on Dawn's head when she starts fidgeting. "I need a cigarette," she says.

Dawn is a heavy smoker. Her house must be enveloped in a constant gray cloud. We don't allow smoking inside, so she hangs out the back door while her color processes.

"I'll be finished in a few minutes," I say. "I can't stop now or half your head will process faster than the other half."

She fidgets some more. "Halloween is coming up," she says.

"Do you have plans?" I ask.

"I hate the holiday now. Brian loved Halloween. It was always his favorite holiday. Even when he got too old to trick-or-treat, he'd dress up and pass out the candy."

"You must have a lot of good memories of those days."

"It hurts too much. Mark and I have been fighting. He doesn't understand."

Mark is Dawn's husband. It's strange that she would say he doesn't understand. Brian was his son, too. "We all deal with grief differently," I say.

"He tells me I need to let Brian go. How can I do that? How can he even ask me to?"

I have no answer. Well, no, I'd actually like to tell her that I agree with her husband. But I know better. I make sympathetic noises and she continues talking. Finally, I get the color on her head and she scoots out the back to smoke a half pack of Winston cigarettes.

A few minutes later, I go out back to check Dawn's color. She has one of Andrea's clients trapped by the door and is force-feeding her Brian's story. I shoot the woman an apologetic look as I slip away.

By the time Dawn leaves, I am wallowing in depression. A giant black void of misery has sucked me into its depths. I should probably call the suicide hotline. Instead, I turn to my next client.

Dennis is 15, blonde, skinny, and devious. He's like an evil Dennis the Menace. He is the only boy in his family, an accident. His two sisters are 12 and 14 years older. People think his parents spoil him for that reason. In truth, his father is simply too old and tired to deal with him and his mother wanted a boy so badly that she has placed him on a pedestal too high for anyone to reach.

As I'm walking with Dennis toward the sinks, I hear one of Roxie's clients say, "I don't ever want my appointment at the same time as that woman again."

That woman she is referring to is Dawn. Roxie's client rants about how Dawn monopolized the entire salon with her loud and depressing talk. She folds her arms across her chest and glares at Roxie. "Make sure I am never booked on the same day with her."

We have a running list of clients who do not want to be in the salon at the same time as someone else. Divorced couples. Ex-wives and current wives. People having affairs. Neighbors feuding. The list is constantly evolving and impossible to maintain.

I wash Dennis' hair while he holds his cell phone up and text messages his friends. Someone sends him a file. A naked girl. He's holding the phone up, so I can see. I want to stick the water hose down his throat and drown the little bastard.

Dennis settles in my chair, still grinning. He thinks he is a stud and that he has shocked me. He's like an annoying little gnat that I want to swat and watch splatter against the wall.

"I broke into my sister Lisa's house yesterday," Dennis tells me.

I lower my scissors because I want to jam them into the side of his head. "You what?"

Dennis laughs. "You can't tell my parents. I'll tell them you're a liar."

"Why would you break into your sister's house?"

"I wanted to."

Of course. What other reason exists for a self-involved, predatory teen? I don't respond. This irritates Dennis. He wants to gloat.

"She's a bitch," Dennis says. "She tries to tell me what to do. She thinks she's so smart that everyone should listen to her."

"Doesn't Lisa have a Master's degree in economics or something?"

"So?"

"That means she is smart," I say. "Maybe you should listen to her."

Dennis glares at me. He flips his phone open and text messages someone. I don't look at what he's typing. It's probably about me. If I see it, I'll definitely want to kill the little shit.

The ever-present background noise in the salon has invaded my nervous system. A dozen voices at once. Blow dryers. The radio. I feel like a guitar string pulled too tight. The sound I make would be horribly high-pitched. Then I would snap in half. If I was a guitar string, that is.

I'm standing here, comparing myself to a guitar string. This indicates problems I am not ready to face.

I finish Dennis and get him out of my chair. As he walks out, I breathe a sigh of relief. Only a few more clients before I get a weekend reprieve.

The four of us – Roxie, Andrea, Renee, and I – are staying to do each other's hair after work. Roxie wants pink streaks. Andrea wants a perm. Renee and I both want highlights. None of us wants to stay in this place after a long Saturday but it's better than coming in on our day off. We absolutely do not want to see the salon on our day off.

When we finally lock the door behind the last client, Andrea rushes out to the back room. She reappears holding two bottles of wine. "I figured, if we have to stay late," she says, "we could at least have some fun!"

"I'm starving," Roxie says. "Want to have pizza delivered?"

We eat pizza, drink wine, rant about our day. And laugh. I laugh so hard my stomach hurts. By the time we get around to each other's haircuts, we're all a little buzzed. Our cuts might be crooked but none of us care.

*

Sunday morning is here and I should be happy. No work. An entire day with my very sexy husband and three spoiled dogs. The sun is out and the temperature is supposed to reach the mid 60s. Not bad for an October day in Massachusetts.

I am not happy. In fact, I've been whining a little this morning. The fact that I am experiencing some serious hormonal mood swings doesn't help. But that is not the cause of my unhappiness.

Scott comes in the door with the three dogs. He's had them out in the backyard. He was tossing a Frisbee for Jack while Neal and Cassady chased the blowing leaves. The dogs run for the water bowl. Scott turns to me and asks, "Are you ready?"

This is the source of my unhappiness. We are meeting Elyse, Scott's daughter, for breakfast. She called yesterday and invited Scott. I was not included in that invitation. As far as Elyse is concerned, I am a piece of baggage that comes along with her father. Since her father isn't exactly high on her list of priorities, that puts me somewhere below ground level.

What's even more unnerving is that Elyse never calls unless she wants something. The last time we heard from her was in August, right before college started. She wanted money for books. And new clothes. She couldn't be seen in college wearing her high school clothes. Working, earning money for the things she wants, is something she has yet to contemplate. Why work when you can put your hand out and someone fills it with cash? Her mother raised her to expect the world to take care of her.

Scott is looking at me, waiting for an answer. "I know you don't want to go," he says. "But I'd really like you with me." He fastens his killer green eyes on me and gives me a devilish grin. "I promise I'll make it up to you later."

Even without that promise, I couldn't say no. Elyse is his daughter, whether I like her or not. And he doesn't ask much of me. But that promise sealed the deal and I plan on holding him to it.

A half-hour later, we are seated at Friendly's restaurant. I'm sipping herbal tea and Scott and Elyse both have coffee. We've ordered and an uncomfortable silence has fallen over our table. Elyse is wearing skintight jeans and a clingy blouse that exposes a little too much cleavage for breakfast with her father. Her dark hair is long and straight, hanging midway down her back. I wonder if she goes to a stylist regularly and, if so, if she treats that stylist like another of her servants in life.

Scott fiddles with his silverware. "How are your classes going?" he asks Elyse.

Elyse has plump lips that are painted burgundy. Those lips now form a childish pout. "That's kind of why I wanted to see you," she says.

Scott and I exchange a look. I keep my mouth shut and stare deep into my tea mug. Scott's voice is calm and relaxed. "Okay," he says. "Something wrong?"

"Nothing's wrong," Elyse says. "Actually, things are great. I'm really excited."

She doesn't look excited but I don't mention that. I wisely remain silent. Scott has a look of confusion. He shakes his head slightly, then smiles. "That's great. What are you excited about?"

"I know what I want to do with my life."

"Yeah? What did you decide?"

"I'm going to be a model."

More silence. Scott picks up his coffee mug, puts it back down. "That's a tough career," he finally tells her.

"I know," Elyse says, in a childish, reproving tone. "Chelsea and I have been talking about it for a long time. We've been wanting to do it. We met this guy at a party a few weeks ago and he said he could introduce us to people. Get us started."

"This guy?" Scott asks. "Does he have a name?"

"Jonathan."

"Jonathan have a last name? And what does Jonathan do that gives him connections in the modeling industry?"

"Jonathan Dyer, I think. Or Dwyer. Something like that. He's into photography. He knows a lot of people in New York."

"New York."

Scott says *New York* like a man who knows he's stepping onto a minefield. I fill my mouth with tea so I won't be tempted to speak.

"Yes, New York," Elyse says with a touch of defiance. "So I'm quitting school. It's stupid, anyway. I'm wasting my time learning shit I don't care about. Chelsea and I are moving to New York and pretty soon you'll be seeing our photos on magazine covers."

Her temerity amazes me. Elyse is a pretty girl, I will give her that. But millions of women are pretty and they don't get their pictures on magazine covers. I look at Scott. His jaw is hanging open. He glances at me, sighs.

"You don't think I can hack it as a model," Elyse says, "do you?"

"It's not as simple as you're making it sound," Scott tells her. "A modeling career doesn't take off overnight. Living in New York isn't cheap. And you're running off because some guy you barely know claims he knows people. What people? Can you be any more vague?"

I am thinking about all the money we will save if Elyse quits college and runs off to New York. The brat only agreed to go to college because she didn't want to work. We're wasting our money. I know this is a bad attitude. I should be supporting Scott, which means supporting his daughter. Guilt sucks me in and, before I know it, I break my vow of silence.

"You should stay in school," I tell Elyse. "Education is important, even for models. There are agencies right in Boston. Get a portfolio done and find an agency here to represent you."

Elyse glares at me with narrowed eyes. Her nose crunches and her lips pucker like she's just swallowed sour milk. I have overstepped my boundaries and given advice. The princess is pissed.

"Jonathan has connections in New York, not Boston," Elyse says through her sneer. "Besides, New York is where all the action is. I don't want small-shit jobs. I want to make it big. And I will."

Scott has had enough. He shakes his head but manages to keep the anger from his voice. "Sounds like you already made up your mind," he says.

"I have."

"What does your mother say about this?

"She had a fit and we're not speaking." Elyse slumps in her chair. A spoiled child. "She's a bitch, anyway. You know that."

"Don't talk about your mother that way."

I glance around the noisy restaurant. Sunday morning church crowd. Where is our waitress? Where is our food? We desperately need a distraction over here.

"Whatever," Elyse mutters. "So Chelsea and I are leaving Thursday."

"You're driving?"

"Yeah, my car is better than Chelsea's. But I'm thinking of selling it when we get there. I won't need it in the city, you know? Everyone takes the subway there."

"Be careful. It's a tough world."

"You can probably get some money back on my tuition for this semester. You know, since it hasn't been that long."

"I'll look into it."

Elyse leans closer to Scott. Her pouty lips and exposed cleavage are more suited to seducing a boyfriend that conning her dad. She says, "I know I'm going to make it huge."

"I hope so," Scott says.

"But mom got all pissy and cut me off. I need some money to get me through, until I land a few jobs."

"No."

Scott's reply is quick and firm. No wiggle room there. He hadn't even glanced my way. No need to confer.

Elyse straightens her spine. "Why not? You'll be getting money back from the college. It's not like I'm asking for money you wouldn't be spending on me anyway."

"No."

"You don't believe in me, either?"

"I don't believe you're making a rational, responsible decision."

Elyse scrunches her face and shoots daggers at Scott. "You don't think I'm smart enough to take care of myself?"

"Obviously not, considering you're still asking me for money."

Elyse grabs her Guess purse from the table. "I changed my mind about eating breakfast with you. And I won't ever ask for your help again!"

Elyse storms off. Scott swipes a hand over his face and looks at me. "She'll get over it," I say.

Scott shakes his head. "I don't think I care anymore."

Our waitress finally arrives balancing a tray full of food. As she sets the plate of French toast in front of Elyse's place, Scott says, "She had to leave suddenly. Can you put that in a take-out box for us?"

"Sure," our waitress says. She sets our plates down and picks Elyse's back up. "I'll package this up for you and bring it right out."

After she walks away, Scott says, "The kids love French toast."

"The kids" are our three dogs and they give Scott a lot more love than his human daughter.

Despite a rocky beginning, Scott and I enjoy a leisurely breakfast. As we're leaving, I say, "I need to stop at PetSmart on the way home. We're almost out of dog food."

"Jack needs new tennis balls, too."

"You know," I say, "if Elyse really does drop out of school, we could use some of that money to go on vacation."

Scott grins at me. "Do you have somewhere specific in mind?"

"Aruba, maybe?"

Scott gives a moan of appreciation. "Endless beaches. White sand. Lazy days in the sun. I'm in."

"We should wait, though. Elyse will probably change her mind once she realizes how expensive New York is."

"Once she quits, I'm done. I won't pay for her to go back to school. And if she takes me to court, they'll have to arrest me because I still won't pay."

He backs me up against our car and kisses me. For a moment, I forget that we are in a public parking lot. When he pulls away, he says, "Let's go to PetSmart, then go home and plan our vacation. I can't think of anything better than a week alone with you on the beach."

⁂

The Mass Avenger parks his van in the crowded lot. He is always annoyed by the quantity of people out on the weekend. He needs his space. Crowds irritate him.

As he steps out of the van, he spots a couple exiting PetSmart. They are holding hands, smiling. The man is tall, rugged, a little too good looking. The type of guy who never experiences rejection. Women flock to him, their power diminished by his appeal.

The Mass Avenger's eyes travel over the woman. She looks familiar. As they move closer, he realizes who she is. His hands absently travel through his hair. His stylist.

Skye is a pretty woman. Sexy, if he is being honest. But she doesn't flaunt it. In fact, she doesn't even seem aware of her power.

Something about Skye had captured his interest from that first moment he'd seen her. Not her looks, though that is enough to draw any man in. He can't name the quality she possesses, isn't even sure if he is right. Yet, his gut tells him that Skye is a lot like him. That she'd understand.

The Mass Avenger watches the couple disappear into the sporty black car. He experiences a brief pang of something like jealousy. Silly, he tells himself. She's probably another dirty tease, just like the rest of them. He shakes his head, as if trying to shake her out of his mind. Then he slams his van door and strides across the parking lot.

PetSmart is jammed with customers. A bunch have brought their dogs. An outing for the spoiled pets. A beagle has taken a shit on the floor. The Mass Avenger turns away in disgust.

He works his way around the throng of shoppers. Against the far wall, he finds what he is looking for. A portable chain link kennel. It is 6 feet long by 4 feet wide. Big enough for most people to lie down and sleep in. Four feet high. Not tall enough to stand, which is good. A person would have to hunch over or kneel and crawl to move around. The thing costs way more than he wants to spend. He frowns but decides it's worth the investment.

The Mass Avenger pays for the cage and takes it out to his van. He's smiling as he loads it into the back. He'll set it up in his garage. Bolt it to the floor so it won't move. Attach a heavy-duty lock to the door.

He climbs into the van, still smiling. He'd been unsatisfied with Sara. The entire process had been too quick. She'd succumbed completely. He could have done anything, taken his time. But he'd had to end it sooner than he'd wanted, simply because he'd had nowhere to keep her.

The cage will be their new home. He can keep them for days. Maybe even weeks. He can get to know them. Play with them. They'll die knowing who really holds the power.

Now all he needs is to find his first guest.

13

It's Monday afternoon and I am at my parents' house. My mother taught four yoga classes earlier in the day. She has also managed to handle eight dogs and chop vegetables for dinner. Despite all that, she is more energetic than I am and all I've done is lie around with my three dogs most of the day. We watched a cooking show on the Food Channel and a documentary on volcanoes. All the excitement put my dogs to sleep, so I left them napping at home while I came to see my mother.

I follow my mother into the living room, where she lights a few candles. Turning to me, she says, "Sandalwood."

"They smell nice," I say.

"The scent is calming. You should take some, burn them at home."

"Are you trying to tell me something?"

My mother gives me that all-knowing look of serenity. "You have been a tad high strung these past few months."

I collapse onto the couch. "I know," I say. Greta, a spunky collie mix, jumps up beside me. Zena ambles over and looks at me. I shove over to the edge of the couch and she joins me and Greta.

My mother chuckles. "Zena doesn't know that she's not a lap dog."

"I've noticed."

"She's really a very good girl. It's been hard to find her a home, though, because she's so large."

"Scott really loves her."

"Zena is quite enamored of him, as well."

I scratch behind Zena's ear. Her beautiful brown eyes are fixed on me. "I think I'll take her home. She and Jack get along well. He'll have a playmate closer to his size."

"Weren't you adamant about not doing that?"

"She's grown on me," I say. "Besides, Scott had a rough weekend. He deserves to be spoiled a little."

"What happened with Scott?"

I tell my mother about our Sunday breakfast with Elyse. My mother scowls as I describe her behavior. My mother has always said that Elyse has bad karma.

My mother sits in a chair that looks a little like a cocoon. She's wearing a dress with long sleeves that flare out at the elbows. The pattern is earth tones with lace accents. The dress stops at her ankles, where it meets a pair of low-heeled boots I know are not made of leather. Her hair is brown but not brown. She has too many shades of gold and red mixed in to define her color properly. Sitting there, my mother looks like some sort of oracle. I feel like we should be on a desert mountain and she should be telling me what my future holds.

"Poor Scott," my mother says. "Is he okay?"

"He's sick of it," I say. "All Elyse does is use him and he knows that. He was hoping that college would be good for her, that she'd grow up. That doesn't seem to be the case."

"It will take a lot more than a paid college tuition to make that girl grow up."

"I agree."

We talk about Elyse a little more. My mother doesn't ask more about Scott. She believes that his feelings are his own and that he should decide when and whether to share them.

"On the bright side," I say, "Scott and I decided that, if we don't have to pay for Elyse's college, we're going to take a vacation."

My mother claps her hands together like a happy child. "Wonderful! You both deserve to get away."

"We're thinking about Aruba. Maybe in January."

"Good for you! Your father and I will take the dogs, of course. They will be fine here."

"Thanks, mom."

Later, I help my mother bread the tofu she'd been marinating. She makes her own breading, with crumbs from fresh whole grain bread and a lot of herbs and spices. As we're lining the pieces onto the baking sheet, my mother says, "I spoke with Marianne yesterday."

Marianne is Scott's mother. Our parents have known each other since before Scott and I got married. Surprisingly, they get along well and occasionally do things together. It's not unusual for my mother and Marianne to speak, although, for some reason, it still makes me slightly wary. Logically, I know that the four of them have better – and more enjoyable – things to discuss than Scott and me. Yet a piece of me can't help feeling like he and I are troublesome teens and our parents have to get together to discuss how to best handle us.

"How is Marianne these days?" I ask. "We haven't been down their way in over a month."

Marianne and Tom live in Hyannis, which is on Cape Cod. Going there means crossing one of the bridges that are always flooded with traffic. As the cooler weather comes, the traffic dies down some. Visiting them in the winter is much easier, since fewer people want to be on the ocean when the air temperature is 30 degrees.

"She's doing well," my mother tells me. "Her neighborhood has been the source of much excitement."

"Really? What's been going on?"

"The police have been there questioning everyone on the street. Someone called in a tip that The Mass Avenger lives there."

"Seriously?"

"Yes, though it turned out to be another false lead. An older man with negative energy had some neighbors worried. Apparently, the police have been getting dozens of this type of call each day. Needless to say, Marianne was terrified for no reason."

"The cops are sure it's not that guy?"

"As sure as they can be. The man allowed them to search his home. The police questioned everyone on the street." My mother gives an uncharacteristic sigh. "That reminds me; how are things with Ken's family?"

I remember that Renee's husband's family lived next door to Sara, The Mass Avenger's last victim. "All is quiet now," I say.

"My heart goes out to that poor girl's family."

"I know. It's awful."

"I wish you'd allow your father to walk you and Renee out in the evening."

"We're fine, mom."

My mother just looks at me. I get a chill up my spine. My mother can be spooky sometimes. "Do you have some sort of premonition?" I ask. "Should I be worried?"

My mother waves her hand as if waving off the very words I'd spoken. "No, no," she says. "Nothing like that. I just worry. No matter how old you get, you will always be my little girl."

"I know, mom," I say. "And I love that you and Dad want to take care of me. But, honestly, I'm fine. Renee and I always leave together. The parking lot is well lit. And, besides, the chance is pretty slim of this serial killer getting his hair cut at our little salon."

My mother concedes, though not happily. I ease out from beneath Greta's warmth and tell her that I have to go. Zena is standing right by my heels. I pat her on the head and ask, "Want to come home with me? Scott will be there soon."

Zena's tail wags frantically. My mother laughs. I manage to fit Zena into my MINI Cooper. She sticks her head out the window while we drive. As we approach my house, her tail wags harder. Scott pulls in our driveway 30 seconds after I do. Zena practically knocks him down in her excitement. Scott's laughter and Zena's frantic tail tell me that bringing her home was the right thing to do. They belong together.

ℛ

I survived Tuesday by a narrow margin. One of my clients didn't show, two were late, and most of them irritated me. One mother dragged her teenage son in. The kid had an expression of absolute defeat on his pale face. As he sat slumped in my chair, the mother told me the kid had mono. I asked why she didn't cancel. The kid should be in bed. She told me that she couldn't stand his scraggly hair anymore and that he could go back to bed when they got home. The kid gave me a weary look. So not only is this lady an incredibly bad mother but she also exposed me to mono. Perfect.

Now it is Wednesday and I am facing another day in hell. Thankfully, I have the morning to recuperate. I'll spend it catching up on laundry and playing with my dogs. I like them better than I like most people.

Scott comes in from an early-morning run. He has both Jack and Zena with him. As he unhooks their leashes, I ask, "How did it go?"

"Great," he says. "They did well together. Definitely kept me moving!"

I give the dogs a chicken treat and tell them how proud I am. Cassady and Neal come running. They hadn't moved from their beds yet this morning, not even to pee. But the sound of a treat bag gets them right up.

I look at my two spoiled little dogs. "You haven't done anything to deserve a treat this morning," I tell them. They sit in front of me, ears perked. I know they are saying please. I give them each a treat.

Scott laughs at me. "What a mush you are."

I give a pointed look at Zena. "Yes, and you are such a hard ass."

"I guess you got me there."

Scott kisses me. He tastes like coffee, smells slightly of sweat. I lean into him. "We could have a quickie," I say.

He playfully bats me away. "I need to shower and get to work."

I give him my best sexy pout. He laughs and rolls his eyes. "Maybe we can combine a quickie with a shower," he tells me.

"I'm all for wet and soapy."

Four short hours later, I am standing behind a client who I want to kill. Denise is in my chair, talking on her cell phone. "I really need to rinse off that perm solution now," I say for the second time.

Denise looks at me and holds up one finger, like I am a child waiting for permission to speak. I want to dump a pail of water over her head. When the perm solution fries her hair because it has been left on too long, I am the one she will scream at. She won't remember that she was too busy talking on her phone to get her ass out of the chair.

I stand close and cross my arms over my chest. I am thinking about cutting the perm rods out of her hair, leaving her with stubby pieces protruding from her scalp. Finally, she punches her phone off and rises. She doesn't look the least bit contrite. In fact, she looks smug.

As I'm rinsing her hair, Denise says, "That was a business call. All kinds of craziness at the office today. They needed me to clarify a few things that couldn't wait."

She says this as if she is the CEO of a major corporation. She is the secretary in a warehouse for a local department store. I can think of no polite response, so I say nothing.

I get Denise back to my chair and squirt the neutralizing solution onto the rods in her hair. I set a timer for five minutes. Then I turn and walk over to the desk. I have nothing in particular to do there. I just need to separate myself from Denise before I knock her out with my blow dryer.

Lorraine is working today. She comes in a few hours a month to do her family and her longtime difficult clients who she doesn't want to inflict upon us. Joan, one of those difficult clients, comes in the door now. She is a tall, dyed-blonde with mean lines slashed deep in her face. Joan swings the door open wide and strides straight for Lorraine. I move to close the door but I keep my eyes fixed on the scene. I don't want to miss anything good.

Lorraine has a very sharp pair of scissors in her hand and is cutting a woman's hair. Joan barrels up to her and says, "I have had a bad day and I'm going to take it out on you because that's what you get paid for."

The entire salon stops cold. I'm pretty sure that no one is even breathing. Lorraine is remarkably skilled at dealing with people. Most times, her treatment borders on coddling them, which is how she built up such a successful business in an area overflowing with competition. But she also has a temper. And Joan's remark might have flipped the switch to set it off.

Lorraine lowers her scissors and slowly turns to face Joan. They are inches apart. Lorraine's eyes are flashing. *Danger, danger*, is what her eyes are saying.

"You pay me to do your hair," Lorraine says. "And that's it. You do not pay me to be your punching bag. Trust me, Joan, you couldn't pay me enough for that. So, if you want your hair done, I suggest you sit down quietly and wait. Otherwise, you are welcome to get the hell out."

Joan takes a step back. She mutters something that might have been an apology, then turns and slinks over to the waiting area. She buries her face behind an issue of *People* magazine.

The salon takes a collective breath. I want to high-five Lorraine but I figure that would be inappropriate. My timer dings and I'm stuck finishing Denise's hair.

The remainder of the afternoon passes uneventfully. By 5:30, the constant buzz of the salon quiets and Renee and I are left alone with our array of male clients. This appears to be my evening for shy men once again. Ross, my 6 p.m. client, struggles to get enough words out of his mouth to tell me how to cut his hair. He sits with his chin on his chest, which makes cutting incredibly difficult. Every time I gently lift his head, he drops it back down again. The thing must be on an automatic hinge or something.

My 6:30 client is Billy, a 17-year-old, acne-ridden, awkward teen. I don't ask Billy about school. I know he doesn't fit in well. He's very smart but no one in high school cares about that. He's a social outcast, a kid who's not sure where he belongs.

"Do you like music?" I ask.

"Yeah," Billy mumbles.

"What do you listen to?"

"Rock."

"Do you have a favorite band?"

"No."

I'm getting nowhere fast. I spend a couple more minutes trying to prompt conversation. Billy continues with his one-word responses. Finally, I decide that this process is too painful for both of us and I let him sit there in silence.

My 7 p.m. client is Kyle. He is one of my newer clients, also shy. He'd been here once before, just a few weeks ago. As I'm shampooing his hair, I'm spinning through the rolodex in my head, trying to remember what we had talked about. I know I'd found a topic that sparked his interest and got him talking. What the hell was it?

Keeping a few hundred clients straight in my head is challenging, to say the least. I remember the details of their hair but the rest turns into background fuzz. Sometimes I give single men wives and children. I forget which of my clients are related and what people do for a living. Occasionally, I add cheat notes next to names on the appointment calendar. I hadn't put anything next to Kyle's name.

Kyle sits in my chair. He avoids looking in the mirror. He also avoids looking at me. I keep my voice soft because I'm afraid of startling him. "Am I just trimming today?" I ask.

Kyle nods. "Last time was perfect."

That remark always unnerves me a little. I know it should be a compliment. But, when I hear those words, I immediately start panicking. What exactly did I do last time? Maybe this time I'll cut it an eighth of an inch shorter. Or use a different gel. Or the stars are aligned differently and the haircut will suffer.

As I'm dealing with my anxiety, I suddenly remember the topic that had put Kyle at ease. My memory occasionally saves me that way. I ask Kyle about his current art project and he lights up. Soon he is talking like we are old friends. I'm much more comfortable when my client is comfortable, so now we're both happy.

I finish Kyle's hair and he books his next appointment. He seems to want to ask me something more when my 7:30 walks in the door. Joe is one of those men who immediately takes over the room. Nothing shy about Joe. Kyle's presence drowns beneath Joe's shadow. He disappears out the door and I am left fighting for air as Joe sucks it out of the room.

The remainder of the evening passes quickly. By the time Renee and I have finished cleaning up, it is 9:50 and I'm beat. We lock up and step out into the night. We linger outside, letting the fresh air clear our lungs as we spout off about our day. I don't think about the serial killer until I am in my car. I remember Scott's warning to lock my doors.

I frown and push the button. Ridiculous. Nothing ever happens in Whitman.

14

I don't sleep well. Weird dreams and nightmares plague me all night. The first time I awake, I had been dreaming that all my clients were in my living room and I couldn't make them leave until I did each one's hair. I doze off and on through various hair-related nightmares. Now I'm awake again. This time, I had been dreaming that we'd turned The Cutting Edge into a drive-thru. Clients would pass their heads through the window. We'd place them on spikes attached to our chairs. Blood and gore from the bloody stumps of the necks leak onto the floor. We'd style the hair, then toss the heads into baskets to be picked up later. One client refused to part with her head. I was reaching for a chain saw when I woke.

Scott is already up. I hear him in the kitchen. The smell of coffee drifts into the bedroom. I put the pillow over my head and pretend to sleep. I don't want to open my eyes. I want the world to leave me alone.

A few minutes later, Scott lifts the pillow from my head. "Don't you need to get up?" he asks.

"What time is it?"

"7:40"

I groan. "I hate today."

"I know."

I still don't open my eyes. Opening them means the day has started and I don't want that to happen. "Maybe I'll cancel the appointment," I say.

"You'll only have to make another. You'll be cranky until you get it over with."

I hate Scott's logic. I open my eyes and frown at him. "Fine. I'll go."

Scott chuckles. "Are you down on all men today or just me?"

"All of you," I say. I shove the covers aside. "You have no idea how lucky you are to have an outtie."

I have an appointment today with my gynecologist for my annual Pap smear. I hate lying there with my feet in stirrups while getting probed with cold metal utensils. My doctor makes small talk while staring into my vagina, as if we're girlfriends hanging out at Starbucks. This is how I'll get to spend my morning. Then I'm doomed to nine hours in a salon that haunted my sleep all night. I continue to frown, feeling vindicated in my crankiness.

Scott wraps his arms around me, pulling me close. He plants sloppy kisses on my cheeks. Zena trots over to join the fun. She's licking one cheek while Scott kisses the other. I finally cave and smile at their silliness.

"For what it's worth," Scott tells me, "I'm very happy that you don't have an outtie."

He leaves me with a cup of coffee and goofy grin. I shuffle down the hall and into the shower. I shave extra close and apply lots of body lotion. I don't even primp this much in preparation for sex.

At 8:50, I am sitting in my doctor's waiting room. The office opens at 8:30 and my appointment is at 9. Three other women are also waiting. This is not a good sign.

I have brought a book but by 9:05 I have given up trying to read it. I'm being force-fed oldies on the radio, while two women across from me chatter about the pros and cons of hormone therapy. A chunky, middle-aged woman to my left takes her cell phone from her purse and makes a call. For the next 10 minutes, I listen to her complain to someone named Marge about her "lazy, sack of shit" husband.

At 9:40, I'm finally called in to the exam room. A nurse weighs me, takes my blood pressure and asks a bunch of personal questions. She hands me a white paper "shirt" with extra large armholes and an opening with no ties, along with a white cotton sheet. She tells me to strip, then disappears out the door. I pull the "shirt" on. It comes to my bellybutton and the armholes are so large that my boobs could fall out. I sit on the exam table and spread the cotton sheet over my naked lap. I realize that these items are meant to offer some semblance of privacy but I just feel silly.

The room is cold. I fidget on the paper sheet that covers the exam table. I hear my doctor's voice in the hallway. She moves past and into another exam room. Fifteen minutes pass. I fidget some more. And now I have to pee. When she finally opens the door, I want to stab her with the forceps.

Eventually I escape from the doctor's office and make it back home. My crotch is slimy with the K-Y Jelly my doctor had smeared onto her torture devices. I shower again, take the dogs outside, and make it to work five minutes before my first client.

I'm cranky and not the least bit happy with the world. Andrea, however, has it worse than me today. She has a bad cold and her voice sounds like something from an alien movie. She is leading her next client to the sinks. The woman says, "Andrea, you don't look well at all. You should go home right after you've finished with me."

I swallow back the nasty comment that threatens to spew from my mouth. As stylists, we do not have the luxury of calling in sick. We are responsible for our own schedules. Calling in sick means rearranging an entire day of clients. This is particularly difficult, since, for the most part, we are booked solid a week or two in advance. Then there are the clients who absolutely must come in on that day, whether the stylist is out sick or not. In that case, the rest of us are left to try to fit these stray clients into our already tight schedules.

Most people have the same attitude that Andrea's client just voiced. I hear it from half of my clients when I am at work sick. *Go home, as soon as you finish with me.* Do they not hear how self-absorbed that sounds? In essence, they are telling us that their haircut is more important than our health. They also judge themselves superior by claiming that their haircut is vital, while everyone else's can wait.

Andrea manages to keep the sarcasm from her voice when she replies, "Unfortunately, my next client will tell me the same thing."

Andrea's client looks at her as if she doesn't quite understand. I turn my attention back to the woman in my chair. Kay is about 50, has a pinched face and an extra chin. She says, "I'm making the most fabulous recipe for dinner tonight. Everyone just loves when I make this! You should really try it."

Judy proceeds to give me precise details of the broiled chicken with strips of bacon and cheese sauce that she will be making. When she finishes, she beams at me and asks, "Doesn't that make your mouth water?"

"I'm a vegetarian," I say.

"Oh, that's right. But you eat chicken, don't you?"

"No. I don't eat any meat."

"Fish?"

"No."

Her eyebrows crinkle. "Then what is it you eat?"

I offer my best tolerant smile. "Vegetables. Beans. Pasta. Rice." I'm cutting her hair and thinking about sticking the point of the blade into her ear. "Anything that wasn't once an animal."

"Oh." Judy purses her lips. "That's an awfully restrictive and boring diet."

Does she not realize that she has just insulted me? And that I am using surgically sharpened scissors to cut her hair? And that I could miss and cut off her ear?

At the very least, her comment doesn't entice me to do my best work.

I do not respond. Debating the merits of my diet with a close-minded, obese woman with absolutely no tact is not in my best interest.

The afternoon passes at an excruciatingly slow pace. All I had time to eat today was a granola bar. That was while driving to work. It is now nearly 6 and my stomach has been rumbling obscenely for the past hour.

My next client walks in the door. His name is Russell. This is his third time here. I remember because each time I hope that he doesn't come back.

Russell is not bad to look at, when you look from a relative distance. Up close, something about his eyes puts me on edge. He has this way of appraising everything he sees, including me. He's polite and soft-spoken. Well-toned but not overly muscular. A boy-next-door face. He's not pushy or demanding.

I don't know why I don't like Russell. For some reason, he gives me the creeps. I think of Jeffrey Dahmer, with his clean-cut appearance and quiet personality. Then I picture Russell making a human stew at home. My stomach does a little flutter.

"Just a trim today?" I ask.

"Please," Russell replies.

I ask Russell how his job is going. He works as a butcher for a local grocery store. His eyes flitter away from mine and he shrugs. "Not the most glamorous job," he says.

I smile. "Neither is mine."

He smiles at me. I feel like he is trying to pass me a secret message. I look back at his hair and somehow muddle through the next twenty minutes.

Russell leaves but my evening does not improve. People annoy me. I have one woman who likes her hair colored brown, with absolutely no hint of red or gold. She practically has a panic attack at the mere hint of a golden hue. Consequently, the color she winds up with is that unenviable mousy brown. That same drab shade of brown other women pay to get rid of.

When I've finished, she studies her hair beneath the lights to be sure no gold or red emerges. "I hate red," she sputters.

I have burgundy streaks in my hair. I glance toward the chair where my next client is waiting. She is a redhead.

I practically flee from the building at 9:30. I'm starving but way too tired to do anything about it. I will probably settle for cereal and something totally mindless and distracting on TV.

Scott is waiting for me. He has the lights turned low and a vegetable stir-fry on the stove. The dogs greet me with quivering tails and sparkling eyes. In that instant, the stress of the day melts away. I wish I could live in this moment forever.

*

The Mass Avenger sits in his van in the Dunkin' Donuts parking lot. The Saturday donut crowd is large but no one pays attention to him. They emerge with their donut boxes and trays of coffee, in a hurry to return home to their families.

He stares through the windshield, watching the building across the street. He likes the name of the business. *The Cutting Edge.* Fitting for so many reasons.

Every now and then, he catches a glimpse of her. Skye. She's older than he normally likes. Older than his victims. Something about her intrigues him.

He sits in the parking lot for nearly two hours. The salon is busy. A constant flow of people. A few of the young women strut, swaying their hips back and forth like pendulums. Looking for attention. Looking to control.

He will teach them all.

The Mass Avenger turns the key dangling from his ignition. Time to move on. He will come back to Skye another time. Decide whether she is a kindred spirit or prey. Not yet, though. He needs more time to study her.

He drives to the gym for his normal Saturday afternoon workout. He's itchy to try out his cage. He'd already set it up, added wire mesh to the top, and bolted it to his garage floor. The soundproof padding in the garage walls and the solid garage door allow him plenty of privacy. And now the cage allows him a way of extending his pleasure.

He is ready for a dress rehearsal.

The gym overflows with people, as always. Muscleheads and gym whores. The Mass Avenger uses the weights first. She approaches, tosses him a smile, then swings her hips as she strolls past. The same routine she's been following for weeks. Getting his attention, teasing him, waiting to see if he will follow like a good dog.

Her name is Caroline. She is about 20 and thrives on the power she holds over the men who ogle her.

He'd asked her out once. Her eyes had widened and for a moment he'd thought she would laugh. She hadn't. Instead, she had invented an excuse about having a boyfriend away at college. As if he'd believe that she is saving herself while the boyfriend is gone.

Caroline continues to tease him each time he comes to the gym. She flirts with the muscleheads. She loves the attention and breaks into a triumphant grin when the muscleheads' eyes follow her.

The Mass Avenger moves to the treadmills. He steps onto the one beside Caroline. She tosses her hair back and smiles at him. He smiles back. He can do that because her power no longer holds him captive.

He leaves the gym and sits in his van. Caroline drives a black Honda. Two cars separate her Honda from his van. He thinks about his cage, about Caroline, and decides that today is the day.

He steps out of his van and opens the rear doors. All that is behind him is a fence. A few hundred yards further is the back of a building. Offices; a lawyer and a chiropractor.

In less than 10 minutes, Caroline steps into the sunlight. She pauses to draw her sunglasses from her purse. Her dark brown hair is pulled into a ponytail. She's wearing the same outfit she'd been exercising in; tight black lycra pants and a short-waisted hooded sweatshirt partially zipped over a black sports bra. Black Nike sneakers.

The Mass Avenger steps out from the cover of the van doors. He pretends to just notice Caroline approaching her car. "Caroline!" he says with relief. "I was going to flag someone down. Could you come here for a second, please?"

She looks at him skeptically. He shakes his head, brushes a hand over his face. "I can't believe I was so stupid!" he says. "Sometimes I swear I am the biggest idiot walking this earth!"

She breaks into a grin. "Oh, you're not an idiot." She walks over, attempting to peer past him and around the van doors. "What's wrong?"

He presses the stun gun against her chest, then catches her as she slumps forward. Within seconds, he has her inside the back of his van. On the off chance that she regains control before he arrives home, the gag will keep her from screaming and the zip ties will keep her from moving.

The Mass Avenger climbs into the driver's seat. He smiles as he drives off.

15

I stretch and yawn and finally crack my eyes open. The digital clock beside my bed tells me that it is 9:35. I don't normally sleep this late on Sundays but it sure feels good today. Last night, Scott and I had gone out to dinner with my best friend Kate and her boyfriend Stephen. I ate too much pasta and drank too much wine. Then we went to a bar to listen to a local band and I drank too many drinks with funny names. I stumbled into bed somewhere after 2 a.m. I think Scott and I had sex, though I wouldn't swear to it. I might have been dreaming.

I glance over the edge of my bed and spot Cassady still asleep in her little bed. She would probably stay there all day, as long as someone stayed in the room with her. I call her name and she opens one eye. I lean over and pick her up. She is warm and soft and smells a little too much like a dog. "You need a bath," I tell her.

I smell hazelnut coffee. Jack trots in, tail wagging, ears perked. "Good morning," I say.

He lifts his front paws onto the bed and stares at me. Scott steps in. His blonde hair is tousled. He's wearing loose flannel pajama bottoms and a smile. He says, "Jack's been in to check on you every few minutes. I think he was worried."

I chuckle, as I scratch Jack's ear. "I'm alive and well," I tell him.

Scott takes Cassady from me. "I'll take her outside."

The house is chilly. I find my slippers, shove my feet inside, then trudge out to the kitchen. As I'm pouring my coffee, Scott brings Cassady inside. She's wagging her tail and prancing as if she's performed a grand feat. "Are you expecting a treat?" I ask.

The other three dogs have already lined up beside me. I give them each a treat and they race off to see who can eat it the fastest.

Scott and I sit at the table, drinking coffee and munch on ridiculously decadent pastries we brought home from the restaurant last night. Scott pushes his plate away and wipes his hands on a napkin. "Another woman is missing," he tells me.

For a moment, I am not sure what he is talking about. Then I remember the serial killer. "They think the Mass Avenger has her?"

"Apparently. They were flashing her picture on the news this morning. Her name is Caroline Robbins. Sound familiar?"

I shake my head no. "Where is she from?"

"Hanson. Twenty-two years old. She was last seen at the Ultimate Fitness gym yesterday afternoon."

"She would be the fifth one."

"Yeah..." Scott frowns. "I don't like the idea of you going anywhere alone until this guy is caught."

"I'm fine. I can take care of myself."

Scott folds his arms across his chest and looks at me as if I am a disobedient child. "You don't think every victim thought that once?"

"I'm very careful. Besides, I'm not his type. All of his victims have been younger women."

Scott simply looks at me. I sigh, roll my eyes. "Fine," I say. "If I go anywhere, I'll take all four dogs with me. No one will be able to get close enough to spit on me."

"Good. Make sure you lock your doors when you're driving. And keep your Mace out."

"Yes, sir."

Scott leans over and kisses me. "I worry," he says. "I   know."

"I'll meet you at the salon on your two late nights."

I know better than to argue. He is in protective mode and the subject is not up for debate.

*

The Mass Avenger carries a carton of orange juice and a cranberry muffin into the garage. Daylight streams into the dark space. He sees

Caroline sitting in the corner of the cage, blinking at the sudden light. She has the checkered blanket wrapped tightly around her naked body. He places the juice and muffin on the table beside the door, then pushes the door shut and twists the locks.

With daylight closed off, the garage is once again plunged into darkness. He hears Caroline breathing. Quick, ragged breaths. The space smells of sweat and urine. He is instantly aroused.

He finds the wall switch and floods the space with light. Caroline blinks rapidly. Jagged red lines crisscross over the whites of her eyes. Her long brown hair is tangled. She pushes back against the cage and makes a little mewling sound.

The Mass Avenger sets her juice and muffin on the floor. He unlocks the cage door and slides her breakfast inside. "You must be hungry," he says. "You missed dinner last night."

He grins at this. He had played with her well into the night, then left her spent and barely conscious on the garage floor. He'd made himself grilled cheese sandwiches before collapsing, exhausted but elated, onto his soft, warm bed.

Caroline glances at the food but makes no move toward it. He swats outside the cage door. He wants to see her naked body but tells himself to be patient. He says, "You should eat. Keep up your strength."

"Please let me go."

Her voice is little more than a croak of a whisper. "In due time," he says through his grin.

"I won't tell anyone about you. I swear."

He almost laughs at this little game they are playing. He pretends he will let her go. She pretends she won't tell. Both lies but he goes along with the pretense. "If you're extra good today," he says. "And you do exactly what I tell you."

"You'll let me go?"

"I don't want to hurt you, Caroline. Remember what I told you last night? You thought you had all the power, all the control. It's not fair that you use that to hurt men the way you do. I need to show you who really has the power."

A sob escapes Caroline's lips, followed by a tiny hiccup. She clenches the blanket tighter. "I didn't mean to hurt you," she whispers.

He knows better. He points to her breakfast. "Eat or I'll take it away."

She shakes her head. "I'm not hungry."

Insolent little bitch. She'll regret that choice. He moves her breakfast out of the cage, slips the knife from his pocket. "Good," he says. "Then we can start right away."

Her eyes widen. He chuckles. "Hand me the blanket now, Caroline."

A tear slides down her cheek. "Please…"

He fingers the blade. "Now, Caroline."

She shrugs off the blanket and tosses it toward him. He tosses it out behind him. He reaches in and takes the bucket he had left her to pee in. He sets that outside the cage. His erection throbs. "Lie down on your back," he says.

She eyes him warily. "Please…"

"Do as I say or it will hurt more."

She stretches out on the cold concrete. He admires her body, as well as the long, thin cuts across her belly. Gifts from last night. He'd only been playing, teasing. The knife hadn't gone deep. He'd yet to mar her beautiful breasts or the youthful skin on her face. He enjoys this; dragging it out, giving her hope. When he is done, she'll be stripped of her power, stripped of her beauty. No one would want her, even if he had intentions of leaving her alive.

↶

The sun is shining and the day has warmed up to an astonishing 61 degrees. Scott and I could be at the park with the dogs. Or in our back yard, raking leaves into piles for Jack and Zena to run through. Instead, we are at the grocery store. And I hate the grocery store.

Scott and I don't normally waste our only day off together in this miserable place. Grocery stores have this stupid rule about not allowing dogs inside, although some of the people I see here are a lot dirtier than my dogs. And Scott's new rule doesn't allow me to go anywhere alone. So instead of doing the shopping by myself tomorrow, when most people are working, we are here today, along with three-quarters of the population.

"Are we going to need potatoes this week?" Scott asks.

We are standing in the vegetable section and I am staring at the widest ass I have ever seen. This ass, and the woman it is attached to, is blocking my access to the peppers, onions, and carrots. She is studying the green peppers, picking each one up and searching for imperfections. I want to shove her out of my way but I'm pretty sure I'd need a forklift.

"Skye?"

I turn to Scott. "Oh, sorry," I say. "Potatoes. Yes, maybe some red ones this week."

He takes my hand. "Why don't you help me."

"You're perfectly capable of picking out potatoes," I say as he tugs me along.

"Yes, but I was afraid that lady might tip over and squash you."

I laugh, despite my irritation. "She took up half the aisle."

"And you looked like you wanted to kick her ass."

"Did I?"

He gives me a smirk. "Don't try acting innocent. It is so not you."

"Well, seriously, does she need to inspect every damn pepper?"

"Pick out your potatoes."

"Fine."

I am standing in front of the dried beans when the lady with the ass waddles down the aisle. Scott inches in close to me. Her ass sways and I am afraid she's going to knock one of us over. She stops on the other side of Scott and turns to examine the rice selection. She leaves her cart in the middle of the aisle. Between her ass and the cart, there is barely enough room to squeeze past.

We escape to the cereal aisle. A child is screaming for a box of chemical-coated sugar. The mother holds out Cheerios, as if the plain oat rings will somehow entice the child away from the sugar rush in the colorful box. The mother caves. She tosses the treasured cereal into the cart. The child drags a sleeve over the snot running from his nose, then gives a triumphant grin. I wanted to slap the mother.

"Do you remember if we need oatmeal?" Scott asks.

I have a wild urge to kick and scream and throw jars of pickles. I give myself a mental shake, turn back to Scott. "I'm sorry. What?"

Scott laughs at me. "We're almost done. Try to relax."

"I hate this place."

Scott nods his head toward the departing monster child. "Did you ever pull something like that in a store?"

"God, no. But I'm thinking of trying it now."

We make it to the end of the store. I grab a pint of Stoneyfield Farms organic vanilla ice cream and toss it in the cart. "I'm eating that whole thing myself," I say. "I deserve it."

Scott leans close and murmurs. "Careful, you don't want your ass to look like that woman's."

I shudder as he grabs a chocolate ice cream for himself.

Caroline is curled in a ball on the floor of her cage. The Mass Avenger fastens his pants, then pulls on his sweatshirt. He'd been rougher with her than he'd intended. He wants her to last but too easily gets carried away with his own excitement. The power soars through him. His true self. No one will ever accuse him of being weak again.

Silent tears stream down Caroline's face, mixing with the blood from the gash on her cheek. Females so easily lose their swagger, their drive for seduction. Teases, all of them. Whores that want to flaunt their power. When challenged, though, they quickly fall back on their little girl tears and pleas to be rescued. Damsels in distress. The other card up their sleeves.

The Mass Avenger doesn't fall for either act. Not anymore.

He leans down and picks his treasure up from the plastic covering the cement floor. Caroline's right nipple. He'd stuffed the gag in her mouth and let her scream into it as he sliced. He'd ejaculated then and his semen had shot into the stream of blood.

He opens the storage freezer and rifles beneath the selection of frozen meat. He finds the metal box and pulls it out. He unlocks it and places Caroline's nipple inside with the others. For a moment, he lingers over the six of them. All unique. He feels like a matador who has conquered the bull and taken its ear as a prize.

16

Today is a raw and rainy Monday. I am babysitting Jonathan, Renee's 4-year-old son. Today is her turn to have her vagina examined.

Jonathan loves to come to my house and play with the dogs. Today he is particularly happy to find Zena, the new addition to our family. The four dogs are gathered around him, clambering for attention. He plops on the floor and giggles like only a carefree child can.

An hour together exhausts all five of them. Jonathan sprawls onto the couch. The dogs drain their water dish, then quickly settle down to nap. "Can we watch cartoons?" Jonathan asks.

"Sure," I say. I scroll through the channels and find SpongeBob, which makes him happy. "Want some juice?"

"Yeah!"

I give him a glass of grape juice and a chocolate chip granola bar. He sucks that down and 10 minutes later he's sound asleep.

When Renee arrives, I tell her that Jonathan has only been asleep for about 20 minutes. "Do you want to hang out awhile, let him sleep?" I ask.

Renee makes a sour face, shakes her head. "No," she says. "I need to go home and wash this goo off my crotch. I swear she used enough lube to keep me moist for a year. What the hell is up with that?"

I laugh. "I don't know but it's gross. I felt like I'd sprung a leak after I left her office."

"Thanks for watching him. Was he okay?"

"Jon is never a problem."

Renee rolls her eyes. "Yeah, right!" She scoops him up in her arms. I help her get him out to her car and buckle him in. He is still out cold when she drives away. What I wouldn't do to sleep that soundly.

I'm in the middle of a major decision – raspberry-flavored or plain green tea – when the phone rings. The caller ID tells me that it is Elyse on her cell phone. I groan. This can't be good.

Elyse doesn't bother with greetings. "Is my father home?"

"He's working."

"He's not answering his cell phone."

"He's probably tied up on a job."

"I really need to talk to him."

"Did you leave a message?" I ask. "I'm sure he'll get back to you as soon as he can."

Elyse sighs into the phone. There are voices in the background but I can't make out the words. She says, "Do you know when he'll be home?"

I'm getting tired of being treated like her father's secretary. "Usually around 5:30," I say. "Is everything okay?"

Another sigh. "I'm really hungry," she says. "I have no money and everything is really expensive here."

"Are you in New York?" I ask.

"Obviously."

She says the word as if I am stupid for even asking. I take a slow breath, remind myself that she is Scott's daughter. "Do you want to come back home?"

"No! That's not what I'm calling for. I said I need food."

"And you expect your father to bring you some?"

I know that was sarcastic and probably uncalled for but I can't help myself. The girl grates on my nerves.

"No," Elyse snaps. "I don't expect him to bring me food. I want him to wire me some money."

"You have no money at all?"

"No."

"Where are you staying?"

"At a motel. Me and Chelsea together. It's not bad, has a little kitchenette. But we have no food."

"You should come home," I say.

"I don't want to come home! I told you that. I'm going to make it big here. I just want money so Chelsea and I can eat."

"We're not sending you money, Elyse."

A short silence. I can picture Elyse mouthing curses and jabbing her fist in the air. Finally, she bites out the words, "I was not asking you. I want my *dad* to send me money."

"I have a news flash for you, Elyse. Your dad's money and my money are the same money."

"I'll just wait and talk to my father," Elyse says. "Thanks for nothing."

The call disconnects. I sigh and replace the phone on its receiver. Neal has woken from his nap and is looking at me expectantly. He wants to go out. I pick him up and kiss his furry little head. Dogs are so much easier than children.

ℴ

The Mass Avenger pulls his van into the driveway. With great anticipation, he walks up the path to the side door of the garage. He has been at work all day, away from Caroline. Concentrating on work had been nearly impossible. Thoughts of Caroline, her naked body caged and waiting, held him in a dizzying distraction all day.

As badly as he wants to see her, he first needs to wash off the stink of his day. The odor traps itself in his nostrils and sickens him. He hurries into his house and stands beneath a steaming shower. Ten minutes later, he is ready to see Caroline.

He unlocks the bolts and steps inside the dark garage. The stink of urine and sweat is strong and is now mingled with the coppery odor of blood. He'll need to air the place out soon, use extra bleach to clean. Maybe he'll buy some of that scented kind this time.

He flicks on the light. Caroline is huddled beneath the blanket. She doesn't look up, doesn't stir.

"Caroline..." He says her name in a singsong voice, like they are children playing hide and seek. "Look at me, Caroline."

She still does not move, does not respond. Could she be dead? He swallows back the sudden fear. He's been building up his fantasies all day. He's not ready to lose her.

He steps close to the cage, squats down and studies the curled up form beneath the blanket. The barest of movements tells him that she is still breathing.

"Caroline!" he calls sharply. "I said look at me. You do not want to make me mad!"

The blanket flutters and falls away from her face. She blinks swollen eyes at him. He smiles. "That's better," he says. "Did you miss me today?"

She doesn't answer. He goes to the sink, fills a plastic cup with water. Then he unlocks the cage and pushes the cup inside. "Here," he says. "Your throat must be dry."

She looks at him but doesn't move. His anger bubbles up. "I'm trying to be nice! Drink the damn water!"

Her eyes grow wide. She inches closer to the cup, sliding along the floor, still huddled beneath the blanket. She slips her hand out, reaches for the cup, and brings it to her mouth. Some of the water dribbles down her chin. She puts the cup down and buries her head into her knees, a round ball covered by a bloodstained blanket.

Her hair is matted, her left cheek bruised. Her lips are dry, cracked, riddled with tiny specks of blood. She is no longer the powerful female that flaunted her sex appeal in his face. He has beaten her.

She broke easily. He is losing interest now. He has nothing left to prove to her.

"Hand me the blanket," he says.

She looks at him, resignation in her brown eyes. She eases the blanket from her skin and pushes it toward him. He admires his work and finds himself aroused. He rubs himself through his pants. "Maybe one last time," he tells her. "A lovely departing gift."

17

Another Tuesday has snuck up on me and once again I am on my way to open the salon. Lillian, my first client, is probably frantic by now, pacing the parking lot and popping Prozac like candy. About six months ago, I did Lillian a favor by starting early on a Tuesday. She'd been a new client and "needed" her appointment in the early morning. I had nothing before 11 for two weeks. And so I did something that I will regret for eternity. I offered to come in early. I have been doing so ever since.

The salon doesn't technically open until 9 a.m. on Tuesdays. The other girls won't arrive until 8:30 or so. We always arrive about 30 minutes before our first client. That way we can get the salon ready, go over our schedules, have tantrums when we see who we must face that day. That alone time is how I psyche myself up for my clients. That's when I stick the plastic smile on my face.

Lillian is my nightmare. She is now my regular 8 a.m. Tuesday client who sits in the parking lot waiting for me. The earlier I arrive, the earlier she comes in. I'm thinking she might have put a tracking device on my car.

Last week I had come in at 7:20. I had client files I needed to update, things I wanted to do before my day started. Lillian walked in the door at 7:25.

Needless to say, I am fed up. If Lillian is going to make me miserable no matter what, I'd much rather be miserable on my terms than hers. Therefore, today I am not rushing. Her appointment is at 8 o'clock. That is when she will get her hair done.

I pull into the parking lot at 7:48. I see Lillian in her luxury model BMW. She is drumming her fingers on her steering wheel, wide-eyed, head spinning back and forth. She spots me and her body slumps as if she's breathed a sigh of relief. I turn away before I'm forced to acknowledge her.

I take my time getting inside the building. The lights aren't even on when Lillian bursts through the door. "You're late!" she announces.

"No," I say. "You're early."

I stride into the back room, leaving her standing there with her mouth open. My behavior is not the best form of customer relations but I can only take so much before I snap. I take a deep breath and compose myself. Then I go back out front to flip on the lights, hang up my coat, and stuff my purse into my cabinet.

Lillian is scrutinizing my every move. "Are you feeling all right this morning, Skye?"

"I'm fine, thanks. How are you?"

She presses her lips together but lets it go. "I'm well, thank you. Happy Halloween!"

I keep my plastic smile in place. "Same to you."

Halloween is not a holiday that I enjoy. I'll no sooner get home, covered in people hair – I don't mind dog hair but people hair is itchy as hell – before we'll be besieged with begging children. The small ones are cute, the teens annoying. After awhile, even the small ones are annoying. The doorbell will receive an aerobic workout and the dogs will wear out their vocal chords.

Scott passes out the candy. He has more patience than I do. My job is to corral the dogs. Zena would knock them down in her excitement, Jack would steal their candy, and Cassady and Neal would probably bite their ankles.

I get Lillian's hair washed. She wants a cut this week. I think she decides that just to punish me for being "late". As I'm cutting, she says, "Did you hear the news?"

Could her question be any more vague? How am I supposed to know if I've heard "the news" if she offers no clue as to what that news is about? I want to poke her with the tip of my scissors.

"Probably not," I say. "I didn't watch or read any news today."

"They found that poor girl."

I am still in the dark. I'm trying to think of any kids that have been reported missing when Lillian says, "Her body was left in a Dumpster behind a CVS. They say she was mutilated!"

"You're talking about that woman who they thought was taken by The Mass Avenger?"

"Yes. Her name was Caroline Robbins. Only 22 years old!"

"That's really sad."

"It's terrifying! We have a serial killer running around loose and the police seem to have no idea who he is!"

"The FBI is working with the local cops now, aren't they?"

Lillian scoffs at that. "For all the good they're doing. They will certainly be of no comfort to Caroline Robbins' family."

I listen to her rant about the inadequacies of our police departments for another 10 minutes. From there, she spends the rest of our time together complaining about her sister. Lillian's husband died three years ago. Her only child, a son, moved to Illinois. Lillian's sister is happily married, her three children are close, and she leads a busy life. This discrepancy fills Lillian with bitter envy. Of course, she doesn't admit this. Instead, she picks her sister apart. Then she wonders why her sister rarely visits.

As Lillian prepares to leave, she asks, "Same time next week?"

I know this is a dig at my imagined tardiness. My plastic smile nearly cracks as I say, "Yup. Have a good week."

Lori, my next client, is waiting. She is in her early twenties, lively, cute, dumb as a doorknob, and speaks only in questions. Her voice rises at the end of every sentence, so she always sounds like she's asking someone's opinion.

I shampoo her hair and get her settled in my chair. Her hair is long, blonde, silky smooth. She wears bangs and the rest is one-length. A simple cut. "Just a trim today?" I ask.

"An inch would be good?" Lori says.

"Okay."

"I'm thinking of growing my bangs out?"

Is she asking my opinion? I'm not sure. "You want to let them grow out so it's all the same length?" I ask.

"I'm thinking of letting them grow long enough to angle into my sides? So it frames my face?"

My head starts to throb. Roxie and Renee come in the door together. They are a good distraction. A half-hour alone with Lori would send me straight to a loony bin.

I manage to work out what Lori would like to do with her hair. Roxie rescues me with a review of the concert she'd been to on Saturday night. She'd seen a band called Breaking Benjamin. Lori practically shrieks with excitement. Apparently she loves Breaking Benjamin but couldn't get a babysitter for her 2 year old.

By 10 a.m., the phone is ringing nonstop and every seat in the salon is filled. The woman in my chair swears she booked her appointment for color and a cut, though she is only scheduled for a cut. That's a big time difference. And she doesn't tell me this until after I wash her hair. Color goes on dry hair.

I'm gritting my teeth so hard that I'm afraid they might break. My smile is frozen, like a bad case of lockjaw. Since her hair is already wet, I decide to do her haircut first, then her color. I will be off schedule the rest of the day. I want to smack her in the head with my blow dryer, as she sits with her red-painted lips pursed in a smug smile.

Why couldn't The Mass Avenger have chosen her instead of Caroline Robbins as his last victim?

ᐟ

The Mass Avenger grips the newspaper in his fists. Front page. He should be celebrating. He is the main topic of conversation on the entire South Shore!

He drops the paper on the table and shoves out of his chair. It topples backward and lands with a thump on the braided carpet. Anger overwhelms him. Suddenly, he feels like a child again; helpless, misunderstood, ignored.

The police have not released any of his letters to the public. Not a word of his mission has been mentioned! With each woman, he has left a note explaining what he does. That is how they know to call him The Mass Avenger. The police released that at the start. But, still, nothing has been printed regarding his letters.

How are people supposed to understand if the police refuse to allow the press to print his letters? They are calling him a sick freak. He's not! He is avenging all the men who have been used, hurt, and laughed at by these women. He is teaching women that they do not hold all the power. They cannot flaunt their sex, simply to get what they want! He has a mission and people need to know.

He paces the length of his kitchen. The Chinese take-out he brought home for dinner sits on the table. The smell makes him nauseous. This was supposed to be his celebration dinner. They would have found Caroline this morning. The note he'd pinned to her shirt would surely make the news this time.

But, no! The police continue to hide the truth. They want people to believe that he, The Mass Avenger, is no more than a sick freak randomly killing young women.

He is not a sick freak!

The women are to blame. They tease. They use their power to control men. Nothing is ever good enough for them. They treat men like dogs, forcing them to do tricks for their favors. They belittle men, get thrills from making all men feel small. Those women are the evil ones!

The Mass Avenger storms through the house. He'll show them all! They think they have him figured out. They don't! He'll show them what happens when they ignore him.

18

My headlights hit my driveway and I pause before turning in. Scott's car is here, parked in his usual spot. Behind it is a silver Lexus. I'm not positive who it belongs to but I have an idea. The thought makes me queasy. I hope I'm wrong.

I pull up beside Scott's car, partially on my dying lawn. It's already dark. The trick-or-treaters will be coming soon. Our front porch light is on but the neighborhood is still quiet.

I push open the gate and step up onto my back deck. Jack catches sight of me through the kitchen window. His barking sets off a chain reaction. By the time I get to the door, all four dogs are creating a welcome-home harmony. I shove the door open and greet them.

Scott is sitting at the kitchen table. "Hey, babe," he says.

I smile at him. "Hi."

I spend another few seconds fussing over the dogs. Knowing I can't put it off any longer, I turn to the woman seated across from Scott. "Hello, Diane," I say.

Scott's ex flicks a glance my way. She looks as if the effort is causing her heartburn. "Hello," she says.

Diane Greer is one of those people who doesn't so much as go out to get the mail without a full application of makeup. Her hair would not move in a hurricane and I'm pretty sure that she doesn't own a pair of jeans with a price tag under $200. She's wearing black leather boots with high spiked heels, black linen slacks, and a silver sweater that is probably angora. Her nails are long, painted red with tiny silver studs on the tips. A gaudy diamond glitters on her right hand, a diamond tennis bracelet on her right wrist, and big diamond studs in her ears. She works at an investment firm and is sleeping with the married owner.

Diane has been in our home five times in the 16 years that Scott and I have been married. Not one of those times was a happy occasion.

I decide to get right to the point. "What's going on?"

Diane ignores me. To Scott, she says, "I expect you to do the right thing."

Scott scowls. Diane lifts herself from my kitchen chair. She has this way of moving, like everything she does is calculated for effect. She doesn't lift a hand before mentally working out how she will look while doing it.

I step aside so she can get out the door. The dogs back away and Neal growls at her. She shoots them a look of disdain, then offers me that same expression. "Thanks for stopping by!" I say. I sound like a greeter at Walmart. "Have a nice night!"

She glares at me. She tosses her head back so that her dyed blonde hair falls over her shoulder. Then she strides out the door without another word.

"What was that all about?" I ask Scott.

He sighs. He has one fist clenched in his lap. I'm pretty sure that it isn't meant for me. He says, "She claims I was terrible to Elyse."

My eyebrows lift. "Oh boy."

Last night, when Scott had gotten home from work, I'd told him about Elyse's phone call. He'd already known, because she'd left three messages on his cell phone. He'd called her back and told her the same thing I had. We would absolutely not send her money. We'd help her get home, if that was what she wanted. But we would not support her while she lived the life of a princess in New York. She would have to learn to work for things, just like everyone else.

Needless to say, Elyse did not take that news well. Evidently, she had cried to her mother about how terrible her father is. And, no doubt, what a bitch her stepmother is.

"Diane now supports Elyse's move to New York?" I ask.

"Oh, sure. In fact, she thinks that I should set Elyse up in an apartment there. After all, don't I want to help my daughter make it as a model? How could I be so selfish?"

"Maybe Diane should tell Elyse to hook up with some rich married guy. It seems to work well for her."

Scott shakes his head. He looks a little sick. "She said that, if I do not wire Elyse money this evening, she will take me back to court."

"For what? No judge is going to force you to support your grown daughter's stupidity."

"She says she'll convince Elyse to go back to school, only this time not a community college. Some private college in New York. Then I can support her while she pursues her dream of being a spoiled brat."

I sit on Scott's lap and kiss his wonderfully soft lips. "I'm sorry," I say.

"She wouldn't win that argument in court," Scott says. "Though she'd probably enjoy the battle."

"Anything to make you miserable."

"Yeah…"

"What do you want to do?"

"Nothing. I'm sticking by what I said. Elyse needs to grow up."

I kiss him again. He pulls me closer and I moan. "Maybe I could do a little something to cheer you up?" I offer.

Just then, the doorbell rings. The dogs go berserk, clambering to the front door and barking like they are trained killers. "Trick-or-treat," Scott says.

I mutter a curse. Then I wrangle the dogs in while he passes out candy. The night goes on this way. I make us veggie burgers, which we eat between doorbell bursts. At 8:30, we shut the lights off. I put my Halloween costume on and prance around the bedroom. In no time, the costume is on the floor and we have completely forgotten about Diane.

*

The Mass Avenger parks his van in the Dunkin' Donuts lot across from The Cutting Edge. The building is dark. Skye, his stylist, is already gone. He isn't sure why he came here. He wanted to see her but it's not her that he wants to take. Not this time.

He jams the gear into drive and pulls out of the lot. Five minutes later, he coasts slowly past her house. The outside lights are on. Kids are on the street, begging strangers for candy. Her husband's car is beside hers in the driveway. A flashy sports car. This pisses him off.

His rage builds but he is also aroused. He grips the steering wheel and escapes her neighborhood. This is no time for stupid fantasies.

A few minutes later, he is driving his van into Brockton. The small, troubled city abuts Whitman and is the perfect hunting ground to fill his needs. Most of the younger kids have gone inside. The older ones and the gangbangers linger on the streets.

The Mass Avenger cruises through the neighborhoods. He finds a hole-in-the-wall bar that might serve his purpose. He parks across the street and watches. Drug deals are taking place in the alley beside the building. A steady stream of young thugs move in and out. Too much activity here.

He moves on and soon settles on a little place on Battles Street. He parks in the lot but is suddenly unsure of himself. He has never done this without a plan. His choice of women has always been of the more discreet, respectable type. The women who flaunt their stuff but don't easily give it away.

The women inside this bar will be different. Trashier. But he is here because they will also be less risky to grab off the street.

He sits in the parking lot, considering his options. A knock on his side window startles him. A woman peers in. He lowers the window. She smiles at him. Her teeth are rotted and chipped. She says, "Twenty bucks will buy you a great time."

His stomach goes sour. He shakes his head, raises his window. This won't do. He can't lower himself to this standard. That would destroy his image. No one cares about these women. They have no power. He needs to send a message, not look pathetic.

He steps on the gas pedal. The foul-smelling whore jumps out of his way as he steers away from the grubby bar. He drives through the city, unsure of his destination. Anger coils in his gut. He wants to show the police what happens when they treat him like a pathetic creep stalking innocent women. He wants everyone to know his mission.

A half-hour goes by. He's been up and down the streets and is quickly losing confidence. He hears his mother's voice in his head, telling him that he is worthless.

As he's passing a convenience store, he sees a woman step out of her car and disappear inside. Aside from her, the parking lot is empty. No one is on the street. She parked off to the side of the building, away from the store's entrance, the bright lights, and the view of the lone cashier inside.

The Mass Avenger takes this as a sign. He pulls into the lot and backs his van into the spot beside the woman's car. He steps into the rear and pulls open the side door. The stun gun is in his hand when she approaches her driver's door. She holds her keys in one hand, a package of toilet paper in the other. Her face registers shock as he steps from the shadowy interior of his van. The toilet paper falls to the pavement. He straps duct tape over her mouth and uses the zip ties on her limp arms and legs. Thirty seconds later, he calmly pulls out onto the street and heads home.

By the time he pulls into the driveway, she is fully conscious. He hears her muffled cries and the slight thrashing as she tries to escape her confinement. Along with tying her hands and feet together, he has strapped her right arm to the heavy-duty metal handle he'd installed on the floor of the van. Her struggles are useless.

He turns the van and backs up close to the garage's side door. The door faces his own house. Darkness swallows the garage, along with his van. He is invisible to everyone, unless they walk up the driveway and around the edge of the garage.

The woman yanks her arms, trying to break free of the strap. He steps over her and squats down. Even in the dark, he can see that her eyes are wide and frantic. "Welcome to my home," he says. "You need to do what I say, so I won't have to hurt you. Do you understand?"

She gives a little nod. He smiles and touches her hair. It's a reddish color, short, and stiff with hairspray. He prefers hair to be soft and natural. Maybe he will wash it later.

"I'll be right back," he tells her. Then, unable to resist, he adds, "Wait here."

He slides open the van's side door. Two steps take him to the garage. He sticks his key in the first lock, then the second, then the third. He pushes the door open and grabs his flashlight from the nearby table. The garage is inky black. He flips on the flashlight and strides over to the cage. Another key unlocks that door. He leaves the flashlight on the floor, where it offers enough light to guide him.

Back in the van, he again squats beside the woman. "I'm going to unstrap your arm," he says. He shows her the stun gun. "If you fight me, I will have to use this. So be good. Okay?"

She nods. He unfastens the strap and releases her arm. She is still tied and unable to offer much resistance even if she wants to. "We're going inside," he says. "I'm going to carry you. Don't resist or I'll have to hurt you."

He slips his arms beneath her and lifts. He picks his way through the dimly lit garage, then stoops down to shove her into the cage. She sees what he is about to do and starts flailing wildly. He slams her inside. Her head bounces off the back of the cage. "I warned you!" he shouts.

He shuts the cage door and locks it. His hands tremble with rage. For a moment, he stares at her. She scoots backward, into the far corner. As if she could possibly escape him. He inhales a slow breath, tells himself to relax. He will break her, just as he did the others.

Outside, he puts the van in the driveway and locks the doors. The brisk night air boosts his energy. This could be a long, interesting evening.

♪

I can't sleep. Scott has been dreaming blissfully beside me for the past half hour. I've been conjuring up ways to kill his ex. The more horrific, the better I feel.

I'm irritated that she was in my house and even more irritated that she is now keeping me awake. I glance at Scott. I'd told him not to worry, that Diane had only been pushing his buttons. I must have sounded convincing because he isn't awake plotting her murder.

I slip out of bed and stuff my feet into my fuzzy slippers. Jack stirs, then follows me into the living room. I grab the remote and plop on the couch. He climbs up beside me and nestles his head in my lap. I might be crazy but I swear that he's trying to comfort me. I pat his head while I surf through the hundreds of channels that offer nothing of interest.

Can Diane force us to pay for some high-priced college in New York? Would she go that far?

I scoff at that. Of course she would go that far. She would be happy to see Scott and me living in a cardboard box in a Boston back alley. Why that is, I've never figured out. She doesn't want him. And I came along a full year after they had tried and failed as a couple. Evidently, being a psychotic, vindictive bitch is reason enough for Diane.

Elyse would absolutely go along with the idea if it meant extending her free ride. I don't think she particularly cares about her father one way or the other. She doesn't want revenge for some perceived slight. She also doesn't respect him or give him credit for all he's done for her over the years. Her only concern is the money tree that comes along with his presence in her life.

We might be forced to once again call our lawyer, to once again fight a ridiculous court battle. Diane is like a leech slowly draining my life. She feeds off my misery. I want to watch her choke on her diamond tennis bracelet.

◆

The Mass Avenger closes the garage door behind him. He secures all three locks, then flips on the light. The brightness stabs his eyes. He blinks several times, giving them time to adjust. Then he picks the flashlight up from the floor and switches it off.

The woman watches him. She is still gagged, still tied, still dressed. Time to remedy that.

He squats beside the cage door and puts on his best concerned expression. "I don't want to hurt you, so you need to do as I say. Understand?"

She nods. Her hair is redder than he'd realized. Under the bright lights, it is a golden auburn. Her eyes are blue. Her skin is milky white. She is somewhere in her thirties, about 20 pounds overweight. She's wearing no makeup and is rather plain. She is not his type, though he is aroused just the same.

He unlocks the cage door, then crawls inside. She remains cowering in the corner. "Slide over here," he says.

She doesn't move. His mood shifts. "I said to slide over here!"

Her eyes widen. She scoots over on her butt, not too close but he is able to grab her arm and yank her closer. He slides his fingers over her face. She stares at him but doesn't struggle.

"Now I'm going to take that tape off of your mouth," he says. "Do not scream or I will hurt you. And no one will hear you, so you'll be hurt for nothing." He gives her a moment to absorb that. Then he says, "This will sting," and rips the tape off.

Her head snaps back and she whimpers. "That's better," he says. "What's your name?"

She stares at him. He waits. Finally, she says, "Holly."

That makes him think of Christmas. His mother would take him shopping and let him fill the cart with all the toys on his wish list. She'd let him bring them home and look at them. The next day, he had to pack them all up for her to bring to a charity. If he cried, she'd get angry and call him a selfish baby.

He blinks away the memory. That kind of reminiscing is dangerous. He couldn't allow Holly to see any weakness, no matter how fleeting.

He runs a finger over her bottom lip. She flinches. "You have nice lips," he tells her. Plump, pouty. Red from the tape. She doesn't respond.

"Now I'm going to cut the ties," he says. "Don't move and don't struggle. That's important. If you don't behave, you will be seriously hurt."

He takes the hunting knife from his pocket. Her wide eyes follow his movements. First he cuts the tie around her ankles. Then he spins her so that her outstretched legs are facing away from him. He doesn't trust this one. He cuts the tie on her wrists but keeps the knife in a firm grip. She looks at the knife, then up at him. "Don't do anything stupid," he says.

He moves backward to the cage door. "Now take your clothes off."

Her left eye twitches. "Please let me go," she whispers.

"Later. Right now, I want you to take off your clothes."

"Please..."

"You're only going to make me angry. You need to do as I say."

She shakes her head. He touches the blade of his knife. "Don't make me do it," he says.

Her eyes fill with tears as she strips off her leather jacket. He holds his hand out. "Toss it over here," he tells her.

He takes the jacket and shoves it behind him. He waits, watching her. She's dressed in plain jeans and a light blue pullover jersey. Generic white sneakers cover her feet. He points to them. "Take your shoes off next."

She takes them off, revealing plain white socks. "Push them over here," he says. "Do not throw them."

She does as he tells her. He gives her a moment to relax. He wants her to think that's the end of it; that he might stop there. He wants her to worry. He wants her to know that he has total control.

"Now your shirt," he says.

She shakes her head. "Holly," he says. "You do not want to make me mad. Remember what I told you?"

She scoots back to the corner. "No."

The word is barely a whisper. Still, it is a defiance he will not tolerate. "Do it now!" he shouts.

She stares at him. The tears have dried. Anger erupts inside him. She thinks she has control! Even now, in her cage, she thinks she has power over him! He pulls the stun gun from his pocket and is on her in no time. Thousands of electrical volts knock her backward. She sprawls on the cold floor. Drool seeps from the corner of her pretty lips.

He takes his time undressing her, allowing his fingers to linger wherever they please. Then he gets new zip ties from the cabinet. He ties each wrist to a piece of the metal cage behind her, so that she is sprawled on the floor with her arms stretched over her head. For a moment, he considers strapping her ankles together. But that would not do. He runs his fingers over her cold flesh and waits for her to be completely conscious.

19

I am an hour into my Wednesday workday and I'm not in a particularly good mood. I'd been up half the night, thinking about Diane the Demon Woman and her Devil Spawn Elyse. The girl can't possibly have any of Scott's genetics. When Elyse was born, Diane must have had the doctor suck out all of Scott's DNA.

If Diane follows through with her threat, that means we will be financing our lawyer's lifestyle once again. The man has a vacation home in Paris, thanks to us. We'll have to forget about our trip to Aruba. No white sandy beaches, no tropical drinks served by tanned pool boys.

To add to my misery, the noise level in the salon is threatening to rupture my eardrums. Clients are yelling across the room to each other, raising their voices over the steady thrum of the blow dryers. The phone won't stop ringing and we've already had three people without appointments walk in wanting haircuts.

Needless to say, I am on edge and now my 12:30 client is 20 minutes late. I'm standing by the desk waiting when Sue strides in the door. She looks at me as she slips off her coat. "Oh," she says, "you're waiting for me."

I nod. "Your appointment was at 12:30."

Sue follows me to the sink. Rather than apologize, she tells me, "I've had a busy morning."

I bite my tongue to keep the sarcastic remark from tumbling out. I rush through the shampooing and get Sue to my chair. She glances at her watch. "I have an appointment for a massage in Hanover at 1:30," she says. "I need you to cut fast."

I'm holding my scissors dangerously close to her jugular vein. Hanover, at best, is a 15-minute ride. She strolls in late, then expects me to jump hoops because she is stupid enough to book her appointments too close together?

"I'll do my best," I say through gritted teeth.

I am a quarter of the way through her cut when she again looks at her watch. "Can't you cut any faster?" she asks.

Her tone is snippy. I can't resist a little snippiness in return. "Since my next client is already waiting," I say, "I would like nothing more than to cut faster. But I'm doing the best I can."

I get through the haircut and don't bother checking to see if it's even. At this point, I don't care. As I'm reaching for the blow dryer, Sue brushes me away. "Don't bother," she says. "I don't have time."

She says this as if it is somehow my fault. I'm tempted to jam my scissors through her eyeball. Honestly, would anyone even miss this woman?

If she had been half as concerned about showing up here in time, she would have had no problem making it to her massage appointment. Of course, being late for me doesn't negatively affect her at all. On the other hand, if she's late for her massage appointment the therapist will likely just shorten her session. Instead of an hour, she'll only get 40 minutes. Maybe I should start implementing that rule. If a client is late, I'll subtract that time from the time I spend with them. Quite a few of my clients would be walking out with half a haircut.

In the next two hours, I apply a color, do three haircuts, answer the phone six times, and call a cab for my 90-year-old client who, thankfully, no longer drives. At 3, Jill walks in the door. She is a somewhat excitable college student. She's sweet and childlike. I think she grew up in an enchanted forest.

Jill is having a highlight. As I'm weaving strands onto tinfoil, she says, "Did you hear that there's another woman missing?"

"No," I reply. "The police think it's that serial killer again?"

"They don't want to speculate." Jill makes quotation marks with her fingers when she says speculate. "But the woman is older than his other victims. I think they said she's 36. So maybe he didn't take her."

Up until now, all of The Mass Avenger's victims have been in their early twenties. That had given me a measure of comfort, since I am 37. It's a little unnerving to think that he might have upped his age limit.

"Where did she disappear from?" I ask.

"A convenience store parking lot in Brockton. Her name is Holly Stevens. Do you know her?"

I shake my head. "I don't think so."

Ellie, Renee's client, turns toward us. "Are you talking about that missing woman?"

"Yes," Jill says. "Have you heard about her?"

"It's horrible!" Ellie says. "She has a teenage daughter at home."

"The Avenger got another one?" Renee asks.

"They aren't sure, yet," Ellie replies. "She disappeared last night."

"It's so creepy," Jill says. "I can't believe there's really a serial killer right here where we live. My father won't let me go to the college library by myself at night. I used to do all my studying there but now I only go if my friends are with me."

"That's smart," Ellie says. "Women need to be extra careful and not trust anyone. This guy could even be a neighbor!"

Jill shudders. "You think he might live here in Whitman?"

"Who knows," Ellie says. "Crazy people are everywhere."

Jill's face pales. I feel like I'm watching Peter Pan being confronted by Ted Bundy. I attempt to interject a level of calm but Ellie is intent on a lecture of women who trust too easily and proper behavior when out alone.

When Paul, my next client, walks in the door, Jill nearly faints. Paul is 6 feet 6 inches tall, with a rumbling voice and penetrating eyes. He also worships his wife and three children. He coaches soccer and teaches a self-defense course to teenage girls. But all Jill sees is a large, boisterous man who could be cutting up women at random. Ellie has done a great job of placing the boogey man into Jill's fairytale life.

I manage to get through the rest of the day without killing anyone. At 8:45, Scott walks in the door. I can't help but drop my sour mood when I see him. Not only is he incredibly good to look at but he is starting the cleanup while Renee and I finish with our clients. Having my husband chaperone me at night isn't such a bad thing after all.

***

The Mass Avenger showers off the stench of his workday. He dresses in old jeans and a sweatshirt. The garage will be chilly. A ripple of excitement gives him a shiver. He'd checked on his guest early this morning. Weak but still defiant, the bitch had spit on him. He'd knocked two of her teeth out with one punch.

Tonight he will break her good. He'll strip her desire to fight. By the time he is done, he will own her.

He is pulling on his old work boots when the doorbell rings. The chimes echo off the living room walls. He hesitates, staring at the front door. Visitors rarely come to his house and never uninvited. A sudden fear grips him. What if it's the police? What if they know?

He shakes this off. The cops aren't anywhere close to figuring out his identity. They're all busy chasing their tails while he shows the world what true power is.

The doorbell chimes again. He goes to the door and presses an eye against the peephole. His heart sputters and his stomach twists. He arranges his face into a welcoming smile, then pulls the door open.

"Mrs. Harland," he says. "What a surprise."

"Rose," she says. "You're all grown up now and need not address me so formally. Besides, I've told you, calling me Mrs. Harland makes me feel like an old lady."

She looks like an old lady, though he doesn't say that. He works on maintaining the friendly smile. "Right. Sorry about that."
Her eyes dart to the space behind him. "I hope I'm not disturbing you."

"No. Not – " He stops himself. He'd been about to say *not at all*. But she *is* disturbing him. And he absolutely does not want her thinking that it's okay to pop in unannounced. He says, "I was just on my way out to take care of a few things."

"I won't keep you, then. I was in the neighborhood and thought I'd pop over to pick up the waffle iron that you said I could borrow. I thought I'd save you the trip to my house. Plus, I'd like to practice with it a bit before Katelyn arrives this weekend. It's been awhile since I've made waffles from scratch."

The dumb bitch! She has no right invading his world this way. Her arrogance infuriates him. The smug, fat whore!

He can't say any of that. He has to continue smiling. Rose Harland had been his mother's best friend. They'd drink coffee and talk about how difficult their lives were. Then they'd go off to get manicures and facials while he stayed at home on a Saturday afternoon and did laundry.

"No problem," he says. "I'll get it for you."

"Wonderful!" Rose exclaims. "You don't mind if I come inside, do you? My nipples are getting frostbitten out here!"

He drops his eyes and turns away. Such a pig. She wants to embarrass him but he refuses to respond to her childishness. He holds the door open and steps aside. "Excuse my terrible manners," he says. "Come in."

Rose steps inside the living room. He feels her assessing the space. A TV, sofa, two matching chairs, and a glass-topped coffee table with matching end tables. The same couch and chairs that his mother had bought for the room two months before she died. The same glass tables she'd made him clean with Windex every afternoon after school.

He'd tossed the old television and upgraded to a 50-inch plasma. The rest of the room remained unchanged.

"I'll go get it," he says. "Be right back."

He hurries to the kitchen and pulls the waffle iron from the cabinet. He practically bumps into Rose as he comes through the doorway. "Sorry," he mutters.

"I was coming to see if you needed help."

"No, I knew right where it was, Mrs. ... Rose."

Rose gives him a condescending smile. "That's much better!"

He squeezes past her, back into the living room. He has never liked her and doesn't want her in his space.

"You haven't changed much about the house," Rose says.

Her tone is almost accusatory. "No," he says. "I haven't."

"I thought you'd have made it your own by now. I know you miss your mother – we all do – but you can't go on mourning her forever."

Mourning her? Ha! If only she knew. "It's fine the way it is," he says.

Rose takes the waffle iron from his hands. "Your mother told me that she used this every Sunday morning to make your breakfast! You're sure you don't mind me borrowing it?"

Bile rises in his throat. He could see himself smashing Rose's head against the hardwood floor. His mother had never made him waffles on Sunday mornings. That had been his job. He'd made breakfast, then cleaned the mess. His mother hadn't done a damn thing. She'd claimed to be teaching him how to be a good husband. Bullshit! She'd been a lazy bitch who'd enjoyed making her son wait on her.

"I don't mind you taking it," he told Rose. "I never use it anymore."

"Katelyn doesn't get to visit often, so I want to do something special for her. Homemade waffles and fresh strawberries for her first breakfast! Doesn't that make your mouth water?"

"Sounds great. I'm sure she'll love it."

"I'll get this back to you in a couple of weeks."

"You're welcome to keep it."

"Oh, no. I could never do that."

"Please," he said. "My mother would like that. As I said, I never use it anymore."

Rose beamed at him. "Such a thoughtful boy!"

He isn't being thoughtful. Not in the least. He doesn't care about Rose or the damn waffle iron. He's only giving it to her because he does not want her coming back. "You can think of my mother every time you use it," he says.

"Oh, I will! Thank you!"

A little more small talk gets Rose out the door. He rushes to the kitchen and grabs the take-out bags he'd brought home. Then, after peeking out to be sure that Rose has gone, he hurries across the yard to his garage.

Holly is curled on her side, the wool blanket wrapped tight around her naked body. Her tangled hair falls over her cheek. Her eyes are open but she doesn't look at him as he unlocks the cage door. The stench of urine is strong. He'd strapped her wrists to the cage wall and gagged her, leaving her just enough leeway to get up and hover over the bucket he'd left her. He hates when they wet themselves.

She remains huddled in the corner as he grabs the bucket. "I'll be right back," he says. Then he takes the bucket out to clean.

Back inside, he finds that she still hasn't moved. "I brought dinner," he tells her.

Holly doesn't acknowledge him. The Mass Avenger swallows back his irritation. He doesn't want her to know how easily she gets to him. "Cheeseburgers," he says. "And a Coke. You're probably pretty thirsty by now."

Her eyes flicker over him. He places her bag of food inside the cage, then slips the knife from his pocket. "I'm going to cut your hands loose and remove the tape from your mouth. Don't try anything stupid."

She whimpers when he rips the tape. He slices the ties off her wrists. Her arms fall to her sides. She wiggles her fingers slowly, trying to bring the circulation back.

Backing out, he closes and locks the door. He moves to the workbench, where he'd placed his own bag of food. He sits in the ratty chair and pulls a burger from the bag. Suddenly he is starving.

Five minutes later, he notices that Holly has not touched her food. He swallows the last bite of his second burger and says, "You need to eat."

She is sitting now, her back against the furthest corner of the cage. She clutches the blanket tight. Her legs are stretched out in front of her. Both ankles are bloody and raw from her struggle with the ties. She'd put up quite a fight last night.

She stares at him. Hatred burns in her eyes. He stares back. "Eat," he says.

A slight shake of her head. He is about to argue but changes his mind. Arguing gives her power. Maybe he'll force-feed it to her later.

"Your choice," he says.

He finishes his meal, then tosses the trash in the covered bin. She watches him and his arousal builds.

"Your family is looking for you," he tells her.

Holly's eyes widen. He smiles. "Your mother was on the news this morning," he says. "She begged for your safe return. Your teenage daughter was with her. What is she, 15, 16? Quite the looker already. Maybe you'd like me to bring her here? We could have a little family reunion."

Terror fills Holly's eyes. Her swollen lips tremble. He laughs. "Don't worry. She's a little young for my taste."

He squats down and unlocks the cage door. "The police have no leads, not even a little clue. They're idiots, all of them. They're so beaten down by women that they can't even do their job properly, anymore. It's sad, really. But soon they'll see that I'm freeing us all."

She has drawn her legs up beneath the blanket. Her eyes don't leave his. He reaches his hand out. "Give me the blanket now."

The blanket tightens around her. He blows out a breath, fighting to remain calm. "Don't make me angry, Holly. You know that doesn't turn out well. One way or the other, I will take the blanket. If you make me do this the hard way, you will suffer a great deal."

Her eyes flicker away from his. A few seconds later, the blanket loosens from her shoulders. She eases it away from her bruised and bloody skin and tosses it to him. Her breasts are large, a little saggy. They sway slightly and her nipples harden from the cold air. He wants the right one. And he wants it hard like that when he cuts it off.

20

Scott and I pass Sunday in blissful solitude. A cold front has rolled in with November. At noon, the temperature hovers at 38 degrees. Scott takes Zena and Jack for a run, while I sit on the living room floor playing with Neal and Cassady. My little ones don't like the cold any more than I do.

Thirty minutes later, Scott comes back with the dogs. His cheeks are flushed. I kiss him and his icy nose gives me a shiver. I make hot chocolate and popcorn floating in butter. The six of us sprawl out in the living room. I share my popcorn with the dogs, while we watch an episode of Chuck on the DVR.

Scott and I go to bed early but don't go to sleep until late. We've had one of those rare perfect days. As I drift off to sleep, I try to ignore that nagging whisper that tells me this is the calm before the storm.

Monday comes too soon. I shuffle out of bed just as Scott's about to leave for work. He's made fresh coffee and turned up the heat for me. My to-do list awaits me; cleaning, laundry, errands. But it's my day off and I feel no need to rush.

I take my coffee into the office and sit down at the computer. I open my homepage and scan the local news. A headline catches my eye. *Holly Stevens' Body Found.* She's the Brockton woman taken from the convenience store. I scan the article, wincing at the details. The description of her body includes "multiple lacerations", "battered", "raped".

A picture of the woman accompanies the article. An average woman whose fame comes through death.

I'm about to switch over to my email when another headline catches my eye. *An Open Letter From The Mass Avenger.* The lunatic has written a letter to the world. I don't know which is worse; the fact that the letter has been printed by news agencies or the fact that I am sitting here reading it.

To the men and women of Massachusetts,

No doubt, you have heard of me. I am the Mass Avenger. By now, you should understand my play on words. I am avenging the masses – I am from Massachusetts. For now, my work is only within the state. But, who knows, in the future I might expand.

I have left a letter with each "victim". I use this word only because it is the term familiar to you. None of my "victims" were innocent. Who, then, is truly the victim?

The police have refused to share those letters with you. Therefore, I have decided to send this letter directly to you, the public. After all, my work concerns you. What right do the police have to withhold relevant information from you?

To all the men who have suffered at the hands of a woman: I do this for you. To all of the women who abuse your power: Beware! I am coming for you.

For too long, women have been pulling the strings that make men dance. They play-act at innocence. We know differently.

Of course, not all women behave this way. Some understand the unjustness of the world and do not use their powers to control. A few even sympathize with the male's plight. These women are safe from me.

All women, each and every one of you, can be safe. The choice is yours. All you need do is learn the lesson before I get to you.

Yours truly,

The Mass Avenger

I continue to stare blankly at the computer screen. The man is crazy. How can it be that no one has found him yet? The police seem to have little in the way of leads. And what about family? Friends? Doesn't anyone who knows this man suspect that he's a nutcase?

Along with the letter, "experts" offer their opinions. I scan the various quotes, which range from the man having been sexually dominated by his mother to him being a frustrated, closet

homosexual. None of the "experts" gives much in the way of
profound insight.   I've finished my coffee and have yet to check my
email. At this rate, my to-do list will still be waiting tomorrow. Only,
by then, it will have grown.

I put my mug in the dishwasher and force myself into the
shower. Thirty-five minutes later, I am on my way to the bank. From
there, it's the dry cleaners – I'd knocked a glass of wine onto Scott's
leather jacket – then a quick stop at the used bookstore to replenish
my stock.

Scott hadn't wanted me going out alone. I'd convinced him that
it is impractical to expect me to remain locked inside until the serial
killer is caught. I'd promised to keep the car doors locked and not to
go anywhere that isn't hugely populated. He'd reluctantly agreed. I'd
felt triumphant then. Now, after having read that creepy letter,
barricading myself inside might not be such a bad thing after all.

Less than two hours later, I am back in my house. Our mail
carrier, who is a sour-faced woman about my age, had just left the
mail as I'd been pulling in. The dogs are clamoring for attention. I
greet them all with hugs and duck medallion treats. They move on to
chew, while I sift through the mail.

The business envelope addressed to me and Scott causes my
heart to sputter. The return address is Robert Madison, our lawyer.
Dread grabs hold of me as I slide the typewritten letter from the
envelope. The words don't surprise me, though I still feel them like a
punch to the gut. He has been contacted by Diane Greer's lawyer.
Elyse plans to attend Columbia University in New York City in
January and Diane expects us to pay. According to Diane's lawyer,
she will be staying in the dorm and will need living expenses as well.

At that moment, I would like nothing better than to feed Diane
to The Mass Avenger. In his letter, he claims to be after women who
abuse their power. What better example than Diane?

Our lawyer closes the letter by telling us not to worry. Easy for
him to say. He's the one with the vacation home in Paris.

He wants us to call for an appointment at our convenience. If
never is convenient, does that mean that we can ignore this whole
thing? I sigh and sputter. The dogs all watch as I pace and swear.
Once I've gotten myself under control, I call for an appointment.
Then I leave a message on Scott's cell phone. He needs to take
Thursday morning off.

So much for yesterday's tranquility. I was right about it being the calm before the storm.

*

The Mass Avenger races inside his house. He kicks the door shut and heads straight for the couch. Holly's photo blazes from the front page of the *Brockton Enterprise*. They'd better have printed his letter!

He doesn't get out of his work clothes or even bother taking off his coat. His excitement hums with a life of its own. Beside Holly's picture is the article about her death. The usual dribble makes for a boring read; grieving parents, a stricken teenage daughter. Maybe the daughter will learn from her mother's death. He'll be creating an improved generation of females!

A note at the end of the article references his letter and informs readers to turn to page six. Page six! His letter should be on the front page! What he has to say to the world is far more important than one dead woman!

He rips off the front page and balls it in his fist. A few slow breaths calm him down. He turns to page six and sees the headline at the top. His letter takes up the left half of the top section. Far from the blazing notoriety he'd expected.

To his relief, the letter is published in its entirety. His words, right there for the world to see! He runs his fingers over the words. Now they know the truth. He is not a sick freak. He is correcting injustices.

He is about to toss the paper onto the coffee table when he notices the article on the opposite side. The headline screams at him. *Experts Weigh In On The Mass Avenger*. Sweat beads on his forehead. Will they understand his message? Will they tell the people that he is perfectly sane?

He puts the paper down, telling himself that he doesn't care what so-called experts are saying about him. People can now judge for themselves. He yanks off his coat and forces himself to hang it in the entryway closet. He needs a shower, then dinner. He hasn't eaten anything all day.

His eyes flicker back to the paper. Scooping it up, he sits on the edge of the couch. Maybe they do understand him. A quick look won't hurt.

The first expert, a psychologist called Stanley Brown, talks about The Mass Avenger's relationship with his mother. Brown cites early abuse and dominance, backing up his words with scientific babble.

Without realizing it, The Mass Avenger had begun to cry. Full out tears, like a stupid child! He swipes at the tears, pushing them off his face with a fury. So what if the psychologist is right about his mother. That doesn't mean a damn thing! If anything, that makes his work more important. He is saving young boys from having to endure what he'd been through.

Angry now, he begins to read the next expert's opinion. This one's name is Arianna Shelby, a psychiatrist at Mass General Hospital in Boston. She starts off by saying that he likely tortured animals in his youth. He'd never harmed an animal! What is wrong with this woman? Obviously, she is not very good at her job!

He tells himself to toss the paper, ignore these so-called experts. Yet, he can't stop himself from reading. As he absorbs the words, he's consumed by a white hot rage like none he has ever experienced. This woman has told the world that The Mass Avenger kills due to sexual inadequacy!

His vision blurs and for a moment he is sure that his heart will explode. Sexual inadequacy? How dare that bitch say such a thing about him! He has no problems with sex!

He forces himself to read on. This woman, Dr. Shelby, claims that he is either unable to please a woman sexually or that he is forcing himself to bury homosexual feelings. His entire body goes icy cold. This psychiatrist, this bitch, has announced to the world that he might be a closet queer!

And what the hell is that about not being able to please a woman? What the hell does she know about him and his sex life? How dare she make such accusations!

A long-ago memory suddenly overpowers him. His mother had caught him masturbating when he was14. He closes his eyes, feeling the shame as intensely as he had that day. She'd laughed at him. In her mocking tone, she'd told him that she hoped he still had some growing to do. She'd laughed, telling him he would never be able to please a woman with what he had. Then she said that he would be doing all the laundry from now on and that he'd better not be getting any of his semen on her pretty towels.

The Mass Avenger shudders. He opens his eyes and blinks at his surroundings. His mother's living room. She's gone. She can't hurt him anymore. His eyes dart back to the paper. Dr. Arianna Shelby of Mass General has accused him of not being able to please a woman. Of being a closet gay. He sucks in a shaky breath. Dr. Shelby is going to learn that spreading such vile lies comes with consequences.

21

More than a week has passed and we haven't heard a word from Elyse. Over the past weekend, I had urged Scott to call Elyse, find out if she's still in New York and what her plans are. It's possible that this whole New York college thing is nothing more than one of Diane's scare tactics. Elyse might not intend to go back to school at all. For all we know, she could be back in Hanover, living in her mother's large and pretentious home.

Scott wanted nothing to do with that phone call. He's pissed at the way Elyse spoke to him the last time and isn't about to let it go. I think he's hit his breaking point with her. Not that I blame him. I don't know how he managed as long as he did. But it would be nice to know if we're still dangling on Diane's hook.

It's 6 on Wednesday night. Renee and I have officially reached the start of yet another of our unofficial men's nights. Mine begins with Craig, who is a pompous ass. He has this slow strut, like he wants you to believe he would never hurry for anyone or anything. When he rises from the chair in the waiting area, he puffs his chest out and hitches his belt. The man watches too many westerns.

Kim, Craig's girlfriend, recently gave birth to their third child. Medicaid has paid all the hospital bills. They have no health insurance, no savings, and live in a tiny two-bedroom apartment. I know this because Kim tells the world all of her personal business. Craig would be mortified if he knew this had become public knowledge. He behaves like he's a combination of Superstud and

Superman – able to leap tall building and mass produce in a single bound.

After I've wash Craig's hair and get him seated in my chair, he pulls a stack of photos from his jacket pocket. I appreciate that all parents think their children are pure perfection and want to show them off, but a couple of photos is plenty. Twenty or thirty gets annoying.

His children are 3, 20 months, and 2-weeks-old. I look at them and see my tax bill going up because these people are producing children they can't afford. That's a pissy attitude but I can't help myself. I make the appropriate gushing noises and tell Craig how beautiful his children are.

As I cut Craig's hair and listen to his self-important drone, I glance up with envy at Renee. The man in her chair is a comedian. He works the clubs in Boston and has had her laughing since he came in. I must have some seriously bad karma.

My next client is Kyle, who is either excruciatingly shy or just the silent type. I have yet to figure out which. I try to remember when he was last in. Judging by the minimal hair growth, it wasn't that long ago. I once had a male client who came in once a week. He said he wanted to grow his hair out but wanted it to grow out straight. My attempts to get him to stretch his appointments to at least three weeks failed miserably. Consequently, I'd pretend to cut his hair three out of the four times each month. He didn't seem to notice, though I experienced a lot of guilt over taking his money.

Kyle gives me a shy smile as I settle him in my chair. "Am I just trimming?" I ask.

He nods. He avoids my eyes as he says, "Yes, please."

"How are your art projects going?"

He breaks into a brilliant smile. "You remembered."

I smile back. "You were working on something with charcoals the last time you were here."

"Yeah. I actually finished that one last night. I haven't had as much time as I'd like to work on my technique but I thought it came out okay."

"You'll have to bring some of your stuff in. I'd love to see it."

"Sure. I'd love your opinion."

I am almost done with his cut when Gail walks in. She's holding a printed sheet and some brochures. "I found a few great deals you might be interested in," she tells me.

Gail is a client and also our local travel agent. Her passion for travel is contagious. Each time I do her hair, I itch to jump on a plane. Two weeks ago, I'd mentioned to her that Scott and I were thinking of going to Aruba. She'd said she'd pull together a bunch of info for me. After all the nonsense with Scott's ex, I'd forgotten about talking to Gail.

"Thank you," I say. "But our trip might be postponed another year. I'm not sure, yet."

"Everything okay?"

"Sure. Our lawyer needs to upgrade his vacation home, so we figured we'd help him out."

"Uh-oh. The ex again?"

Gail knows the story of Diane. We share ex horror stories. Her ex left her with three kids, so that he could pursue a lifetime of shirking responsibility. Every time she catches up to him for child support, he quits his job and moves on.

"Unfortunately, yes," I say. "She won't be happy until we're living in a cardboard box."

Gail leaves the papers on the desk. "You know my thoughts on exes. Just let me know if things work out and you want to book the trip."

"I will. Thanks."

After she leaves, Kyle asks, "Problems with your husband's ex-wife?"

I roll my eyes. "They were never even married. A very brief fling tied him to this woman forever. She's truly evil. Their daughter is 18 and decided to take off to New York City to pursue a modeling career. We're now expected to finance her lifestyle there."

"That's ridiculous," Kyle says.

"You'd think, right?"

"The girl doesn't work?"

"No. She has been raised to expect Daddy to pay. Diane, his ex, hooked up with some rich married guy, so that's the kid's example for getting what she wants in life."

"Wow. That must really piss you off."

I chuckle. "To say the least. Sometimes I wish that serial killer, The Mass Avenger, would get hold of her."

Kyle laughs. "Yeah, I can see why you'd feel that way."

I've finished Kyle's cut. Like many men, he doesn't like it blow-dried because it makes his hair too puffy. My next client is already here waiting. My stomach does a little flip-flop at the sight of Jason. His piercing stare grates on my nerves. I want to stick my scissors through his eyeballs.

Jason stares up at me as I wash his hair. I try holding one arm over his face while I scrub. Let him stare at my forearm for awhile. I get him to my chair and ask, "Just a trim today?"

"Right," he says. "I heard you talking about your husband's ex. Sounds like she's a real prize."

I don't like the idea of sharing personal information with this guy. He's staring at me with his x-ray eyes. He has a sharp nose and jutting jaw. Even his cheekbones stand out like they are carved from stone. "She definitely has some issues," I say.

"Must be pretty bad, if you want her dead."

"What?"

"You said you'd like that serial killer to get his hands on her."

"Oh. Well, sometimes I think about it when I'm really mad. But, you know, it's just one of those stupid thoughts. I don't really wish she'd get murdered."

Jason smiles, which does nothing to soften the sharp lines of his face. "Nothing wrong with a little fantasy now and then."

If only he knew. Right now, I am fantasizing about ramming my scissors through his unblinking stare.

I am just finishing with Jason when my next client walks in. My evening immediately goes from bad to worse. Russell greets me with a polite hello. He's freshly shaven and dressed neatly. His presence is not overpowering, as Jason's is. His creep factor, though, exceeds even Jason's. I'm uncomfortable around him in a way I don't understand.

Jason schedules his next appointment. As he's leaving, he says, "Good luck with the ex. With some luck, maybe you'll get your wish and she'll disappear off the face of the earth!"

I try to laugh off that remark. This whole serial killer thing has me way too edgy. I'm suddenly taking everything too seriously.

I bring Russell to the sink. As I'm shampooing, he asks, "Problems with an ex?"

I shrug. "My husband's ex, yeah."

"They have kids together?"

"One. She's 18, so we thought the court battles would be over. Evidently, we were wrong."

"She's taking you to court?"

I wrap a towel over Russell's hair and lead him to my chair. "It's Diane's life mission," I say with forced humor.

He shakes his head. "Too many women use their kids as pawns that way. It's sad."

I don't want to follow this line of conversation. I keep the tone of my voice light. "I suppose we all have our reasons for the things we do. Just a trim tonight?"

"Yes, please."

"How is your job going?"

Russell is a butcher. The idea of slicing off an animal's body parts grosses me out. But it's better than talking about Scott's ex. He gives me that boy-next-door smile. "It's a way to pay the bills," he says.

"That's all work is for most of us, I guess."

"I suppose we can't all be rock stars, right?"

I chuckle. "Sadly, no. I sing along with the radio at home and my dogs howl."

This makes Russell laugh. "You can't be that bad."

"Oh, yes I can. Trust me!"

I manage to keep the conversation light, while avoiding Russell's creepy gaze. Russell departs as my next client comes in. Thankfully, John is a 60-year-old, laid-back electrician who works with Scott. Finally, I have a client I can be myself with. Well, almost anyway. I'll still keep my murderous fantasies to myself.

The Mass Avenger sits on the couch with his laptop. He is curious about the woman who is Skye's husband's ex. He's looking for court records or anything that will tell him the woman's name. Skye's husband's name is Scott but he finds no Scott Summers in any court records. Isn't all this stuff available to the public now? He should be able to find something.

Skye would like the woman dead. He'd seen it in her eyes. Eighteen years and the bitch is still making Skye's life miserable. Even worse, the woman is teaching her daughter to use men for their money. Another generation of females being raised to abuse their power. She needs to be stopped.

Skye had tried to laugh it off but he could tell that she felt the same way. He'd known, right from that first time they'd met, that she is different from other women. She gets it. And she is being unfairly tormented by a self-serving bitch.

He'd do this for Skye. He'd teach the bitch a lesson about using men. Maybe he'd even be able to tell Skye about it. Share the details.

Or bring her in and let her watch. The world would have to take him seriously if he had a female partner.

He pushes his hands through his hair, then shakes his head and sighs. He is getting carried away. Having a partner would be dangerous. Plus, he isn't sure that Skye could follow through. She might not have the stomach for his type of work.

Just the thought of having her there with him, teaching women what true power is, arouses him. He touches himself but stops before he gets carried away. He has work to do. He will find this ex and make her pay. First, though, he has his own revenge to carry out. Dr. Arianna Shelby of Mass General is going to find out how wrong she had been about his supposed sexual inadequacy.

22

When Scott arrives at The Cutting Edge on Thursday night, I can tell by his forced smile that something is wrong. I have just finished up with my last client. Renee is doing a blow-dry, so I grab the bin of dirty brushes and lead Scott out to the backroom. As we de-hair the brushes, I ask, "What's wrong?"

"Elyse called," Scott says.

"And?"

"She said she wanted to offer me one last chance."

"Last chance? You're kidding."

"Nope. That's exactly how she worded it. One last chance to do the right thing before her mother's lawyer files the papers to bring us to court."

"And, according to Elyse, the right thing is to give her money?"

Scott uses a little too much force to rip the hair from a brush. "She and Chelsea found an apartment and she thinks it's reasonable to expect us to pay for six-months' rent."

I suck in a quick breath. "At New York City prices? Are either one of them even working, yet?"

"Of course not. They're getting portfolios made to hand out to modeling agents. That's the other thing. We're supposed to foot that bill as well."

I mutter a not-so-nice word. "Her mother has taught her well."

"Tell me about it."

"What do you want to do?"

He looks at me as if I have said something absurd. "Is there even an option?" he asks. "No way am I going to give in to her blackmail tactics. Even if we had the money, I wouldn't give it to her. She's a spoiled brat who needs to grow up and learn about responsibility."

"Yeah…" I lean over and give him a quick kiss. "I'm sorry."

"I'm the one who's sorry. It doesn't look like Aruba will be happening anytime soon."

"That's okay. We'll make a slide show of Aruba for the computer, then spread a blanket out and kick back with frozen margaritas while we look at the beach scenes."

Scott laughs. "I'm not sure what I did to deserve you."

Renee comes out back, huffing a loud sigh. Her last client left seconds ago and Renee is on a tirade. The woman had been in having her color redone because she'd said Renee had made it too light the last time. Renee darkened the formula a half-shade and the woman had spent the past 20 minutes complaining that it is now too dark.

Renee spouts off a string of curses. "I took an hour of my time," she says, "didn't charge her a dime, and she can't even say thank you, much less tip me!"

We spend 15 minutes trading complaints while we clean. Scott has a silly grin on his face as he listens. Evidently, Renee and I amuse him.

We go home and I shower all the people hair off me. The amount of hair that finds its way through my clothing is truly astounding. Sometimes it's like having tiny splinters stuck in my skin. I put on a button-down flannel pajama shirt and nothing else, then climb into bed beside Scott. We stay up late discussing Elyse and Diane. We can do nothing to appease either of them, so all that's left is to sit around and wait for the court summons.

Scott feels he is somehow to blame for Elyse's behavior. I don't agree. He spent as much time with her as Diane would allow. He always supported her financially and did what he could to offset Diane's insanity. I remind him of this but he just shakes his head.

"Genetics is a powerful thing," I say. "And Diane's seem to be way stronger than yours."

"Yeah…"

"Besides, she sees her mother using men to get designer clothes, jewelry, vacations. She figures that's the way to go."

"I should have fought for custody."

"You never would have gotten Elyse," I say. "You know that. Corrupt values aren't enough to prove a mother unfit."

Scott sighs. I cuddle close and we lie that way for awhile. I'm drifting off into a sleepy haze when he says, "I don't like my daughter."

"I know."

"I think the sex lasted twenty minutes," he says. "We were both so drunk. Twenty minutes of sloppy sex was not worth a lifetime tied to Diane."

I laugh. "Sloppy sex, huh?"

He chuckles. "Oh, yeah. She threw up afterward."

This makes me laugh harder. "You never told me that!"

"It's not exactly something I'm proud of."

"So was the sex that bad that you made her puke?" I tease.

He gives me a nudge. "No! Well, maybe. Hell, I don't remember. But I knew right then that her throwing up all over the place was a bad omen."

"If only she'd thrown up a few minutes sooner, you might never have completed the act."

"She was a beautiful baby."

"Yes, she was," I say. "And someday she might be a beautiful and nice adult. Give her time to grow up and figure things out for herself."

Scott pulls me closer but doesn't say anything. A few minutes later, he is asleep. It's almost 2 a.m. and we both have to get up early for work. I think about Diane and The Mass Avenger and I wonder if the serial killer has an ex-wife who drove him over the edge. I think about putting Nair in Diane's shampoo and Rogaine in her Estee Lauder foundation. This makes me smile as I drift off to sleep.

Saturday afternoon finally arrives and once again I am free from clients for two whole days. My parents are having a going-away party for Hendrix, the little Pug they have been fostering. And, yes, Hendrix is named after Jimi Hendrix, whose guitar playing my Dad still worships.

My parents do these parties up in style. My mother makes the dogs a "cake" with dog-friendly ingredients. She makes a separate cake for the humans to eat. Hopefully, we will never confuse the two. She puts together goodie bags for all the dogs, filling them with treats free of byproducts and chemical-free toys. We wear party hats and take the dogs on a final walk as a group through the neighborhood.

Scott has prepared our dogs for the party. They are bathed and brushed, looking quite dapper for their evening out. Scott is also looking good in his faded jeans and green Henley shirt. The green matches his eyes and his smile makes his dimples pop. I invite him to join me in the shower but he claims we have no time for that.

When we get to my parents' house, Kate is already there. She has brought Stephen, her boyfriend of two years. He proposed a few months ago. She is still considering her answer.

Kate, my best friend, was married once. She'd been 19 and Tom had been 32. She'd been a confused girl, searching for a daddy figure to replace her father, who had become a second mother. Unfortunately, Tom had been an ass and they'd gotten divorced a year later. Kate was left with a baby to raise on her own, which she has done an amazing job of. Bryan, her 17-year-old son, is a great kid. He's a senior at Whitman-Hanson Regional and plans to go to ITT Tech next year. He'd opted out of the party, claiming he had a date and he did not want to bring her to a dog party. I can't imagine why not.

My mother's friend Teresa is also here, along with her husband Charlie. They volunteer as foster parents with the same rescue organization as my parents and have brought their three dogs with them. Renee, her husband Ken, and their son Jonathan will be here with their Husky, and my parents' next-door neighbors are bringing their pimped out Poodle, Reggie. All together, we will have 15 dogs and 13 humans.

Kate is helping my mother in the kitchen. The goodie bags are lined up on one counter. Each one has a dog's name written in red marker. Both cakes are on the table. I only know which one belongs to the dogs because it's in the shape of a bone. They both look good enough for human consumption. My mother has made a fresh vegetable tray with four different flavors of dip, which Kate is gathering together to bring into the dining room.

The smell of homemade spaghetti sauce draws me near. I lift the lid on the Crock-Pot and sniff the heavenly scent. Tiny meatballs float in the sauce. The meatballs are not actually made with meat but no one here has a problem with that.

"What can I do to help?" I ask.

My mother dances through the kitchen. She's wearing faded jeans with a large black peace sign on one thigh. Her psychedelic-print shirt is loose and flowing. A matching scarf holds her hair away from her face. She hands me two bags of rolls from the natural food store's bakery. "Would you mind slicing these for me?" she asks.

My mouth waters at the scent of freshly baked bread. Jack, Cassady, Shiloh, and Taffy are right by my side. Their tongues are hanging out and their eyes are wide with excitement. They know this party is for them.

Before long, everyone has arrived and both dogs and humans are enjoying the food. When my mother cuts the dogs' cake, we all sing "for he's a jolly good fellow" to Hendrix. Each dog gets a plate. The challenge is in making sure they stick to their own and don't try to steal each other's. Then the humans get their cake, while the dogs lie around and sleep off their meal.

Later, we all grab a leash and a dog. It's dark and cold and the neighborhood is dead silent until we all step outside. Jonathan leads the way, with his Husky, Nemo. Jonathan is a big fan of the movie *Finding Nemo* and insisted on the name. Fifteen dogs of all sizes trot, sniff, and amble down the sidewalk as we humans attempt to keep them in line. We're bumping into each other and tripping over leashes. Despite the absurdness of the situation, we are all laughing so hard that tears are running down our faces.

Back at my parents' house, the dogs drain three bowls of water, then drop into immediate slumber. Renee and I are cutting up the remaining dog cake to put in the goodie bags. She asks, "What's with that Jason guy you've been doing? Does he ever blink, for Christ sake?"

"Isn't he creepy?" I say. "I want to poke his eyes out!"

"Who is Jason?" my mother asks.

"One of my newer clients," I reply. "The man stares at people like his eyes are glued open."

"At people?" my mother asks. "Or at you?"

"He stares at everyone," I say. "I don't get special attention."

My mother looks like she doesn't quite believe me. Jeanette, my mother's neighbor, comes in to tell us she's leaving. Her poodle is yapping behind her. I'm rescued from my mother's interrogation as she gathers Reggie's goodie bag and walks her neighbors to the door.

Soon, everyone has left and it's only Scott and me with my parents and our 10 dogs. I'm in the kitchen, helping my mother with the last of the clean-up. "Tell me about this Jason," she says.

I sigh. "He's just a client, Mom."

"I'm sure The Mass Avenger is 'just a client' somewhere."

"He's not The Mass Avenger," I say, though my voice doesn't hold as much conviction as I'd like.

"You're sure about that?"

"I'm only cutting his hair. I'm not dating him."

"If he's that strange, then perhaps you should send him elsewhere."

I laugh. "If I sent all my strange clients elsewhere, I wouldn't have a job!"

"Do you get bad vibes from him?"

My mother is a firm believer in instinct and vibes. When I was 15, I wanted to date a 17-year-old from our neighborhood. The guy was clean-cut and a good student. She wouldn't allow me near him, claiming that he gave her bad vibes. My mother was never one to keep me in tight restraints, so her emphatic "no" was unusual. Two months later, that same boy was arrested for raping a 12-year-old girl down the street. I've learned to listen to my mother's vibes, if not my own.

"Lots of people give me bad vibes," I say. "That doesn't mean they're serial killers."

She gives me a look. "Stop cutting his hair. You should refuse clients who make you uncomfortable."

I'd be working one day a month if I only did the people I liked. I don't tell my mother that. Arguing is pointless. I mutter an agreement and slip out to the dining room to gather the remaining coffee mugs.

By the time we get home, I'm wrapped in a heavy blanket of fatigue. The dogs immediately go to their beds. They don't even crack an eye to look at Scott or me as we move around the bedroom. Scott decides to help me undress, then he does a funny little striptease that makes me laugh. His hands are rough and his lips are soft. For a little while, I forget all about Elyse, Diane, The Mass Avenger, and my creepy clients.

Later, as Scott sleeps beside me and Neal snores in his bed on the floor, I can't get the image of Jason's creepy eyes out of my head. What if he is The Mass Avenger?

♪

The Mass Avenger follows the pristine BMW to a fancy restaurant with valet parking on the North Side of Boston. He coasts through the back of the lot, watching while the couple steps out of the shiny car. The man hands his keys to the young valet attendant, then places his hand on the small of the woman's back as they stroll inside.

Arianna Shelby and her husband, Stuart. The Mass Avenger has followed the couple from their cookie-cutter mansion in Revere, which is a suburb of Boston. Stuart is an accountant with a private practice not far from his and Arianna's home. He's an average-looking man, with a thin mustache and wire-rimmed glasses. An inch shorter than Arianna, everything about Stuart seems small next to his wife. The woman carries herself in a way that would overshadow the President.

Arianna Shelby is a bitch. Does she emasculate her husband with words, as well as appearance? The Mass Avenger ponders this as he watches.

No doubt, the man has been browbeaten all his adult life. Perhaps throughout his youth, as well. Stuart wears a look of defeat that sticks to him like clingy plastic wrap. Soon he will be freed from the woman sucking the masculinity from the very core of his being.

Not yet, though. As much as The Mass Avenger would like to take Arianna tonight, he isn't ready. He needs to catch her alone, at a time when no one will be expecting her. That way, he allows himself time to get her comfortable in her new home.

The image of her in the cage makes him chuckle. He leaves the parking lot, content, for now, to head back home. The esteemed Dr. Arianna Shelby will soon be learning what happens to women who abuse their powers over men. The thought arouses him and he shifts uncomfortably in the seat.

He turns his thoughts to Skye. His arousal builds. He shifts again, surprised by his body's reaction to the mere thought of Skye.

He hasn't fantasized about Skye sexually, though he does consider her somewhat of an ally. Is he suddenly confusing kinship with sexual attraction?

The Mass Avenger gives himself a shake. He stops at a red light and reaches down into his pants. The intensity of his arousal borders on painful. Could he and Skye ever be a team, in both body and spirit?

Earlier today, he found the name of Skye's husband's ex. Scott's last name is not Summers, which is where his confusion came from. His name is Scott Skyler. Summers is Skye's maiden name. Normally, The Mass Avenger has no tolerance for a woman who does not take her husband's name. In this case, however, he can understand why Skye chose to keep her maiden name. Skye Skyler is not a name any woman would want.

Is that an omen? Does Skye not belong with Mr. Scott Skyler?

He tries his own last name after Skye. The two names go well together.

The light turns green. He yanks his hand from his jeans and steps on the gas. Once he is finished with Arianna, he plans to take care of Diane Greer. As he thinks about sharing the experience with Skye, his erection throbs.

23

I wake up Monday morning with my period. This explains the uncontrollable mood swings. Yesterday, I'd had more ups and downs than a see-saw. Poor Scott. Sometimes I swear an evil gremlin hijacks my body.

I open the blinds. Gray gloom greets me. I wrap myself in my thick robe and call for the dogs to come. Zena and Jack are right on my heels. The two little ones aren't budging. I pick them up and carry them out the back door. A blast of arctic air steals my breath. I set the dogs down and tell them to go pee. Then I scurry inside and close the door.

By noon, I have managed to shower and dress. Cramps threaten to rupture my internal organs and I'm cranky. I make tea and wrap myself in a blanket. Neal and Cassady join me on the couch, while Jack and Zena sprawl out on the carpet. I channel surf while I tell Cassady how lucky she is to have been spayed. "No periods," I say. "I need to be spayed."

Nothing on the television interests me. I've sifted through hundreds of channels and I wind up right back where I started. A somber-faced newscaster speaks in her broadcasting school-polished voice. Her tailored suit is as gray as the day. I'm about to switch the TV off when I tune in to what she is saying.

"According to her husband, Dr. Arianna Shelby left her home at approximately 7:15 this morning. Dr. Shelby's secretary claims that she never made it to the office. Concerned when Dr. Shelby did not arrive in time for her 8 a.m. appointment, the secretary contacted Mr.

Shelby, who immediately alerted police. So far, there is no information on her possible whereabouts.

"Dr. Arianna Shelby recently gave a scathing statement as to her opinion of The Mass Avenger, the serial killer running loose on the South Shore. Police are unwilling to speculate as to whether the statement might have placed her on The Mass Avenger's radar."

A little chill races down my spine. I punch the button on the remote and the TV goes silent. The police might be unwilling to speculate but it isn't a giant leap to make. Dr. Shelby's statement had been the talk of the salon. She'd publicly emasculated a guy who already has an issue with women.

Jason's penetrating eyes jump into my head. I shake off the image. Part of me thinks I should call the cops but that's just plain stupid. What would I tell them? *I have a creepy client who likes to stare without blinking. You might want to check him out.* Yeah, like they'd take that seriously!

Besides, Jason is far from the only creepy male client. Russell is right up there with the creep factor. As my mother would say, he has negative energy. I can't very well tell the cops about every creepy guy whose hair I cut.

I pull the blanket tighter. If The Mass Avenger did take that doctor, then she is probably being tortured this minute. From the little I've read, this guy takes his work seriously. His victims pay an enormous price for being female.

I'm queasy and on the verge of tears. Damn hormones. I don't even know the woman. I certainly have no reason to cry about her disappearance.

Too bad that reporter hadn't interviewed Diane. Maybe she'd be the one missing right now.

I give myself a mental slap. As much as I can't stand Scott's ex, I shouldn't be wishing for a serial killer to abduct her. I would, however, like to drown her in a vat of hot wax. Or put poison gas in her blow dryer.

Cassady cracks open one eye and looks at me. "It's the cramps," I tell her. "They make me vicious."

I curl on my side. Cassady nestles against my chest. I drape the blanket over us and drift off. Dreams suck me right in to a world of pleasant revenge.

r

The Mass Avenger hurries home. He goes straight into the house, though he is tempted to first detour through the garage. He showers off the stench that follows him home from work each day. Dressed in jeans and a flannel shirt, he goes down to the kitchen and makes four sandwiches with roast beef and ham cold-cuts. He grabs two Cokes from the refrigerator and the bag of chips from the cabinet, then, humming to himself, heads to the door.

Fumbling with the armload of food, he manages to get outside and lock the door behind him. Darkness has settled, turning the late afternoon a dusty black. He crosses the yard and sets the food down while he unlocks the garage door.

Her scent fills the space. Expensive perfume gone musty with sweat. Stale urine. Fear. He finds the flashlight on the table and flips it on. She is squatting in the corner of the cage. The gag remains in place. He'd been worried that she would find a way to work it loose. The bitch doctor had wanted to do a lot of screaming this morning. The garage is soundproofed but he doesn't want to test its limits.

He carries the food inside, then closes and locks the garage door. Only then does he turn the lights on. Arianna blinks at the sudden brightness. She has been locked in darkness all day and the light is probably blinding her, burning her eyes. The Mass Avenger smiles at this. That little bit of pain is only the beginning.

He'd wanted to stay with her today but he couldn't risk taking the day off. As it was, he'd been late. None of that mattered, though. He is home now and has all night to break the bitch doctor.

He squats down in front of the cage and waits for her to meet his eyes. "Are you ready to cooperate?" he asks.

Her eyes narrow but she nods. Streaks of black mascara stain her cheeks. Her lipstick is worn, smeared in spots. Her short, bleached hair stands on end. Arianna Shelby no longer looks like the sophisticated, powerful psychologist she portrayed to the world.

She still wears her clothes. He'd had no time to strip her this morning. The designer suit is wrinkled, the nylons have a tear along the right calf. Her slut shoes cover her feet. He becomes aroused as he thinks about stripping her naked. Along with her clothes, he will take her power.

"Do you know who I am?" he asks.

Arianna nods. He smiles. "Good," he says. "Then you also know what I will do to you if you don't cooperate."

The fear in her eyes gives him childlike pleasure. Of course, he's going to kill her whether she cooperates or not. If she behaves, it will simply hurt less. Maybe she knows that. Most likely, she is holding on to that hope of rescue. Or of him changing his mind and letting her go. They all hold onto that at first.

"I'm going to untie you now." He shows her the stun gun and the knife. "If you even twitch, I'll make you sorry."

The fear in her eyes gives him an electric jolt of arousal. He slices the tie around her ankles first, then releases her wrists. After freeing her, he backs up to the doorway of the cage, out of her reach. "Take your shoes off," he says.

She stares at him. He waits but she doesn't move. Already she has forgotten about cooperating. "I said take your shoes off," he tells her. "I'm not asking again."

She blinks at his abrupt tone. A second later, she slips out of her shoes. Her feet are long and thin. Probably a size 9. Toenails painted red beneath the sheer nylons.

"Slide the shoes over here," he says. "Do not pick them up."

Arianna does as she is told. She doesn't try to throw the shoes at him. She's learning. He tosses the shoes out behind him and offers her a smile. "I brought sandwiches and drinks. You're probably pretty thirsty by now. I want you to scoot over toward me. Stay on your butt and scoot backward. Understand?"

She nods, then turns and scoots. When she is close enough, he tells her to stop. Before he unties the gag, he says, "If you scream or even speak too loud, I'll knock all your teeth out. Do you understand me?"

He waits for her nod, then removes the gag. "Now scoot back to where you were."

"Why are you doing this?" she asks.

Her voice is hoarse and crackles with the effort to speak. He chuckles at her question. "You're the psychiatrist," he says. "You claimed to have all the answers."

She doesn't respond. He pushes a napkin with a sandwich inside the cage. Then he fills a paper cup with Coke and puts that inside as well. "Eat," he says.

"I can help you," Arianna says. "You don't have to do this."

He glares at her. "I don't need your help! Now shut up and eat or I'll stuff that gag right back in your mouth."

He closes and locks the cage, then sits at the workbench with his dinner. Fifteen minutes later, he turns to find that she has eaten all of her sandwich and drank her Coke. She is the first to so quickly eat the food he offers. A clear sign that she is a fighter and believes she will find a way out.

The stun gun sits heavy in his pocket. The weight comforts him. While he has no doubt that he could handle her physically, he does not want to risk a wrestling match in the cage. He squats down and unlocks the door once again. For a moment, he simply stares at her. The muscles in her throat work up and down. Her jaw clenches. She can't stand being the subject of his scrutiny.

"You're hurting," she says. "But you don't have to resort to this. I can –"

"Do *not* try to psychoanalyze me!"

Arianna stops talking and bites down on her bottom lip. The Mass Avenger blows out a long breath. She pisses him off like no woman ever has. He'll take tremendous pleasure in breaking her into little pieces.

24

I am miserable. I don't just have menstrual cramps; I have a team of gremlins playing soccer with my ovaries.

I've managed to get through my Tuesday-morning clients without killing anyone. Considering my emotional state and the type of clients I've had to deal with, that is no small feat. Twin 4-year-olds spent five minutes fighting over who got to go first. Then the winner, Samantha, changed her mind halfway through the cut and wanted out. She squirmed, kicked, then promptly screamed when I didn't let her down right away.

Mary, my 10 o'clock, had a serious case of the farts. She sat in my chair, all prim and proper, as if the eye-watering, toxic fumes were not drifting up from her ass. I had to take shallow breaths through my mouth and find an excuse to walk away for air every few minutes.

Now it is noon and I have an entire half-hour of client-free bliss. An actual lunch break! This is a rare occurrence and I intend to take full advantage. I need to sit down, put my feet up, and swallow a bottle of Advil. First, I go across to the donut shop for a hot chocolate and a blueberry muffin. I also get a hot chocolate for Renee, a tea for Roxie, and a bagel for Andrea. The one lucky enough to get a break also gets to be the errand girl. I step back into the salon at 12:05 and my 12:30 client is waiting for me. The urge to dump my hot chocolate over her head is incredibly strong.

Jean is the touchy-feely type. She's always hugging me, grabbing my hand, pressing her fingers against my arms. I'm not a particularly touchy person, unless it's my husband or a dog. Needless to say, Jean makes me uncomfortable.

"Hello, Skye!" Jean says with ridiculous happiness.

I can tell she wants to hug me but I'm balancing a cardboard box filled with goodies that forces her to keep her distance. The groan almost escapes my lips. I bite it back and paste on my plastic smile. "Hi, Jean. You can have a seat at the sink and I'll be right with you."

"Oh, no hurry. I'm early."

"That's okay."

"Did you have lunch? I'm in no hurry. I don't mind waiting. We can chat while you eat."

Yeah, that's exactly what I want to do. Does she really think that this is some sort of social hour for me? I know that neither my doctor nor my dentist would invite me to hang out for lunch if I arrived early. And I'm pretty confident that Scott doesn't fix a customer's electrical problems, then stay for lunch afterward.

"I only have a hot chocolate," I say. She doesn't need to know about the muffin. "I'm ready for you."

"Are you sure?"

I want to smack her. The plastic smile is threatening to crack. "I'm sure. Have a seat and I'll be right there."

I put my hot chocolate in front of my chair and carry the rest of the order to the back room. Roxie flashes me a little smirk. I refrain from rolling my eyes as I meet Jean at the sink.

I finish Jean with about 15 minutes to spare until my next client. Naturally, Jean wants to linger and chat. By the time I get her out the door, I have maybe three minutes to pee before my next client arrives. Forget the muffin.

Time creeps by. Four o'clock comes and I've managed to keep from killing anyone. My scissors, however, are doing obscene things in my fantasies. Little ten-second clips run through my mind every now and then. Killer scissors that come to life. These fantasies keep the soccer-playing gremlins from taking over my body.

The day is winding down. Andrea raced out the door ten minutes ago. She has a parent-teachers conference to attend. Renee is applying a color to her last client and Roxie is waiting for her last group; three young children. My 4 o'clock is Donna, a retired nurse. She's nice, usually quiet. I've been doing her hair for more than a year and she only recently began sharing any sort of personal information. Last month she'd confided that her daughter and teenage granddaughter were moving in with her and her husband for a few months. She didn't seem happy about that.

As I'm cutting Donna's hair, she asks, "Did you hear about the latest missing woman?"

"Yes," I say. "That psychologist who'd been interviewed."

Lea, Renee's client, chimes in with her blustery voice. "She called that serial killer sexually inadequate! They think he took her for revenge."

Donna startles. Lea's volume can be unnerving. Donna had been a nurse in Boston and I try to remember which hospital she'd worked for. "Did you know her?" I ask.

Donna nods. "Not well. She occasionally did psych evaluations on my patients."

"You know the woman!" Lea exclaims.

Donna's muscles tense. I would like to snip off Lea's tongue. Renee shoots me an apologetic look. Of course, it's not her fault that her client is a loudmouthed busybody. I have more than a few of my own to contend with.

"Is there any news?" I ask.

"No," Donna says.

"The FBI is involved," Lea announces. "I never thought we'd have the FBI hunting a serial killer right in our back yards!"

Roxie's next client opens the door. The harried-looking mother practically shoves three children under 7 inside. Renee tosses a look at the children and says softly, "This is probably not a good topic to discuss right now."

I know that she is directing her comment at Lea. Thankfully, Lea nods her agreement. "We wouldn't want to scare them," she murmurs.

We pass the time listening to Lea's Thanksgiving Day lineup. The holiday is a week from Thursday. I haven't thought much about it, yet. My parents do most of the cooking. My aunt Elizabeth, my father's sister, brings a turkey and my mother refrains from talking about the factory farm it came from. My uncle Alan, Elizabeth's husband, wrinkles his nose at the Tofurky and makes snide comments about how the dominant species is supposed to eat meat.

My cousins will also be there. Victoria is a lunatic. She has a Bachelor of Arts degree in classic literature from Princeton that evidently entitles her to act superior. The fact that she hasn't worked since leaving college is irrelevant in her world. She's addicted to Vicodin, a painkiller given to her for migraines she might or might not have. Daniel, her husband, runs an insurance company and their two daughters are spoiled brats.

Benjamin, the gay surgeon, remains in the closet. He might or might not bring Todd, his best friend and co-homeowner. Everyone aside from his immediate family knows that the two of them are lovers.

My father's parents will also be joining us. My grandmother will complain about the food, while pretending not to really complain, and my grandfather will drool in his salad.

Sadly, my mother's parents died a few years ago. They were both quite old and died within months of each other. My mother has two older brothers. One lives in Florida, the other in Hawaii. We don't see them often. That means we don't have any cool family members to offset my father's crazy side.

I've been drifting off, tuning out Lea's chatter. Donna's eyes are slightly out of focus. She has zoned out as well. I give her a quick blow-dry and smile at her obvious relief as I release her from Lea's presence.

My last client is a teenage boy who has his head shaved to almost bald. I don't even have to wash his hair. As I'm pulling the clippers out of the drawer, Lea is preparing to leave. She leans into me and says, "I think that woman deserved it."

I must have missed something while I was contemplating Thanksgiving. "What woman?" I ask.

"That psychologist," she replies with disdain. "She had to know that her remarks would get that serial killer's attention. She was showing off and should have known better."

I don't know how to respond. Our clients, including Lea, say stupid shit all the time. That doesn't mean they all deserve to be tortured by a psycho killer. If words were an excuse to kill, most of my clients would be dead and I wouldn't have to worry about going to prison.

Renee interrupts, saving me from fumbling for an appropriate response. This doesn't stop Lea from offering unsolicited advice.

"You should be very careful about what you say to the men in here. You never know where this serial killer is going to turn up!"

*

Daylight has faded by the time The Mass Avenger arrives home. He loves this time of year, when darkness overpowers the day before most people have left work. The night sky offers him invisibility. His guest waits for him in the cage, within the inky black garage.

He goes up to his bathroom and strips off his clothes. He would like to have gone straight to see the esteemed Dr. Arianna Shelby. All day he has wondered how she is holding up. But he hates the smell he wears at the end of the day and must shower first.

As he soaps himself, his mind replays his time with Arianna the previous evening. She'd done her best to hold on to her female power. She'd claimed that she could help him, while tossing out her psychoanalysis of his behavior. Even after he'd told her to stop, she continued with her superior tone. The stun gun had shut her up fast.

He'd used the zip ties to secure her wrists to the cage wall. Then he'd sliced off her clothes. He smiled now, as he recalled the look of terror that had filled her eyes. She'd learned then just how wrong her assessment of him had been. He is far from sexually inadequate.

The memory has him aroused. He hurries through his shower, dresses, and jogs across the yard to the garage. Last night had been about proving himself, about breaking her sexually. Tonight would be something else entirely.

*

Scott meets me at the door. He doesn't look happy. The dogs clamber around him, trying to get to me. He sighs and steps aside.

I give the dogs a quick greeting. Then I give them each a chicken strip and they happily scatter to their favorite chewing spots. I wrap my arms around Scott and kiss his lips. "Bad day?" I ask.

He shakes his head. "The day was fine, until I got the news. We have a court date. January 6."

"She's going through with it."

"Looks that way."

Diane is a bitch. But, then, we all know that. "Has Elyse actually enrolled in a college up there?"

Scott shrugs. "Hell if I know."

"No court is going to make us pay for her to live like a princess in New York."

"Probably not. Small consolation, though. We'll still have to pay Madison a fortune to fight this. That's what Diane's counting on."

"You think she's hoping we'll cave? Give Elyse money?"

"That's exactly what I think."

"I'd rather eat canned beans for a month."

Scott laughs. "That might be all we can afford!"

"Oh, it's not that bad. We're far from broke."

"I know. It just pisses me off."

"Me, too."

Scott takes my coat from me and brushes his lips over mine. "How was your day in the loony bin?"

I tell him a few of the highlights. "I was too queasy for breakfast and, thanks to Jean, missed lunch. I am starving! Feel like Chinese tonight?"

"Sure. But you remember that your parents are stopping by, right?"

I sag against him. "Tonight?"

"Your dad is dropping the birdhouse off for Charlotte."

"Right. I forgot."

Charlotte lives next door to us. She has wrinkles deeper than the Grand Canyon and no teeth. Her granddaughter moved in last year, supposedly to take care of her. But the girl spends all of her time partying with her friends. Scott mows Charlotte's lawn and we try to check on her at least once a week. But Charlotte is lonely and only has her finches for company. I mentioned her to my father a few weeks ago and he volunteered to make her a nice birdhouse.

"What time are they coming?" I ask.

"Six. Your dad called just before you got home. Your parents are going to meet us here, so we can go over with them."

"Okay."

"Why don't we all go out for dinner? We can bring Charlotte."

Scott has a wonderful soft side. I need him to balance my irritation with the human race. "That's a great idea. I'm sure

Charlotte would love it. Feel like giving her a call? I want to take a quick shower."

"Take your time." Scott gives me a long kiss that makes me want to put a 'Do Not Disturb' sign on the door. Then he nudges me in the direction of the bathroom and says, "We'll get back to this tonight."

Forty-five minutes later, I'm stuffing my face with vegetable egg rolls. I'm so hungry that I could swallow them whole. Scott smirks at me as I devour another before reaching for the vegetable lo mein.

Charlotte is seated on the opposite side of the table, beside my father. She beams as she gums a forkful of vegetable fried rice. She'd cried when my dad gave her the birdhouse. Tears slid into the crevices on her cheeks. Charlotte is a sweet old lady and it sucks that she got stuck with such a selfish granddaughter.

My mother is sitting across from me, on the other side of my father. She has been eyeing me with motherly concern all evening. Now she leans across the table and says, "What's bothering you tonight?"

"I'm tired," I say. "Long day. And I have raging PMS."

"It's more than that."

"Sometimes you're creepy with this psychic thing, you know that?"

My mother grins at me. "I'm not psychic. I'm just a mom."

"We got a court date," I say on a sigh. "Diane's determined to drain our bank account."

"I'm sorry," my mother says.

For once, she doesn't give me a speech about karma and the universe. My dad leans in and asks, "What's all this serious murmuring about?"

"I have PMS," I say.

My dad rolls his eyes. "Poor Scott!"

Thankfully, my mother says nothing about Diane and we move on to other topics. As we're leaving, my mother grabs my hand and pulls me close. "I know this will work out in your favor," she says. "But, if you need anything, you know that all you need do is ask."

I smile and kiss her cheek. "I know," I say. And I do know. I look at Charlotte and realize that, sometimes, that's all that matters.

25

The Mass Avenger brushes his fingers lightly over Arianna's left cheek. Her makeup wore off long ago. Shades of purple stain her cheek. Her fault. Last night, she'd fought him and he'd been forced to slam her face into the cement floor. Fascinated, he traces the outer edge.

Limp, platinum strands of hair fall over her forehead. The dark smudges beneath her eyes are a mix of old mascara and fatigue. She stares at him through those wide brown eyes.

He holds the stun gun an inch from her exposed neck. Her fingers clutch the checkered blanket tight around her shoulders. Bright red fingernails curl around the edges. Three have jagged breaks. He wonders how many hours she'd spent trying to work the zip ties loose. Her wrists are raw and she'd flinched when he'd sliced off the ties.

"I'm going to remove the gag," he tells her. "If you scream, I'll zap you until you're unconscious. Then you'll spend the rest of the night paying for your mistake. Understand?"

Arianna's eyes bulge. She nods. He keeps the stun gun in one hand and uses the other to work her gag free. She doesn't make a sound.

"So," he says, "did you enjoy last night?"

Arianna's eyes widen, though she doesn't respond. The Mass Avenger chuckles. "Not so sexually inadequate after all, am I?"

He moves away from her, squatting by the cage door. The stun gun remains in his hand. "Now, toss me the blanket."

She licks her cracked lips. "Please..."

"Don't piss me off, *doctor*."

She drops her eyes and shudders. The blanket comes loose and she pushes it over to him. He shoves it outside the cage, then lets his eyes roam over her bare skin. He'd bitten her harder than he'd realized. Perfect teeth impressions sink into her flesh. He'd have to remove that section before disposing of her body. If the police ever did find reason to suspect him, the last thing he wanted was to be convicted because of something so stupid.

Arianna sucks her bottom lip into her mouth. She huddles in the corner, trying to cover herself with arms and legs. She no longer looks the part of the professional, know-it-all doctor.

"I know you're probably hungry," he says. "I was going to stop to pick something up but I was in too much of a hurry to get back to you. I'll go out later."

"Could I have a glass of water?"

Her voice is soft and full of cracks. "Sure," he says. He slips out of the cage. "Do not move. Understand me?"

He waits for her to chirp out a yes. Then he crosses the garage to the utility sink. He keeps an eye on her as he fills a plastic cup with water. Back in the cage, he forces her to move to the center to reach the cup. She gulps greedily. He runs a finger along the inside of her thigh and she chokes on a mouthful of the water.

She arouses him more than the others. She's tougher, which makes breaking her all the more rewarding.

"I was wrong," she says. Her eyes meet his. "I had no right to claim that you were sexually inadequate. You've certainly proven your sexual prowess. I need to make it up to you; tell the world how wrong I was."

"Your lies are hurtful."

"I realize that. I apologize. I promise that I will correct my error."

He smiles. She is bargaining; her release for his redemption. But he will get his redemption when her body is found.

"A public apology would be nice," he says, leading her on.

She nods, encouraging. He smiles again. "But first," he says, "we have other things to discuss."

"Of course. Whatever you want to talk about."

Her voice betrays her fear. He slides his fingers over the muscle in her calf. "Do you know what it's like to exist under the thumb of a woman like you?" he asks. "You dangle your femininity, then rip it away when we show interest. You make demands along with your promises, make us believe we never quite measure up to your standards. You use us to suit your needs, always dangling your love just out of reach. You want people to believe you're strong females but you're nothing more than manipulative whores!"

"Someone has hurt you," she says. "I'm so sorry. I can help you. I –"

He cuts off her words with a vicious slap. Within seconds, she is pinned beneath him. His mouth close to her ear, he says, "I'll show you what it's like to be at another person's mercy."

*

The Mass Avenger places the nipple in the container with the other six. He runs his finger over them, smiling at his growing collection. Women show off their nipples through sheer blouses. They wear low-cut tops that barely cover their nipples; teasing, enticing. Those same nipples that are meant to nurture become objects of sexual desire that women taunt men with.

He'd been nurtured once. His mother had told him that she'd held him to her breast, allowing him to take her nipples into his mouth. Her breasts were large and sagged low on her chest. She'd blamed the sagging on him. Within a few months, she switched him to a bottle. She claimed that he'd begun to suck too greedily.

One summer night, when he was 12, he'd been out behind the garage with a neighborhood girl. The girl was 15 and had a reputation for teaching the younger boys. He'd had his hand up the girl's shirt when his mother shined a flashlight in his face. She'd called him a filthy pig and dragged him inside the house. Beneath the harsh kitchen lights, she'd glared at the erection still straining against his denim shorts. He could still hear her shrill voice.

Did touching that slut's little boobs make you horny? You want to see boobs? Is that what you want?

His mother stripped off her shirt and her lacey bra. She lifted one large breast in her hand. *You sucked these nipples. You were a greedy little monster, sucking until I was sore! Do you want to suck them now? DO YOU?*

His erection throbbed. He did want to suck them, though somehow he knew he wasn't supposed to feel that way. *Did you think that little slut's nipples would feel better in your mouth than mine? Did you even think you'd know what to do with them? Or would you still suck them like that greedy little monster you'd been as a baby?*

She reached under his baggy t-shirt and found his right nipple. She squeezed hard. He winced and tried to back away. She squeezed harder, until tears sprang from his eyes. *That is what it was like to nurse you!*

A frail whimper from across the room brings The Mass Avenger back to the present. He'd forgotten about Arianna. He shudders as he closes the container and returns it to the back of the freezer.

Arianna lay just as he'd left her. Blood spatters cover the plastic on the cage floor. He'd been rougher than he'd intended. Sadly, she won't last much longer.

He glances at the clock. Ten after midnight already. Precious few hours remain before he needs to be at work. Fatigue grips him but he can't give in. He needs to shower, then dispose of her. He's sure she won't last another day and he doesn't want to risk finding her dead when he returns from work. Touching cold, dead flesh makes him queasy. And the stench is nearly impossible to get rid of.

He walks to the cage. She is sprawled on her back, too weak to move. Her once attractive face is now barely recognizable. He sees the bite mark on her breast and remembers that he needs to slice off that chunk of flesh. He'll toss it in his fireplace, burn away the evidence.

He doesn't bother to gag or tie her. He locks the cage and leaves the garage, careful to secure all the locks before crossing the yard to his house. He showers off the blood, then dresses in jeans and an old sweatshirt. His grumbling stomach reminds him that he hasn't eaten since breakfast. The kitchen offers him nothing. He'll have to find a late-night drive-thru on his way back home.

Twenty-five minutes later, he has Arianna's body wrapped in plastic. She wasn't quite dead when he'd put her there. The plastic suffocated her. He likes that she watched him as she died.

The chunk of flesh with his teeth marks is also wrapped in plastic. He stuffs it in his pocket to dispose of later. He drags Arianna's body out of the garage and heaves it into his van. He'll have to clean the garage when he returns. Leaving any trace of Arianna behind is too risky.

A wide yawn cracks his jaw. He'd been foolish to get so carried away tonight. He'd be lucky to get an hour's sleep before he needed to leave for work. As much as he'd like to take the day off, calling in sick is not an option. He needs to keep up appearances. If, by some slim chance, the cops start asking questions, he'd be able to show that his time had been consumed with work.

He climbs into the van. The faint scent of death tickles his nose. This makes him smile as he pulls out of his driveway.

26

The two hours I've been at work feel more like a month. Everyone is in a hurry but no one is on time. I'm waiting for my 2 o'clock client, who is currently eight minutes late. I stare at my schedule on the computer screen. The name Robyn Lansing glares out at me. Robyn misses every third or fourth appointment, which means I'm probably standing around waiting while she's off shopping or having a late lunch with friends. At this point, I'd rather she didn't show. I'm tired of playing catch-up.

What I'd really like is to start charging Robyn for all the appointments she blows off. I don't get paid when I stand around, which means that Robyn's behavior is not only inconsiderate but it also costs me money I can't afford to lose. I frown at the computer screen. Robyn puts me in a foul mood.

My 2:30 appointment is Penny Sims. Perfect Penny. Her life story begins with "Once upon a time..." and will likely end with "And she lived happily ever after." Penny has been married to Brad for three years. Brad holds Penny's jacket and her doors. They would probably be a cute couple if they weren't so nauseating.

Penny had a baby six months ago. A daughter, Jennifer, whose big blue eyes and dimples are only exceeded by her brilliant smile. I'd like to say that I hate Perfect Penny and her perfect family but, honestly, they are nice people. And this pisses me off. Anyone with such a perfect life should have at least one thing that you can latch onto and hate.

I can always count on Penny to be early. She steps inside at 2:15. Robyn has not shown up or called. Not that I expected her to. I greet Penny as she's hanging her coat on the rack. "Where's Jennifer today?" I ask.

"Brad's mother wanted to stay with her," Penny says. "It's only the second time I've left her. I'm not sure I'll ever get used to it."

I feel that way about my dogs, though I don't tell Penny this. Instead, I say, "I know it's hard but it's good for you to get out on your own now and then."

I wash Penny's hair, then get her settled in my chair. "What are we doing today?" I ask.

Penny looks at me with bright blue eyes. Her face is a portrait of innocence. "Whatever you want. Be creative."

Of the several hundred different clients who sit in my chair each year, Penny is one of only two who ever tells me to do what I want. What's even more amazing is that she's always happy with whatever it is I decide to do. Not only is Penny perfect but she makes my job fun. Sadly, there aren't enough Perfect Pennys to offset the Bitchy Barbaras and Impossible Irenes.

Penny tells me about Jennifer, who is just starting to crawl. Brad has put padding on all their furniture, including the kitchen cabinets. He's an overprotective, doting dad. He'll probably have a nervous breakdown when Jennifer gets her first bump or bruise. Penny's stories make me laugh and I'm actually in a good mood when she walks out the door.

I'm sweeping the hair from around my chair, a smile still on my face, when Diane walks in the door. I blink twice. She's still standing there looking at me. I must be hallucinating. Scott's ex has never set foot inside this salon. I blink again. Diane is now glaring at me.

My smile long gone, I step closer to Diane. I'd like to slam the broom against her temple. "What are you doing here, Diane?" I ask.

"Scott refuses to answer his phone."

She says the words as if it is somehow my fault. "He's probably busy," I say.

"He's avoiding me!"

She might be right, though I'm not about to admit that. "Is something wrong?"

"Elyse needs help."

Her snippiness has me clenching my jaw and the broom too tight. I don't like that she's here or that my coworkers and their clients can hear our conversation. "Let's go out back," I say.

She stomps off toward the back room. I finish sweeping the hair. Renee gives me a look, her eyebrows raised in a silent question. I shrug and drag myself out to the back room to see what the evil bitch wants.

Thankfully, the back room is currently empty. I keep my voice down and ask, "What's wrong with Elyse?"

"She has no money for food and will soon be without a roof over her head."

Diane is standing in the center of the room. Her manicured nails rest on her hips, which are covered by a black pencil skirt that must have some overpriced designer's name attached. She glances at the waxing chair, then the small table with the coffeemaker and tin of cookies. I don't offer her a seat and I'm absolutely not going to offer her coffee.

I stifle a sigh and ask, "Does Elyse want to come home?"

She huffs at me. "That would be your solution, now, wouldn't it?"

"Well, yeah, it would be."

"Perfect. Then Elyse can live with you!"

"Excuse me?"

"I do not want Elyse moving back in with me. I've already turned her bedroom into a sewing room."

"A sewing room?" My eyes move over Diane's outfit, from the fancy silk scarf draped around her neck to the four-inch black heels she has her feet crammed into. We both know she's lying. Diane wouldn't know what to do with a sewing machine. "What is it you want, Diane?"

"As I said, Elyse needs help."

"And you've taken up sewing."

She glares at me. "Elyse is Scott's responsibility as much as my own. He conveniently forgets that."

"He's never forgotten that." I want to say more. In fact, I want to slam my fist into her face. But I'm all too aware of the curious glances coming from the next room.

"Scott has had it far too easy these past years."

"Too easy? You can't be serious!"

"I'm sure that Elyse will adjust to your… quaint little home."

"Quaint?"

"Of course, she'll be devastated that her father did not support her modeling career. She'll likely blame him for having to give up her dream. That could make her somewhat difficult to handle." She scrunches her face into a frosty smile and adds, "You would understand this if you'd had children of your own. I suppose some women simply don't have mothering instincts."

"Yes, and it's too bad those women decide to have children anyway."

Diane folds her arms over her chest. Her expensive bra has her boobs propped up like a shelf to rest her arms on. I'd laugh if I wasn't so pissed off.

"Perhaps," Diane says, "you can convince Elyse's father that it's time he did the right thing and supported his daughter's dream."

"By sending her money," I say. "Isn't that what all this bullshit is about?"

Diane reaches inside her Prada purse and produces a slip of paper. She hands it to me and says, "There is a Western Union not far from where Elyse is staying. This is the information you'll need. You can wire the money there."

"Scott and I are not sending Elyse money, Diane."

"Then I suppose she will be moving in with the two of you."

"No, I suppose she'll be getting a job."

"I rather doubt that Scott wants to be responsible for his daughter living on the street."

"Because you have a sewing room now and no place for your daughter."

Diane rolls her eyes. "Have Scott contact me. After all, Elyse is his daughter and this decision has nothing to do with you."

"And yet you came to my work to dump it on me."

She lifts her chin, sticking her nose high in the air, and brushes past me. Her cologne washes over me and I feel nauseous. She strides toward the door. A few heads turn toward me. My next client is waiting. I want to grab my scissors and jam them into the side of Diane's silk-wrapped neck.

"She did what?"

Scott's deep baritone bellows through our kitchen. The dogs cower. "Calm down," I say. "You're scaring the kids."

"Diane was at the salon demanding money? You're serious?"

"Well, not demanding, exactly. More like blackmailing." I tell him the story, stopping every so often to let him sputter and swear. I hand him the slip of paper with the Western Union information. "Diane said you are to wire Elyse the money here."

My stomach is grumbling. I've been home less than five minutes. I should have eaten before getting into this discussion but it's late and I figured Scott would need time to work out his anger. Maybe we can relieve each other's tension in the bedroom.

Scott grabs his coat and car keys. I step in front of the door. "Where are you going?"

"To talk to Diane."

"That's not a good idea."

"Why not?"

"You might kill her."

"You're right," Scott says. "But there is no way in hell I'm going to let her get away with harassing you at the salon."

I take the keys from his hand and kiss his lips. "First, you need to calm down. Going at her like this will only make things worse."

Scott spouts off a few things about Diane that would make a sailor blush. "Okay," he says. "I'll wait until tomorrow. I'll stop at her place after work."

"Do you want to send the money?"

His eyebrows rise on his forehead. "Absolutely not. I'll call Elyse after I talk to Diane. This shit has to stop."

"What if Elyse decides to move in here?"

Scott finds this amusing. "Right, Diane has a sewing room now. That's not going to happen, either."

"You'd tell her no?"

"Elyse doesn't want to live here and Diane would never allow it. Hell, Diane didn't even like Elyse staying with us on weekends. She's not about to take the chance of Elyse finding out that you're not really the evil stepmother from storybooks."

"Yeah, you're probably right."

Scott wraps his arms around me and pulls me close. "Hungry?" he murmurs.

"Starving."

"Go ahead and shower. I'll heat some pasta for you."

His lips find mine. He tastes like butterscotch candy. "After I eat," I say, "I'll help you work out some of that aggression."

"I was hoping you'd say that."

27

Thursday morning brings icy rain. I pull the covers up to my neck and stare at the ceiling. Scott left more than an hour ago. He'd brought me tea but I'd dozed off again and now it's cold. I should get up. I have errands to do before work. But the gray gloom outside makes me want to stay under the covers.

Jack has commandeered the bottom of the bed. He takes full advantage of the space. I stretch and he lifts his head to look at me. His expression is one of annoyance, like I've disturbed a good dream.

A full half-hour passes before I convince myself to move. Another hour goes by before I find my way to the shower. At 11, I'm finally dressed and have consumed a sufficient amount of caffeine to hold my eyes open. Scott's aggressions took a long time to work out last night. I'm exhausted and my body still tingles. But don't get me wrong. I'm not complaining.

I've wasted away the morning with my laziness. Errands will have to wait until the weekend. I feed the dogs, then take them outside. The rain has stopped but the gray sky remains. Jack isn't bothered by the cold, wet day. He scampers off into the backyard. Zena steps cautiously, lifting her feet high off the grass. I have to literally shove the two little ones off the deck to get them to pee.

At 11:30, I am in my car and on my way to my daily prison. Renee meets me out front and drags me across the street to the donut shop. "So did Scott freak?" she asks.

"Oh, yeah," I say. "I had to stop him from going straight to Diane's. Hopefully, he's calmed down enough to talk to her today."

"You think he can reason with her?"

"No. She's enjoying this too much."

Renee orders a fancy mocha thing and I get a hot chocolate. The sky starts to spit rain as we cross back to the salon. We're stepping onto the sidewalk when Renee says, "Roxie thinks she's pregnant."

I stop short. "Oh, no."

Renee rolls her eyes. "Morning sickness and all."

Not only is Roxie young and unmarried but she is barely attached. She's been dating her current boyfriend for less than six months. The guy is a mediocre drummer in a local band. He doodles naked women on cocktail napkins and collects Matchbox cars. Those things are bad enough but they're Roxie's problems to deal with. Her being pregnant means we'll be short a stylist for at least a few months. My frustration is purely selfish.

"Is she happy about it?" I ask.

"She's a wreck, terrified to tell her parents. Hell, she hasn't even told her boyfriend, yet."

The clouds let loose and the rain drives us inside. Roxie is occupied with a retired teacher who speaks in an incessant monotone. No wonder so many kids are failing in school. Andrea follows me into the back room and asks, "Did Renee tell you?"

"About Roxie? Yeah."

"She's not ready to be a mother."

"I don't think most women are."

"I mean she's really not ready. When I came in this morning, she took one look at me and burst into tears. I can't do nine months of this."

"Yeah, that's probably what she's thinking as well."

Andrea fishes her lunch from the refrigerator. I go out to the desk and check my schedule. I'm starting my day with Anita, who is one of the most insecure women I've ever met. She's in her late forties, has two teenage daughters and is the office manager for a local dentist. She's also active in town politics. Anita is not a woman who anyone would accuse of being meek or shy. Yet, she wears her hair one-length, past her shoulders, because that's how her husband likes it. She once told me that she asked her husband if she could cut it. She actually asked his permission! He'd told her to go ahead; however, he would not sleep with her until it grew back.

I'm often amazed at the things people tell me. I don't think I'd ever admit that I had to ask my husband's permission for anything, much less to cut my own hair. Of course, I can't imagine myself married to a guy whose permission I would need.

I move through the day like I'm wading in three feet of molasses. Roxie's eyes glisten with the threat of tears. Her 3 p.m. client brings her baby and Roxie nearly loses it when the kid starts to cry. Roxie corners me in the back room later and tells me that Andrea suggested she give the baby up for adoption. "How could I send my baby off to be raised by strangers?" she asks me.

I have no answer for her. Instead, I say, "You need to do what's right for you. Don't worry about what other people think."

"I haven't told Bryce."

"That's the first thing you should do. The two of you need to talk about this, make these decisions together."

"I know."

Her bottom lip trembles and she sucks it into her mouth. I give her a hug because I don't know what else to do. She wipes tears from her eyes and scurries out to her next client.

I go back out front just as Becky, my next client, flings the door open. She's one of those women who requires center stage. "Have you heard?" she asks.

I hesitate. Becky can be crude. But I can't ignore her, so I take the bait. "Heard what?"

"They found that missing psychiatrist."

Andrea turns. "Dead?"

"Mangled!" Becky says. "Her body was left in a shallow ditch in vacant lot. The smell finally got the neighbors' attention and they called the cops."

By the time I get Becky to the sink, she has announced a few gory details. Arianna Shelby had been tortured and raped. The Mass Avenger had left a note behind, though the police have not disclosed the details.

"In all honesty, she was asking for it," Becky says.

"Asking to be raped and tortured?"

"Well, you know what I mean. She ridiculed the guy. What did she expect?"

I don't respond. What is there to say to people like Becky?

I get through the haircut with fantasies of snipping off the tip of Becky's tongue. She chatters away, completely unaware of my intense dislike for her. I'm almost finished with the cut when she says, "After what happened to Arianna Shelby, maybe psychiatrists will think twice about making assumptions. They're not gods, after all."

She is looking at me, waiting for me to respond. All the words on the forefront of my mind are totally inappropriate. I scrape deeper and finally come up with, "I'd like to think that most psychiatrists have good intentions."

"They all have messiah complexes. Why the hell else would that woman publicly say something so derogatory about a man she's never met?"

"I don't know, but that man is a serial killer. Maybe she had a point."

"I suppose she found out the hard way whether she was right or not."

Well. Interesting. I'm jumping out on a limb and assuming that Becky has gotten some unwelcome feedback from one or two psychiatrists. I can see why that would happen. I'd like to slice her tongue off to keep her from saying another word. Otherwise, I might be compelled to aim for her jugular.

I finish with the cut and pick up the blow dryer. Becky fingers the wet strands and starts preening in the mirror. Her hair is chin-length, with long layers and a side part. She'd asked for a half-inch off all over. I'd done that and checked with her twice along the way. Now she looks at me and says, "I think I'd like another half-inch off. I guess it's a little longer than I realized."

I'd just spent twenty minutes cutting her hair. Now I'd have to spend another twenty doing it over, after which I'd still have to blow-dry the mop. In the meantime, my next client will be waiting. We schedule cuts on half-hour slots. We foolishly count on people to know what they want when they come in.

I bite back the reply that threatens to bubble over. I also resist the urge to shave her bald, as I meticulously do the cut over with another half-inch off. While I'm blow drying, Becky tangles her fingers in her hair and pulls on it. She must realize how hard it is to dry hair she's yanking on, so I don't bother to point that out to her. When I finish, she says, "It's shorter than I expected."

My grip on the blow dryer tightens and my arm threatens to slam the dryer into Becky's temple. Could I claim justifiable homicide? Temporary insanity?

Would they make me work in the prison's hair salon?

That thought makes me shudder. Being locked up in a prison full of clients I can never escape from would be the ultimate torture.

I ignore Becky's comment and move toward the desk. Becky is still tugging on her hair and studying herself in the mirrors while I run her credit card. She finally leaves me with a $2 tip, a vicious tension headache, and a schedule that I am now 25 minutes behind on.

My 6 o'clock client walks in the door as I'm taking my 5:30 client to the sink. My 6 o'clock is 17 and has three of her friends with her. They all have massive diva attitudes and like to hover over one another while getting their hair cut. I breathe a sigh of resignation. The night will go no better than the afternoon.

⚕

The Mass Avenger stares at the building across the street. He sips the coffee he'd bought at Dunkin' Donuts and watches through the brightly lit windows as Skye fusses with the blow dryer and a big round brush. She's wearing jeans that caress her curves and a snug t-shirt that says *The Cutting Edge* across the front with a pair of scissors beneath the words. Her hair is messy in that sexy way. He wonders if she is happy with Mr. Scott Skyler and if she would get pleasure from killing Skyler's ex-girlfriend.

Skye is different from other women. The Mass Avenger is comfortable with her in a way that isn't typical for him. Would she understand him? He'd like to find out.

Diane Greer lives on a quiet street in Hanover. He assumes that she lives alone now, since the daughter took off for New York. However, he's not positive. She could have a man living with her or one who stays on occasion. He has to find out for sure. He also needs to know where she works and where she hangs out. Not getting caught means having all the information at his fingertips.

He sits in the darkness, nursing his coffee. Customers move in and out of the donut shop's parking lot. No one pays him the slightest attention. It's late and he's been here a while. He should head home. But he continues to watch, fascinated by Skye's movements.

The other woman, Renee, is working with Skye. They are alone, the two of them, with their two clients. A man approaches the building from the parking lot. Skye turns to him as he steps inside and her face breaks into a bright smile. Seconds later, he has the broom in his hand and is sweeping the waiting area by the windows.

Scott Skyler is tall and rugged. The Mass Avenger's lips curl into a snarl. He could never compete with a man like Skyler.

Then again, he'll soon have a gift for Skye that Mr. Scott Skyler would never be capable of offering. This makes him smile as he starts the van and heads home to plan.

28

The Mass Avenger follows the Lexus along the tree-lined roads. The driver had spent three full hours inside a fancy spa. The sign out front claimed they could transform a woman with their facials, manicures, pedicures, and full body massages. The woman had emerged looking no different from when she'd walked in.

He'd followed her through the traffic, out to the quiet, small-town back roads. Dead leaves blow across the pavement. The trees are nearly naked now. Nature is preparing for the long winter. The weak will die, the strong will survive. A cleansing of sorts. In his own way, he is helping nature along. Correcting its mistakes.

The Lexus turns onto South Ave. He sucks in a quick breath. He hadn't expected her to come this way. Minutes later, Diane Greer parks in the lot behind The Cutting Edge. What is she doing here?

He slows to a stop along the side of the road. He doesn't pull into the lot. Instead, he hovers at the curb, engine running. His windows are darkened. A Patriots cap pulled low over his eyes and dark sunglasses obscure his face. He feels safe watching. No one will pay him the slightest bit of attention. No one ever does.

Diane steps out of her car and smoothes her pants. She brushes away hair from the animal pelt she wears. Then she strides up the walk and around the corner.

The Mass Avenger lets out a shaky breath. What is she doing here? Does she have business somewhere else on the street and parking here is merely a convenience? Why would she be going to Skye's salon?

He grips the steering wheel until his fingers ache. Is Skye secretly working with Diane in order to ruin her husband? Is Skye another manipulative whore, like the rest of them?

The urge to run inside the salon to find out is almost overwhelming. Skye couldn't have deceived him so completely. She isn't like the rest of them.

Or is she?

He stares at the building. His muscles constrict and his breathing grows shallow. If Skye and Diane are friends, that changes everything.

*

Saturday afternoon and I've almost made it through another week. Thanksgiving comes in a few days, then Christmas rides in soon afterward. This year will pass, turn into another, and I will have survived my job into a new year. Providing, of course, that I don't kill anyone between now and then.

The salon is busy in that crazy, loud way that comes with Saturdays. Renee's client is carrying on a personal conversation with Andrea's client. Renee is on my left, Andrea on my right. I am caught in the middle of the voices, which are clashing with the radio, the waiting clients, the ringing phone, and the hum of Roxie's blow dryer.

I'm winding Kaye's hair into perm rods when the front door pops open. Through the mirror, I see Diane step inside. Her glossy lips are pursed in a smug smile. She's wearing black slacks, black pumps, and a caramel-colored fur coat. Animals were sacrificed for her comfort. Definitely not a fair trade-off.

Something twists and yanks at my intestines. I choke on the air and disguise it with a cough. Evidently, whatever Scott said to her the other day served as an invitation to further harass me. "Diane..." I say. The air is sucked out of the room. I can find no appropriate words.

"We need to discuss Elyse," Diane says.

She hikes the strap of her Gucci purse back onto her shoulder. She's staring at me with a dare in her eyes. I have no doubt that she'd love to create a scene, to embarrass me in this place that is slowly eating my identity.

"Now isn't exactly a good time, Diane. Have you tried calling Scott?"

She offers up a smile, showing the others how perfectly reasonable she is. "You know that he refuses to compromise even the slightest bit. He punishes his daughter with his vengeance for me."

I sigh. "Give me five minutes."

Diane flashes a predatory smile. If snakes could smile, that's what they would look like. She moves to the waiting area and picks up a magazine. "I'll be right here," she says. As if I could possibly overlook her.

I finish winding Kaye's hair into the gray rods, then drizzle perm solution over them. After setting the timer, I step over to Diane and say, "Why don't we go out back?"

She smirks but says nothing as she stands and follows me. The back room has a couple of clients milling about. Roxie has someone in the waxing chair. I motion to the back door. "Let's step outside a minute," I say to Diane.

I am amazed at how calm my voice sounds. No one would guess that I'd contemplated grabbing my scissors so I could slice Diane into little pieces. We step out the door and I hover close to the building. I'm afraid that, if I am alone with her too long, I will wrap my hands around her neck until her prissy face turns purple.

I hunch against the cold air. "You can't keep coming here, Diane," I say. "If you want to talk to me, call when I'm home. I'll meet you someplace. But not here."

"It bothers you that I come here?" Diane asks in a mockingly sweet voice.

"You know it does. So, unless you want me to start hanging out at your workplace, then I suggest that you knock off the shit."

She blinks. Apparently, it had not occurred to her that I could play her game. She sidesteps my comment and says, "Scott has not sent Elyse the money."

"He told you he wasn't going to. Why would you expect otherwise?"

"I thought that perhaps you would talk sense into the man. He is her father, after all. I know that has always bothered you."

I hold my hand, palm up, near her face. "Stop," I say. "I'm not doing this dance with you."

"Of course. I understand why it would upset you that another woman gave Scott what you haven't been able to."

My hands clench into a fists. "If, by that, you mean that I haven't been able to give Scott a lifetime of heartache, headaches, and misery, then you are absolutely correct. Now cut the shit and tell me why you're here."

Her eyes narrow and her face contorts. "Elyse is a godsend! Just because you are barren –"

"Save it, Diane." I blow out a long sigh. "Look, I'm busy. I have no time for your crap."

She straightens up and takes a half step closer. Diane is tall, around 5 feet 10 inches tall. I hit 5 feet 5 inches if I stand on my tiptoes. Standing closer forces me to look up at her. She flaunts her height like she flaunts her daughter. Something I should be envious of.

"Elyse received a modeling contract," Diane says.

This startles me. Good news? There has to be a catch. "That's great," I say. "Scott will be thrilled for her."

"She needs that money by Monday morning."

I frown and bite back a string of swears. "Why does she still need the money if she's working?"

"Obviously you know nothing of the modeling world."

I think about my scissors. The edges are razor sharp. I could filet Diane's tongue so that it would wag in the wind. "Enlighten me," I say.

"Elyse requires a professional portfolio, a new wardrobe, fashion accessories, and, naturally, a hairstyle by one of the best stylists that New York has to offer."

"But she did get a job?"

"The representation is contingent on Elyse satisfying these requirements."

"Representation? So it isn't an actual job."

"Of course not! One must first get the proper agent. This is the most vital part of the process."

I reach for the door. "Thanks for stopping by, Diane. Scott and I will see you in court." I take a step, then turn back. "And, by the way, if you show up here again, I'll call the cops. Then I show up at your work and make sure everyone knows that you're trying to extort money from Scott. Afterward, I'll file for a restraining order."

Diane's jaw drops. I close the door on her face.

The Mass Avenger lowers his passenger window a few inches when Skye and Diane step out the back door. They stand about 30 feet from where he sits idling. He doesn't dare move closer. Even shutting the engine off so that he can better hear their conversation would risk drawing their attention.

Skye's expression is one of restrained anger. He recognizes it as if he is looking in a mirror. That expression is one he often wears.

Bits of their conversation float in the air. At one point, he is sure that Skye will punch Diane and he is instantly aroused. The punch doesn't happen but he sees the murder in Skye's big brown eyes. His right hand finds his erection as he watches.

Soon Skye disappears inside the building, leaving Diane gaping after her. The designer woman is no match for Skye. Turning on her expensive heels, Diane stomps off to her Lexus.

Giddiness bubbles in The Mass Avenger's throat. He suppresses a giggle. He never should have doubted Skye. She is nothing like the others. She is like him, before his first. Maybe he can teach her how to unleash those urges. They would make a perfect pair.

29

Today is the Saturday before Thanksgiving and the salon has been a madhouse since 7:30 this morning. Everyone is primping, wanting to look his or her best for the big event. For many people, Thanksgiving has taken the place of the family reunion. Distant relatives get together once a year over turkey, too much pie, and enough alcohol to make them forget that they don't like each other.

Earlier in the day, I had a client tell me that she'd spent $500 on a dress and $200 on facial and makeup products, just so she could finally outdo her "golden-haired, diva cousin". I doubt that the dress and makeup will make much difference. I could spend two grand on makeup and buy a one-of-a-kind gown from a famous designer I've never heard of, and still not outshine Victoria in my grandparents' eyes.

Marilyn, the client currently in my chair, has been rattling on about how much work she has to do for the holiday. She's in her early forties. Her two kids are away at separate colleges and she hasn't worked since before they were born. Her husband is either a banker or a loan shark, depending on who you talk to. They live in a big house with horse stables. A maid comes twice a week to do the "heavy stuff", which probably includes cleaning the toilets and hefting the laundry basket. Yet, Marilyn feels vindicated in her complaints to me about having to prepare the guest room for her husband's brother and sister-in-law.

"Everything has to be perfect for Brian and Laura," Marilyn says. "Of course, I'll have to put the Egyptian cotton sheets on the bed and I need to buy new pillows. We only buy goose down and they simply don't last more than a couple of months."

I nod, snip her hair, consider what her head would look like minus one ear.

"The children will be home on Tuesday," Marilyn continues. "I need to freshen up their rooms and buy fresh flowers for all the bedrooms. At some point, I must get with the caterer to verify the menu. Al needs his suit cleaned and I haven't a clue what I'll wear. I committed to making a blueberry pie for our church. They do wonderful work with the unfortunate at this time of year and I simply couldn't refuse. However, I don't know where I will find the time!"

Marilyn is nearly breathless when she concludes her speech. Comments roll through my head. I sift through them and find none appropriate. Marilyn watches me through the mirror. I offer a sympathetic smile and say, "The holidays are a busy time for most of us."

Marilyn sighs as if I have missed the point entirely. I finish cutting her auburn hair and politely ask if the cut is short enough. She asks for the hand mirror and gets up close and personal with her image. Finally, she says, "It seems fine."

I grab the blow dryer and a round brush, thankful the noise helps drown out the sea of voices surrounding me. Marilyn continues to talk about herself. I miss half of what she says but all I have to do is nod and appear sympathetic to her plight. I wonder what would happen if I stuck the blow dryer in her open mouth and left it on high.

I get Marilyn out the door just as my next clients are walking in. Ashley, Alexis, and Devin – ages 9, 7, and 3 – are high up on my favorites list. They are adorable and love getting their hair done. Their visits are among those rare times when I think that having kids might be fun. I savor their enthusiasm and bright smiles. The girls are a much-needed bright spot in my day.

Unfortunately, the fun doesn't last. The girls are soon replaced by Brandon, who does not want to be anywhere near my chair. Brandon is 15 and has a mother who treats him like he is 5. I could hear her lecturing him when they were out on the sidewalk. She would make a great drill sergeant.

"Cut his hair short," Ann, Brandon's mother, tells me. "Above the ears. Clean him up good."

"I don't want my hair that short!" Brandon shoots back.

"You're going to look respectable for the holiday!" Ann says.

"It's my hair!"

They are standing by the desk. Brandon still has his coat on. I half expect him to run out the door screaming. They continue their power struggle for a few minutes. Most of the shop has tuned in. Ann looks at me, irritation pouring from her eyes, and says, "Tell him how much better he looks with short hair."

I blink. My mouth opens but I can't form the words. In truth, I think Brandon is cute the way he is. His hair isn't overly long. It's thick and wavy and, from his mother's perspective, unruly. I hold my hands up in surrender. "Not my call," I say.

Ann flashes me a narrow-eyed glare. "Get your coat off," she tells Brandon. "And get your hair cut. Otherwise, I take your X-Box, computer, and cell phone away."

"Mom!"

"You heard me!"

Brandon shakes his head in disgust. He yanks his jacket off and shoves it at his mother. Then he follows me to the sink as if I am leading him to the gas chamber.

"I'm sorry," I tell him as I shampoo his hair. "Your mom only wants what's best for you."

"No, she's worried about what other people will think. She doesn't care what's best for me."

"You know that's not true," I say. But, even as I mouth the words, I hear how false they sound.

Ann stands behind me as I cut Brandon's hair. When I'm halfway through the cut, she says, "Cut it shorter."

"Jesus," Brandon mutters.

I shoot him an apologetic glance before I give him what could pass for a military cut. Seconds after I've finished, he bounds out of my chair, grabs his jacket, and storms out the door. "You're lucky you don't have kids," Ann says to me.

I don't know what to say to that, so I say nothing. She pays me. The $5 tip feels like bribe money. I tuck it in a separate pocket in my jeans, to add to the donation fund for the animal rescue.

My last client is due in 10 minutes. The salon is a mess. Dirty brushes overflow from the bins. A carpet of hair stretches across the floor. My coworkers are all busy and voices continue to rise in competition for airtime. I grab the broom and make one short sweep before the phone rings. A glance at the clock reminds me that the day is almost over. Then I will have two days of freedom before I have to come back to this place.

⌁

The Mass Avenger carries his coffee out to the van. He sits in the driver's seat and stares across the street. The place is jammed with people. He can barely see Skye through the crowd of bodies.

Today her t-shirt is red, with *The Cutting Edge* logo across the front. Her faded jeans wrap around her in a way that he would like to experience.

He shakes his head, irritated with himself. His arousal is almost painful. The coffee is too hot and burns his tongue but at least it takes his mind of Skye's body.

He has found where Diane Greer works. The building is busy and offers no privacy. He's pretty sure that she lives alone in the raised ranch in Hanover. Watching her there has been difficult. The neighborhood is full of suburban busybodies.

Taking Diane won't be as easy as the others. She's often surrounded by people. He might be forced to break his own rule and go to her home. He could do it late at night, use the stun gun and get her out to the van. It's cold now and people won't be outside. If he did it right, made sure her outside lights weren't on, he could get her out without being spotted.

But how would he get her to let him in?

His attention is drawn back to Skye. She is cutting a teenager's hair, while the mother hovers. Even from this distance, he can see the irritation in the crinkles around Skye's eyes. The mother is obviously micromanaging her son's existence. Another controlling whore, wielding her power over the helpless.

Skye knows that it is wrong. He can see that. Yet, she is just as powerless as the boy.

He needs to remember this woman. He'll ask Skye about her. Maybe they can grab the whore together, make her pay for her behavior.

First, he needs to work on his gift to Skye. Diane will be served on a silver platter, for Skye to do with as she pleases. She'll see that they are kindred spirits and he'll never have to be alone again.

30

My family is crazy. We would make a great sitcom, maybe in cartoon form like *The Simpsons*. Thanksgiving at my parents' house would be a smash hit at the box office. We could call it *Holiday Madness*. Or *An LSD Thanksgiving*. Lilly Skye Destiny's LSD, not the stuff discovered by Albert Hofmann. Though, to be honest, anyone watching us would be hard-pressed to know the difference.

Today is Thanksgiving. Scott and I have been at my parents' house since 11 this morning. We also brought our four dogs. They never stay home alone on a holiday. My parents are back to having six dogs now. Yesterday, they took in a new refugee from the rescue. This one's name is Reggie and he's a one-eyed collie. A sociopathic teenager poked out the missing eye. The parents opted to keep the kid and get rid of the dog. Personally, I would have gotten rid of the kid and kept the dog.

Ten dogs is a lot to have inside one house, especially when cooking food that makes them drool all over the kitchen floor. Earlier, Scott and my father took them out in the backyard. They chased Frisbees and balls and exhausted themselves. Only two of them bother to lift their heads and bark when my Aunt Elizabeth and Uncle Alan show up.

Elizabeth is carrying a huge roasting pan. She's wearing pink speckled oven mitts on both hands. My mother leads her into the kitchen. The smell of turkey floods the air and my father cracks open a window.

Alan hands my father a bottle of wine. "You have scotch?" he asks.

My father points to the dining room. "On the side table," he says. "We bought it just for you, Al."

"I'll get you a glass," Scott says. "Do you want ice?"

Alan grunts something unintelligible as he barrels past us, following Scott through to the dining room. "You bought him scotch?" I ask. Elizabeth rarely allows him to have hard liquor.

My father looks at me, his eyebrows dancing on his forehead. "We're hoping he drinks it all and passes out cold."

The doorbell rings, causing six of the 10 dogs to bark. My grandparents are standing on the stoop. They look indignant, as if we have left them there for hours. My father ushers them in. I take my grandfather's coat and help him to a chair. He's wearing a crooked blue paisley silk tie and black dress slacks with razor sharp creases. My grandmother stands by my father, eyeing the dogs warily. "How many of those things do you have?" she asks.

"Ten," my father says.

"Why 10?"

Disgust overflows from her voice. My father smiles as he takes her coat. "Because 11 would be simply ridiculous," he replies.

I suppress a laugh and turn back to my grandfather. "Can I get you something, Grandpa?"

"Wine," he says.

"You haven't eaten dinner, yet!" my grandmother snaps.

"I bet Jesus had wine before dinner."

"And you are not Jesus!"

I leave them to bicker and go out to the kitchen to help my mother. My cousin Victoria and her family arrive while I'm mixing the salad dressing. Victoria is wearing an ivory tailored suit with a deep green turtleneck that is probably cashmere. A child clings to each leg and each foot teeters on a four-inch spiked heel. "The girls are afraid of your dogs," Victoria announces.

"None of them bite," my mother says.

"Must you allow all of them inside?"

"Well, no, but I don't have to allow you inside, either."

My mother turns back to the melons she is slicing for the fruit cups. Victoria's eyes attempt to burn a hole into my mother's back. My aunt huffs a sigh. She takes the girls by the hand and says,

"Come with me, girls. You can watch TV with your great-grandfather."

The girls are 10 and 7. They are dressed in matching frilly, pink ruffled dresses and have had their hair curled and pulled up on top of their heads. These angelic children snub their noses at me. The older one sticks up her middle finger as my grandmother leads them away.

Benjamin is the last to arrive. He is dressed in black slacks and a soft, gray cable knit sweater. He's carrying a bottle of Chardonnay. And he is alone. I want to ask about his boyfriend-slash-roommate but he looks so sad that I would get no pleasure from harassing him.

Halfway through dinner, my grandfather starts farting and blaming it on the dogs. The girls refuse to eat because we don't have plates with dividers and the gravy ran into their vegetables. Benjamin politely sidesteps his parents' interrogation about when he will settle down and have children. And my uncle Alan and Victoria's husband Daniel nearly empty the bottle of scotch.

I catch Scott's eye and he grins at me. I don't know how he manages my family so well. His family is stoic by comparison. Holidays with them are calm to the point of boredom. At least I can say that my family is never dull.

A

The Mass Avenger shovels cereal into his mouth while he watches the parade cross his TV screen. Thanksgiving Day. The rest of the country is sitting at large tables, surrounded by family, eating turkey with homemade gravy. He is here alone, on his mother's sofa in the house he'd grown up in, eating Cheerios.

He has no family. His mother is dead. Not that she was ever much company, anyway. He doesn't miss her. Not really.

His father is probably alive, somewhere out there in the world. He'd never met the man. Doesn't know who he is, not even his first name. His mother had refused to discuss the subject. She'd taken his identity to her grave.

He'd had grandparents once. They'd lived in an old farmhouse in Vermont. He vaguely remembers the smell of cows and chickens. They'd been killed in a car accident when he was 4. His mother hadn't cried.

His mother had been an only child and so is he. And now he is truly alone.

Smiling faces fill his TV screen. A man and a woman huddle close against the cold. He slurps the milk from his bowl, then sets it on the coffee table. He'd never had a real girlfriend. That hadn't been possible around his mother. He couldn't risk bringing anyone home.

The faces on the screen mock him. *Happy holidays*, they say. Their teeth gleam white and their eyes shine.

He could have a girlfriend now. No one is here to stop him. But the women he meets are all teasing whores. Manipulators. They use their sex as a power to control.

All except Skye. She's not like the others.

She doesn't look at him the way she looks at Scott Skyler. She doesn't see him, not really. Not the way he wants her to. Soon he will give her his gift and that will change everything.

31

The day after Thanksgiving and here I am at work once again. I'd walked in the door at 8:30 to a ringing phone. The thing has been ringing steadily ever since. Schools and colleges are closed and lots of people have the day off. Apparently, everyone in Whitman with nothing better to do has decided that it's a great day to get their hair done. The problem is, even more people had planned ahead and we are booked solid today. The people calling do not want to hear that. Some of them plead; others get pissed and all but accuse us of lying. As if we're all sitting around eating leftover pie instead of working. We work on commission. We don't get paid to eat pie.

Barb, my 11 a.m. client, strolls in 10 minutes late. She collapses into my chair with a great sigh. "Did you want any changes to your color?" I ask.

"No," she tells me. "I really like what you've been doing."

I go back to the cabinet and mix her color. The noise level in the salon threatens to pierce my eardrums. The ringing phone has become a contest of wills. We all ignore it, waiting to see who will cave first and answer the damn thing.

As I'm applying Barb's color, she says, "I am exhausted! I almost didn't make it here today."

"Busy morning?"

"It's been crazy! My girlfriend and I were out the door at 5 a.m.!"

"Shopping?" I ask. Today is *Black Friday*, the busiest shopping day of the year. I've never shopped on Black Friday, partly because

I'm always at work. Even if I had the day off, I don't know of any sale good enough to get me to stand in line at 5 a.m.

"Yes," Barb says. "We picked up some amazing deals! The crowd, though, was insane! People were fighting over things. I actually saw one woman slap another woman! Can you imagine?"

"No," I say. "I can't."

"You have to push your way through but the sales are phenomenal. Did you get any shopping done this morning?"

"No. I'm always here fairly early. I've never fought the crowds on Black Friday."

"Oh, that's too bad," Barb says. "You miss out on a lot. Fortunately, I didn't have to work
today. At least you're lucky that you have an easy job."

"Easy?" I don't manage to keep the irritation from my tone. I bite my lip to keep from saying more.

"You girls are always laughing and having a good time. And you get to play with hair all day!"

Barb must have missed the irritation in my voice and the daggers shooting from my eyes. I don't know how to respond politely to her statement. Instead, I change the subject. "Did you manage to get your house painted?" I ask.

The last time Barb was in, she'd sputtered for a good 15 minutes about the painters who were supposed to do the outside of her house. They'd had to postpone once because of rain and another time because of illness. Barb's understanding is on a level with a 2-year-old being told "no cookies" before dinner.

"Yes, finally!" Barb says. "You would not believe what I went through with those people."

Barb rattles on about the painters while I finish applying her color. Afterward, I happily escape to answer the phone. Barb traps Andrea's client in a conversation about the quality of workmanship these days and I slink out to the back room.

Roxie is there alone, sipping from a juice box. "I'm having a baby," she tells me. She says the words as if she's trying them on to see if they fit.

"I know," I say. "You told your boyfriend?"

"Yes. He wants to get married."

"That's good, right?"

"I don't know. My parents told me I'd be destroying my life."

"They don't like him?"

Tears seep from Roxie's eyes. "They don't think he'll be able to provide for me and the baby."

"What do you think?"

"I think I'm going to throw up."

Roxie races to the bathroom. I had come out here with the intention to pee. Instead, my headache increases and I'll have to cross my legs while I cut Barb's hair.

I rinse Barb's color and get her back into my chair. Renee's client has brought her 5-year-old twins with her and they are now fighting over the bowl of lollipops. Renee is doing her best to get them to pick a color and move on. One of the boys takes a handful, sticks his tongue out, and runs to his mother.

"Have you heard anything new about that serial killer?" Barb asks as I cut.

"Not a thing," I say.

Andrea says, "Yesterday's paper had a small blurb about him. Apparently, the police don't have many leads."

"But he hasn't taken any more women," Barb says. "Maybe he's moved on to some other area. It's terrifying to think there's a madman right here in our town, kidnapping and murdering women!"

Isabel, Andrea's client, says, "I won't go anywhere by myself. Not even during the day. My husband drives me wherever I need to go."

"That's wise," Barb says.

The serial killer talk continues for a few more minutes. Then it turns to Christmas shopping. Three of the five clients I've had so far today have been late because of Black Friday. One woman got into a fistfight at 4 this morning, while waiting in line at a toy store. That's Christmas spirit for you.

The day continues along with late clients and holiday talk. At 3:15, Karen is in my chair telling me about her wonderful family and their wonderful holiday. In reality, I know that her husband rarely speaks to the two older girls, who are Karen's by a first marriage. And their son Dennis is hell on wheels. He's the teen I call Dennis the Menace, who recently told me he'd broken into his sister's house just for the fun of it.

"Dennis kept us laughing all day," Karen says. "His sisters adore him."

I clamp my mouth shut, smile and nod. Dennis is 12 years younger than one sister and 14 years younger than the other. The older one has a 1-year-old daughter who she won't let Dennis anywhere near. She once told me she is afraid Dennis will deliberately drop the baby. He doesn't like competition.

Of course, I don't tell Karen any of this. I continue to listen to her fantasy as I snip away at her hair. Her ears are small and she's wearing tiny gold hoops on her lobes. I think about snipping them off.

What is wrong with me?

"Have you done any of your Christmas shopping, yet?" Karen asks.

"No," I say. "But I don't have a lot to buy."

"That's right. You have no children to spoil. Vic and I are buying Dennis a computer for his room. He wants one for gaming, which is apparently a big thing with the kids these days."

Karen drones on, sounding like a buzz saw in my ear. If I slice her lips off, would she still be able to speak? I wonder about the importance of lips and contemplate the razor edge of my scissors.

I know this is not a healthy thought process. The phone rings again and I use the excuse to step away. The scissors in my hand have become an extension of my arm and I want to ram them into the next person who irritates me.

I need a vacation. Badly.

32

I am reveling in a quiet Monday when the phone rings. The caller ID tells me that it is Elyse's cell phone. This can't be good news. I consider letting the call go to the answering machine but duty takes over and I pick up on the fourth ring.

"My father isn't answering his phone," Elyse says.

Elyse has never been one for the social niceties in life. No, *Hello, how are you?* from her. We get straight to the point, with her tone accusing me of some wrongdoing I'm not yet sure of.

"He's working," I say. "I'm sure he'll get back to you as soon as he can break away from what he's doing."

"I left two messages almost an hour ago."

I want to tell her that some people don't keep checking their voicemail while at work. Some people are expected to work instead of socialize. Instead, I say, "Is there something I can help with?"

"I can't find my mother."

I'm momentarily stunned. Elyse gives no further information, so I ask, "She's not at work today?"

"Would I be calling you if she was?"

I bite back a snippy reply and refrain from hanging up. "Maybe she took the day off and went shopping or something."

"She's not answering her cell. She always answers!"

Elyse's voice rises into near panic. "Okay," I say. "Maybe she's not feeling well and is home napping."

"I'm at home, so I would know if she was here!"

Hanging up is oh so tempting. Elyse's shrill voice creates an instant tension headache. I take a slow breath, then say, "I didn't know you were at home."

"I came back for the long weekend. It was Thanksgiving, you know."

"I'm aware of that, Elyse."

"I was going to drive back to New York yesterday but I hooked up with this guy at a party and thought I'd spend a few extra days here."

"How long has your mother been missing?" I ask.

Elyse hesitates. "I'm not sure."

"Is her car gone? Maybe the battery on her phone died."

"Her car is here." Elyse's voice breaks. She sniffles, then adds, "She was here yesterday morning. I haven't seen her since. I came in about 4 this morning and crashed. I woke up a couple hours ago and haven't been able to find her. She didn't leave a note or anything." Another pause, then, "I'm worried, Skye."

These last words get me. Elyse sounds like a scared little girl. And this is the closest she'd ever come to asking for my help. "I'll leave another message for Scott," I say. "Do you want me to come over?"

"Please."

"I'm on my way," I tell her.

*

The Mass Avenger trembles with excitement as he steps from the shower. He'd washed away the odor of work and, with it, the stress of the day. Now he is ready for what awaits him.

He goes to his kitchen and retrieves the take-out bag containing two meatball subs. He stuffs the 2-liter bottle of Pepsi under his arm and exits the house. She's waiting for him and he can barely contain his excitement.

The air is cold and damp. Rain had come down in torrents earlier. He sloshes through the puddles, unlocks the garage door, and steps into the darkness.

Her muted scream is barely audible. The noise vibrates in her throat but travels no further than the gag. He locks the door behind him before flipping on the light switch. She flinches at the sudden brightness.

The Mass Avenger carries the food to the table by the cage. She sits inside, knees tucked up tight to her chest. Zip ties hold her feet together and attach her wrists to the cage. A gag keeps her quiet. He'd been extra careful with this one. First, he'd strapped her mouth with duct tape. Then he'd wrapped a scarf over that, tying it tightly behind her head. He'd left just enough room beneath her nose for her to breathe.

He squats by the cage door. "Hello, Diane," he says. His voice holds a happy lilt. This is by far his biggest prize.

Diane tries to look defiant. She doesn't know better. Yet.

He'd been anxious to get her; in a hurry to please Skye. He'd followed her when he could, tracked down her whereabouts at night. She worked with too many people, never left the building alone. Her routine took her nowhere out of the way. Her married boyfriend stayed with her for a few hours after work twice a week. No cheap motels. No late-night rendezvous.

He should have waited, been more patient. The daughter had been at the house over the past weekend. Spoiled brat drives a brand new Mustang and shakes her ass like a prostitute when she walks. He'd wanted to kill her right then in the driveway, simply because he knows what she will do to men as she grows older.

But he wasn't there for the daughter. Not this time. Maybe later.

Elyse, the daughter, had taken off late Sunday morning. Diane was alone in the house. He'd never taken a woman from her home before. That is a risky endeavor.

Diane grunts and squirms. He smiles at her. "Trying to tell me something?" he asks.

She tries to stare him down. Something in his eyes must tell her that she'd lost. She shudders and looks away.

Yesterday afternoon, after watching Elyse leave, he'd driven in circles for almost two hours. When it finally got dark, he'd smudged dirt on his license plate and driven straight into Diane's driveway. When she opened the door, he claimed to be friends with Elyse. "She told me to meet her here at 6," he'd said.

He'd counted on Diane inviting him in, rather than turning him away and telling him to wait in the driveway. She'd pulled the door open further and he stepped inside. A second later, he'd pressed the stun gun against her neck.

Now he has his prize in the cage. His next dilemma is getting Skye here, so he can present his gift.

He grabs one of the subs from the bag, then pours Pepsi into a plastic cup. Setting the food on the floor, he unlocks the cage door. "Hungry?" he asks.

Her eyes flicker his way. He hasn't touched her. Not yet. He'd brought her here, taken the stun gun to her again, then forced a sedative down her throat. As he'd tied her limp body, he'd fought the temptation to undress her. To touch her. To show her what power is.

She isn't his, though. He wants his gift to be in perfect condition for Skye. Presentation is everything.

"I'm going to untie you so you can eat," he says. "Do not try anything stupid. Understand?"

Diane watches him but doesn't move. He sighs. "I asked if you understand."

Still, she makes no attempt to respond. He slips the stun gun from his pocket and shows it to her. "Don't make me use this," he says. "I'm trying to be nice."

Her shoulders slump and she nods at him. A tear slips from her left eye.

He says, "One wrong move and I'll slice you into little pieces. So behave."

He slips inside the cage. As he slices the zip tie from her ankles, he wrinkles his nose at the smell of urine. A large wet spot darkens the crotch of her designer running suit. He slices the tie from the right wrist, then moves around to the left. Her arms fall limply by her side. "Pins and needles?" he asks.

Diane nods. He'd known that having her arms in that position all day would cut into the circulation. Little does she know that this is only the beginning of her misery.

"I'm going to rip the tape off now," he says. "Do not scream. Do you understand?"

She nods and he rips the tape from her mouth. She moans but is otherwise silent. His fingers travel over her red, raw lips. His arousal is instant. He backs away before he goes too far.

He slides the food in toward her, closes and locks the cage. "Screaming with get you zapped," he says. "And will be a total waste. The building is soundproofed and there's no one around to hear you, anyway. So don't make me do anything to hurt you."

"Why are you doing this?" she croaks.

He grins at her. "Eat your dinner."

◊

I meet Scott outside in Diane's driveway. He climbs out of his little black Solstice, looking grimmer than I've ever seen. "Have you heard anything?" he asks.

"No." I wrap my arms around him and plant a quick kiss on his lips. "The police took a half-assed report. She's an adult, there's no sign of so-called foul play, and no one is really sure how long she's been missing. But the detective I spoke to agreed to look into it, since the situation is odd."

"Odd how?"

"Elyse found her mother's purse, with her cell phone and car keys inside, on her bedroom bureau. If she left the house with a friend, she would have taken her purse."

"Jesus…" Scott mutters.

"Elyse and I have called everyone listed in her address book. No one has heard from her."

"Neighbors see anything?"

"Elyse spoke to the couple across the street. They didn't notice anything unusual or anyone here yesterday. The people on both sides aren't home, yet."

Scott nods and blows out a heavy sigh. "How's Elyse doing?"

"She's a wreck. Kept mentioning The Mass Avenger and thinks her mother got abducted by a serial killer."

"That's a stretch."

"That's what I told her."

"I guess I should go in."

Scott says this as if he is walking to his death. I take his hand and we head inside. Elyse is curled up on the couch, looking like a lost little girl. Scott sits beside her and she crumbles into his arms. This is the first time I've seen her display affection toward him in many years. The scene would be touching if not for the situation with Diane.

Scott says, "I'm sure your mother is fine. She probably stepped out with a friend. Lost track of time."

"She's not with Henry."

"Henry?"

"That married guy she sleeps with. I know about him and they're not together."

"Oh. Well, she does have other friends."

"I called them all."

"Maybe a boyfriend she hasn't mentioned?"

Elyse shakes her head. "She'd tell me. And she would've taken her purse and phone."

I sit in the chair across from them and we all listen to the grandfather clock ticking. A half-hour passes. Elyse wipes tears from her eyes. "I'm going to see if the other neighbors are home, yet," she says. "Maybe they saw something."

"I'll come with you," Scott says.

Elyse turns to me. "Can you wait here by the phone? In case she calls. Please?"

"Sure," I say.

She offers me a sad smile and follows Scott out the front door. While they are gone, I check the kitchen cabinets. I find canned tomato soup and some crackers. I pour the soup into a saucepan and set it on a burner. The soup bowls appear hand-painted and expensive. I set them on the table, along with spoons and the crackers. I fill the teakettle with water and hunt down the teabags. I take three from the box of Darjeeling, although I would have preferred chamomile. It's better for relaxing.

Scott and Elyse are gone about 15 minutes. Elyse runs in the door first. "We need to call that detective!" she says. "Did he give you his card?"

"A neighbor saw something?" I ask.

Scott closes the door behind him. "A white cargo van was here early yesterday evening. The lady next door saw it in the driveway but she isn't sure how long it was here and she didn't see the driver."

"So she didn't see Diane leave in it?"

Scott shakes his head no. Elyse says, "But she must have left with whoever it was! Where else would she be?"

"Do you know anyone who drives a white van?" I ask Elyse.

"No. And I know she didn't leave willingly. She wouldn't disappear like this!"

"I'll call Detective Clark." I say. "You two go in the kitchen and eat. I made soup and tea."

"I'm not hungry," Elyse says.

Scott puts his arm around Elyse's shoulder and leads her to the kitchen. "You need to eat something. You won't do your mother any good if you fall apart."

I get Detective Clark on the phone. When I mention the van, he starts peppering me with questions. "Has this happened before?" I ask.

"I can't comment," Clark says. "This neighbor is at home right now?"

"Yes."

"I'm on my way."

❧

The Mass Avenger fills a bucket with warm soapy water. He puts it inside the cage, along with a wool blanket, and says, "Give me your clothes."

Diane glares at him. She actually has the temerity to narrow her eyes disapprovingly! He has all he can do to rein in his temper. He reminds himself that she is Skye's prize and he needs to deliver her in perfect condition. Afterward, when he has Skye here with him, they can decide how to handle this manipulating whore together. He will take great pleasure in stepping aside and watching, if that's what Skye wants.

"Don't piss me off!" he snaps. "I'm being as nice as possible and, trust me, you do not want to make me mad. So take your clothes off and clean yourself up. You stink."

"Please let me go."

"Do you want me to take those clothes off for you? Because I can guarantee that you won't like how I do it."

Diane's eyes fill with tears. Black streaks roll down her cheeks. "You have two minutes," he says.

He turns away and grabs a bottle of bleach from a shelf against the wall. He fills another bucket with bleach and hot water, then drops a sponge inside. The floor inside the cage is stained with urine. He doesn't want Skye to see the place this way.

He wishes she was here with him now. If she knew what he'd done for her, he had no doubt that she would drive straight to him. The bitch inside the cage had tried to destroy Skye's life. Now, together, they will destroy hers.

The problem remains as to how he will tell Skye. And how will she react? He can't call her at home. Her husband will be there and he can't be a part of this. Can he risk calling in sick to work tomorrow? He could go to the salon, get to Skye before she goes inside for the day.

How will he tell her? You don't walk up to someone you barely know and announce that you have the woman she most despises waiting in a cage. She doesn't know him well enough to trust him. Not yet. He can't spring that type of thing on her out of the blue. How will he get her here?

As he mulls this over, he becomes aroused. The thought of Skye being in his space, sharing in his mission, makes him nearly euphoric.

He shakes himself from his daydream. Lots to do before Skye arrives.

ᴧ

Scott and I arrive home shortly after midnight. Elyse has a couple girlfriends spending the night. One brought Xanax. Since it helped Elyse relax, neither Scott nor I questioned the half-dozen pill bottles in the girl's purse.

Detective Clark had spent about twenty minutes with the woman next door. Then he came in and looked around the house. The white cargo van held much interest for him. I couldn't get him to tell me much, though I did eavesdrop on a conversation he had outside with another cop. The Mass Avenger, our local serial killer, is thought to drive a white cargo van.

I lie in bed contemplating this. I despise Diane. That hasn't changed because she's missing and is likely in trouble. But do I want her dead? Tortured first?

I try to picture this. I'd read and heard that The Mass Avenger likes to use a knife. He slices the women up in a gruesome fashion.

Diane's smug expression would be replaced with one of horror. Maybe those lips that so often spouted awful lies would be removed with surgical precision.

None of these thoughts particularly bother me. I don't believe any of it will happen. Diane is too evil to die. Ten minutes with her and that serial killer will likely commit suicide.

What if she is murdered? Would I care?

"Are you awake?" Scott asks.

"Yeah."

"Elyse will fall apart if something happens to her mother."

"I know." I snuggle close to him. "Maybe the person in the van is a friend and she'll go walking in her front door tomorrow morning."

"You don't really believe that," Scott says.

I don't. Diane isn't the type to disappear. I try to put hope in my voice as I say, "Stranger things have happened."

"I've wished her dead before."

"Me, too."

"It's a stupid thing to wish for."

33

The Mass Avenger rises early, then does something he hasn't done in five years. He calls in sick. The act is liberating. Maybe he'll never go back to that wretched job.

He dresses in faded jeans and a blue chambray shirt. His heart races. He is both excited and terrified about the day ahead of him.

Downstairs, he pours himself a bowl of cornflakes. When he finishes eating, he washes his bowl and spoon, dries them, and puts them away. Then he takes two granola bars, grabs his jacket, and leaves the house.

The garage smells like fear. Most people don't realize that fear has a scent. Your own fear is difficult to smell. Someone else's fear, when powerful enough, is intoxicating. He savors the pungent odor.

After carefully relocking the garage door, he flips on the lights. His guest is huddled beneath the wool blanket. Her eyes blink rapidly at the bright light. She shields them with her hands.

He smiles at her. "Good morning, Diane. Are you ready for your big day?"

He had left her untied. The garage is well soundproofed. She can scream at the top of her lungs and no one will hear her. Still, he isn't always comfortable leaving them this way, particularly before they have been broken. At night, he knows no one will approach the garage. During the day, however, he needs to be more cautious.

The scent of urine is strong at the cage. He squats down and sees that her bucket has been used. "I'm going to unlock the door," he says. "Don't do anything stupid." He shows her the stun gun. "You won't win."

He takes the bucket out of the cage and tosses her the granola bars. "Eat," he says. Then he takes the bucket and relocks the cage door. "I'll be right back."

After cleaning out the bucket, he sets it beside the cage. He fills a paper cup with water and sets it beside the bucket. Then he unlocks the cage door again and hands the cup to Diane. She reaches out from beneath the blanket and takes the cup with trembling hands. Her red nails are split and broken. No doubt, she had been trying to pry her way out of the cage. That won't ever happen and the knowledge makes him giddy.

She is still naked. He'd considered giving her an old pair of his sweats to wear but he preferred her this way. It kept her vulnerable. Plus, her body wasn't bad to look at. The time she spent in the gym with her personal trainer paid off.

She guzzles the water. Her eyes are fixed on him. Purple smudges beneath make them look worn and old. "You could still let me go," she says. "I won't tell anyone about you."

He laughs at this. "I have a special surprise for you today, Diane."

Her eyes widen briefly, fear pinning her pupils open. "What kind of surprise?"

"If I told you, it wouldn't be a surprise, now would it?"

She clutches the blanket tighter and tries for an edge of defiance. "My family will find me. I'm sure that my neighbors saw you and they're all busybodies. You should let me go, before this all goes too far."

He snorts a laugh. "Come closer."

She remains huddled beneath the blanket. He sighs, takes the stun gun from his pocket, and slips inside the cage. "Don't make me do this the hard way."

"What do you want with me?"

He grabs a handful of her hair and yanks her toward him. She loses the blanket as she flails her arms and legs. The stun gun instantly makes her go limp in his arms. For a moment, he gazes at the naked body sprawled across his lap. He brushes his hand over her right nipple. His arousal is almost painful. He could take her now, just this once, before Skye arrives. He squeezes the nipple and thinks about biting it off. Then, with a sigh, he shoves her aside. This is Skye's prize and he must respect that.

He spreads the blanket on the floor, then props Diane against the far wall of the cage. He ties each wrist to the metal above her head. Then he ties her feet together. After securing the gag, he tosses another blanket over her body and locks the cage door.

The sky is brighter now, though it's still early. He isn't sure what time Skye starts work and he needs to be waiting. He climbs into his van and drives to The Cutting Edge.

Many of the local businesses share the parking lot, though it actually belongs to the town. He pulls in and is dismayed to see a Nissan parked in the area normally used for the salon. An old lady sits inside. She is craning her neck back and forth, as if she is waiting for someone. Maybe her husband or a friend ran out to do an errand and she is awaiting his or her return.

He parks across the lot, by the dance studio. It's 7:12 a.m.

⚡

Tuesday morning comes all too soon. Scott takes the day off. He doesn't want to leave Elyse alone all day. He drives off to Diane's house, with a promise to keep me updated. I drive the short distance to The Cutting Edge.

Lillian is waiting for me in the parking lot, as usual. I fumble with my travel cup and ignore her as I climb out of my car. She is right on my heels as I'm unlocking the door. It is 7:52 a.m.

"Good morning, Skye!" she practically shouts in my ear.

"Good morning, Lillian," I mutter.

"Did you oversleep this morning?"

"No. Actually, I barely slept at all."

I flick on the lights and jack the heat up. Then I flip on the radio, hoping to drown out Lillian's squawking.

"Insomnia?" Lillian asks. Without waiting for my reply, she says, "I use Sonata. Knocks me right out but there's no hangover feeling in the morning. You should try it."

"Thanks, but I don't have insomnia."

I shrug out of my jacket. Lillian follows me to the coat rack. "Then what kept you up all night?" she asks. She gives me a smug look. "Burning the candle at both ends?"

"No, my husband's ex is missing. We spent most of the night with his daughter and the police."

"Oh. Oh, my. I'm so sorry. What happened?"

"We don't know. Elyse was gone over the weekend and came home to find her mother had disappeared. No one has seen or heard from her."

Lillian continues to pepper me with questions as I shampoo her hair. Her voice grates on my raw nerves and I want to dump shampoo into her open mouth.

I get her to my chair and she informs me that she needs a haircut this week. The blades of my scissors gleam and I want to stab Lillian with them. This makes me think of Diane. I experience a moment of guilt at my murderous fantasies.

Ten seconds later, Lillian's self-absorbed monologue erases the guilt. I don't know why the old biddy needs to come here every week. Doesn't she have running water? I know she can't own a bottle of shampoo, since she's never washed her own hair.

Renee saves me from a murder one charge by coming in the door. I tell her about Diane and she promptly decides that I need to leave early. We make phone calls and rearrange my schedule. Lillian says, "You know if that serial killer does have her, it's too late for you to do anything."

I stare at her openmouthed. Renee says, "They don't know where she is or what happened to her. Whatever the case, Skye needs to be with her husband and his daughter."

Lillian turns a shade of pink. "I didn't mean that quite the way it sounded."

I turn away to answer the phone. Luckily, I didn't have my scissors in my hand.

ᴧ

The Mass Avenger slams his fist against the steering wheel. That old crow has ruined his plan! Why did she need to be here so early? He should have killed her for getting in his way.

He stares at the salon. The lights blink on. Soon Skye's coworkers will arrive and he will have no chance of talking to Skye alone.

Now what?

He sits for a moment, willing himself to calm down and think. This isn't the end. He'll come back. He'll find a way to get to Skye.

Maybe she goes out for lunch? Would she do that alone? Surely, all the ladies can't leave the salon at the same time. For now, he'll go home and check on his guest. He doesn't want to call attention to himself by staying too long.

He's about to twist the key in his ignition when he has a thought. A backup plan is always best. Something to stall her, in case she doesn't come out for lunch or he isn't able to catch her alone. He flips open his knife and tucks it into his coat sleeve. Then, as casually as possible, he strolls toward Skye's little red MINI Cooper.

The day is cold. A raw wind blows. Not many people are walking through town in this weather. Across the street, the donut shop parking lot is full and a line snakes around the drive-thru. But no one is looking his way.

He bends down and rams his knife into Skye's rear tire. Then, just to make himself feel good, he walks past the old crow's Nissan and lets his blade slide across the entire passenger side. She probably won't notice right away, since she's parked so that she can slip right into the driver's side without walking around the car. Perhaps it will be days before she notices. She'll have no idea where it happened. She will, however, wonder who did it and why. She might even be afraid that someone is out to hurt her. And she might be right.

34

My last client walks out the door just before noon. The salon is in a state of disarray. We've had a typical Tuesday morning; the phone ringing incessantly, people walking in off the street, and a full schedule of clients for each of us. Consequently, things like sweeping and cleaning the dirty brushes get neglected.

I'm reaching for the broom when Roxie snatches it away. "Get out of here," she says. "I'll take care of this."

"Are you sure?" I ask. "I don't want to leave you guys in a mess."

"We'll be fine," she says.

"Go," Renee adds.

"Get out while you can," Andrea chimes in.

I thank my friends and grab my purse and jacket. A twinge of guilt nudges at me as I slip out the back door. As much as my job irritates me, I don't like leaving early at my friends' expense. Though I've cleared my schedule and I know they'll be fine, the guilt remains like an itch I can't scratch.

The wind bites into me as I cross the parking lot. I'm walking around the van parked beside my car, thinking about picking up three hot chocolates from the donut shop, when I notice my rear tire is flat. I sputter a bunch of words that shouldn't be said within 500 feet of a church or daycare center.

"Hey, Skye!"

I jump and make one of those stupid sounds when you suck in air using your vocal cords. Kyle steps out of the van. His cheeks are flushed pink and his eyes skitter away as he says, "I'm sorry. I didn't mean to startle you."

"Not your fault," I reply. "I didn't notice you in the van."

"Off for lunch?"

"No, actually I'm leaving for the day."

"Oh? Lucky you!"

"Not really," I tell him. "I've got a family situation to deal with." I motion to my tire. "And I came out to find this."

Kyle shuffles his feet back and forth. He can barely meet my eyes. His shyness must make dating impossible.

"Do you have a spare?" he asks.

"Yes. It's just a nuisance. And it's so cold out here!"

"I'll change it for you."

"No, I couldn't ask you to do that."

"I don't mind. You could sit in my van and stay warm. It'll only take me a few minutes."

"Are you sure? I know how to do it. My dad taught me years ago, though I haven't actually done it since I was a teen."

Kyle gives me that shy smile. "I don't mind at all. In fact, I have a couple of those charcoal drawings I was telling you about in the back of the van. Maybe you could give them a quick look while I change your tire? Tell me what you think?"

"Sure. I'd love to."

Kyle opens the side door on his van. I climb inside and, for some reason, Kyle gets in behind me and pulls the door shut. Now I'm annoyed. I don't have time for this. "What are you doing?" I ask.

"The family situation you referred to, that's about your husband's ex?"

"Yeah..." He is suddenly making me nervous. His eyes have changed. He watches me carefully now, no longer averting his gaze.

"You wanted her to disappear, right? You hated her."

"I ..." I try to put space between us but Kyle grows eager in a childlike way.

"It's okay," he says. "You can be honest with me."

"Kyle, I really need to go now."

"I have her."

"Who?" Even as I form the word, I know. Kyle has Diane. My stomach flips. Is he also The Mass Avenger? Shy Kyle, who paints and draws? Kyle, who only stands out in his shyness? Kyle, who sat in my chair and talked and laughed like a normal guy?

"I have Diane," he says. "I took her. For you."

"For me? Why would you do that?"

"Because you wanted her dead."

He says this so calmly. I hear the tremble in my voice when I ask, "Have you... Is she dead?"

"No. No. Of course not."

I experience a shred of relief before Kyle adds, "I kept her for you. So you can do it."

I shake my head slowly. My mind scrambles for words but nothing comes. What does a person say to a psychopathic lunatic?

"I can see why you hate her so much," Kyle says. "She is a manipulating, disrespectful whore. She uses her sex as power to control men. Women like that need to be punished. They aren't real, like you." He is beaming now, gushing his words to me as if he's speaking to a favorite rock star. "I knew right away that you are different. I knew you would understand me and my work. You and I, we're kindred spirits."

I look past him at the closed door. The front seats and the other doors seem so far away. The windows are tinted dark. I have no idea what to do but it's a pretty safe bet that he's not going to let me walk away.

"What is your work, Kyle?"

A boyish grin lights up his face. "I want to tell you all about it! I've been waiting to share it with you." His gaze slips away and the shyness returns to his voice. "I was hoping that maybe you and I could become partners."

"Partners in what?"

"I'll tell you all about it, Skye. I promise. But don't you want to see Diane first? I've been saving her special for you."

If I say no, that will piss him off. I don't need a degree in psychiatry to know that. I could try fighting him and maybe I'll be lucky enough to get out one of the doors before he kills me. Would he kill me? And, if I do manage to get away, what happens to Diane? I don't know Kyle's last name. I have no idea how to find him. He would kill her before the police found either of them. He would get away and continue killing. Do I want to live with that?

"Skye?" Kyle's eyes narrow as he watches me. "Have I made a mistake? Did I misunderstand your signals? You're not like the rest of them, are you?"

"Of course not, Kyle," I say. Somehow, I manage a smile. "I'm worried, that's all. My husband is expecting me. Maybe I should call and tell him I'll be late."

"That's not a good idea," Kyle says. "I don't want you to talk to him right now. I've done this for you, Skye. Don't you care?"

"Yes, yes, I care. No one has ever done something so... personal... for me before."

He is beaming again. "We'll go now. Okay?"

"Yes. Sure."

Kyle ushers me to the passenger seat. "Buckle up!" he says. Then, with a giggle, he adds, "We wouldn't want to get pulled over by the cops."

ℴ

Kyle drives the speed limit through Whitman and into the town of Hanson. While at a stop sign, I consider jumping out and screaming for help. But that would leave Diane to die at this lunatic's hands. I'm not sure why I care. Maybe I don't care about her at all and I'm just too afraid to move.

Ten minutes later, we are on a dead-end back road where the homes are older and sit on a minimum of a half acre. At the very end, Kyle pulls into the driveway of an old but well-kept farmhouse. A pale yellow garage sits in front of us. At least an acre of land stretches around the two buildings. The space across the street holds two grazing horses. I've seen no humans around.

"This is it," Kyle says.

I'm clutching my purse, thinking about the cell phone inside. Will I get the chance to call Scott? If I play this right and keep Kyle's trust, will I be able to walk away?

I reach for the door handle but Scott holds my arm. With his free hand, he points to my purse. "Is your phone in there?"

Lying would be stupid. Any second, it could ring, then Kyle would never trust me. "Yes," I say.

"You'd better leave it here, please. I don't bring phones into the garage, just in case one of my guests manages to get loose briefly." He grins at me. "No sense in taking chances, right?"

I can't get beyond the fact that he calls them 'guests'. "Right," I manage to say. "Smart thinking."

I drop my purse on the floor at my feet and push the door open. I could run now, head to a neighbor's house. Someone might be home. I might make it there ahead of Kyle. Unless he has a gun. Would he shoot me? Of course he would shoot me, particularly if I run and he thinks I am betraying him.

He comes around to my side and motions for me to follow. "This way."

The side door on the garage has three deadbolts. As he unlocks them, he tells me, "I kept her perfect, just for you. Earlier, I told her that I would be bringing a surprise but she has no idea that the surprise is you! I hope I don't sound cocky about this. I wasn't sure you'd come. I hoped. I knew you were different and that you and I shared certain desires. I wanted to believe that you'd see that I did this as a gift for you." He removes the key from the last lock and puts his hand on the knob. Before he turns it, he looks at me with bright, happy eyes. "I've never had a real friend. No one ever understood me. I still can't believe we've found each other and that you're here!"

I smile. In a crazy, sick way, I almost feel bad for the guy.

I have no idea what I'll find inside this garage. Will Diane be tied up? Has she been beaten? Drugged? Are there other women inside? All these questions swirl in a confusing mess through my mind.

Kyle pushes the door open. The first thing that hits me is the smell. Bleach. Lots of it. Some other odor as well; something more human, though I don't know what exactly.

We step inside and Kyle shoves the door closed. "Be careful," he says. "I'll get the light in a second."

I stand still and stare into the darkness. I hear the locks turning, though I don't how Kyle can see what he's doing. I feel him move away, then light floods the room. This catches me off guard and I blink rapidly against the intrusion.

"Surprise!"

Kyle yells this like he's hosting a child's birthday party. I turn toward his voice and that's when I see the cage. It's one of those large metal dog cages that people use in their backyards. Wire mesh covers the top. Heavy bolts protrude from the floor, holding the cage in place.

I haven't fully processed this when a lump beneath a blanket inside begins to move. The lump is connected to a head and that head belongs to Diane.

A gasp escapes my open mouth. Kyle watches me through narrowed eyes. "You're not happy."

"No, I..." I can't help but stammer. Heavy gray tape covers Diane's mouth. Plastic ties hold her wrists to the cage. A blanket covers some of her body. I don't think she's wearing clothes.

I have to get through this, which means that I need to play along. I stare at Diane and let myself feel all the hatred for everything she's done to Scott and me through the years. If she'd been a better person, neither of us would be here right now. I'm here with a madman because of her.

"This is just overwhelming," I tell Kyle. "You have a remarkable setup here. I'm impressed."

"Really?"

He's like a little boy seeking approval. What am I supposed to do next? What do I say to this madman? I wish I'd spent more time studying psychology.

"Yes!" I say with as much enthusiasm as I can muster. "You've got that bitch right where she belongs. And this place is perfect! No windows. No close neighbors to be nosey. Do you live alone in that house?"

Kyle grins at me. "Yes. Everything is mine." He holds his arms out, gesturing to the entire room. "I even soundproofed this building with the highest-quality materials. You could be standing right outside and you wouldn't be able to hear a thing!"

Diane is staring at me. Tears stream down her face. I do a form of yoga meditation that my mother taught me. I will my muscles to relax, my breathing to steady. I hope my voice doesn't betray me as I say, "Then why do you have her tied and gagged in there?"

He gives a boyish shrug. "I guess I'm overly cautious. I wasn't sure how long I'd be gone and I didn't want to take any chances that she'd manage to make enough noise to attract attention."

"That's smart," I say. "Do you think it's safe to untie her now?"

"Yes. I'll do that for you."

"Thank you, Kyle."

"Do you know what you want to do to her? I'm sure you've thought about this thousands of times."

I want to vomit. Bile has risen into my throat and is burning a hole there. "I'm not even sure this is real, yet," I say truthfully. "I think I need time to process it all."

"I understand," Kyle says. "I'm just so happy that you're here!"

Kyle unlocks the cage and crawls inside. I wish I could slam the door shut and lock him in there. I don't care that Diane would be with him. I want to run away, find help, escape this nightmare. But Kyle has the keys in his pocket and a stun gun in his hand.

He warns Diane to keep quiet before he removes her gag. Her eyes are fixed on mine. I see pleading there. I give her no sign of encouragement because I don't trust her reaction. He cuts the ties on her ankles and turns back to me. "I should probably leave her hands tied for now," he says. "Until you wear her down. I know you're strong but she's really feisty and I don't want her to hurt you."

I'm hesitant to argue the point. I don't want to contradict him or appear as if I'm defending Diane. "Okay," I say. "But I'm not afraid of her."

"Oh, I know that. I bet you're not afraid of anything!"

If only he knew. I am terrified of him.

35

Kyle can barely contain his excitement. He slips out of the cage and stands beside Skye. She has a faint chemical scent from the salon. Beneath that, he smells her. His arousal embarrasses him. He doesn't know how she will react if she notices.

He has all he can do to keep from gushing. He wants to share the stories of all his conquests. He wants to tell Skye about each of the vile women and how easily he was able to break them. His secret box in the freezer holds their right nipples. Does he dare share that with her? If he tells her his story, would she understand why the nipples are so important to him?

Has she realized that he is The Mass Avenger? Should he tell her now?

He takes a long, slow breath and tells himself to relax. Skye is here with him. There's no need to rush things. She must be eager to get her hands on that controlling whore in the cage. They can talk about everything else later, when she is satiated.

"No need to hold back," Kyle says. "Go ahead. Do what you want to her. Just let me know if you need help. Otherwise, she's your gift to do with as you please."

I stare into the cage as my heart slams against my chest. I don't want to go in there. What if this is some sort of sick joke he's playing? What if he locks me inside with Diane?

I swallow the bile that rises into my throat. It's like swallowing a mouthful of battery acid. I can't keep the quake from my voice when I say, "I don't want to go in the cage."

Kyle's eyes narrow. "Why not?"

He looks so normal. Nothing about Kyle screams serial killer. Even his eyes are nice, until he gets mad. And he's starting to look mad now.

"I cleaned it thoroughly, just for you," Kyle says. "And I haven't touched her the whole time she's been here. But now you're telling me you don't want to be in there with her? Why? You don't trust me? Is that it?" His eyes narrow and bore into me. "Do you think I'd do something bad to you? You think I'm crazy, right? Is that it?"

"No, Kyle, no. Of course not. It's just that..." My eyes are welling up with tears. I struggle for something, anything, that will make him trust me. Then the words suddenly spill from my mouth. "My father used to lock me in the closet after he beat me. Sometimes I'd be in there for days." I can't stop the tears from sliding down my cheeks but maybe that's okay. "I'm ashamed to admit that I'm still terrified of confined spaces."

Kyle's face softens. He pats my arm. "I'm sorry that your father was mean to you. I never knew my father but my mother was as mean as any man."

"So you understand," I say.

"Yes. I have emotional scars from my mother, as well. I can help you get over them."

"You can?"

He grins at me. "We can be a team."

I don't want to ask for details. I'm afraid I won't be able to handle what he tells me. Instead, I say, "Okay. That would be great."

"For now, do you want me to take her out of the cage? I can tie her to the outside of the bars instead."

"I would really appreciate that, Kyle. Thank you for understanding and for not making fun of me."

Kyle gives me the sweetest look. "I would never make fun of you, Skye."

He slips back inside the cage. After a stern warning to Diane, he cuts the ties from her wrists. Initially, she remains docile as he shoves her out of the cage. But as he pockets the knife, she immediately scrambles to her feet and tries to run. He slams her to the floor and pulls the stun gun from his pocket.

I don't want to see him use it on her. I might need her help somehow and I want her conscious. I touch his arm and say, "Could I?"

Diane continues to struggle against him. She curses at both of us, screaming louder than I've ever heard any human voice. Kyle hesitates and I reel back and punch Diane below her right eye. My fist connects with her cheekbone and I feel the sting like a slow burn. Diane yelps. She goes limp and Kyle slips new plastic ties around her wrists.

After he has her wrists secured to the cage, he turns to me and says, "Wow! That was a hell of a punch."

"That was 17 years of pent-up hostility," I say. "And man did it feel good!"

I realize that I sound too happy about this. I look at Diane, strapped to the side of the cage, and I remember all the times I'd wished her dead. Those fantasies I had of using my scissors to slice up body parts could now be my reality. But I am not that person. I despise Diane and many of my clients infuriate me beyond my ability to express in words. However, I don't want them dead. I don't want to see their blood. I don't even want to see them cry.

This realization is comforting. I'd been starting to wonder if I was crazy. If maybe I had the ability to kill without remorse. Hell, I don't eat meat because I can't stand the thought of it having been alive once. I don't even kill spiders! When they get in my house, I trap them and bring them safely outside.

I'm not a killer. This is good. But Kyle is. This is bad.

Kyle is elated. This day has already far exceeded any fantasy he'd dared consider. Skye is truly his soul mate. When she'd punched Diane, he'd thought his erection would explode. He can't wait to see what she will do next.

When he'd first laid eyes on her, he'd known they belonged together. Now she is here and he can barely contain himself. He wants to share everything; the details of his mission, his collection. He knows now that she will understand. They're partners.

He reminds himself to take it slow. He doesn't want to scare her off with his enthusiasm. He doesn't want to appear weak or needy, either. Skye is a strong woman and will want a strong man. But she was abused too, so he can talk to her. They can help each other. His mother is gone now. If her father is still alive, they can take care of him together. Give him what he deserves.

He smiles at her. He isn't alone, anymore.

ᴧ

Diane's right eye is swelling. She stares at me. I feel a twinge of guilt but it doesn't last. She deserved the punch.

She struggles against the ties. Her breasts sway. She's a little too clean-shaven and naked for me. I turn to Kyle and say, "Where are her clothes?"

"I had to take them," he says. "She wet herself and the smell was awful."

"Oh. Do you think you could get her something to put on?"

"Being naked usually keeps them more docile."

"I understand," I say. "Plus, you're a guy, so of course you'd like looking at her. She's got a great body. But I'd rather not look at her and be reminded of what she did to Scott with that body."

Kyle shakes his head in disgust. "She doesn't deserve that body. She used it to manipulate men. That body gave her too much power."

"I agree. But I'd still rather not see it."

Kyle gives a soft chuckle. "Okay, I'll get her some sweats to put on."

"That'd be great."

"Why don't you come in with me? I really did want to show you my drawings. Your opinion is important to me."

How am I supposed to refuse? He seems to trust me and keeping that trust is my only chance of getting both myself and Diane out of this alive. "I'd love to see your work," I tell him.

His eyes sparkle. "Cool. I'll put her back in the cage for now."

Diane continues to wriggle against her restraints. Her right eye is now a mere slit. She's crying. I consider sending her some sort of message that I'm on her side but decide her emotional comfort isn't worth the risk.

"Do you think that's really necessary?" I ask. "You have an incredible setup here. She can't get out of that. Besides, we won't be long. I'm looking forward to making her left eye look like the right."

Kyle grins at this. "Okay. I should probably gag her, though. And tie her feet together, just to be safe."

I know when to stop arguing. I give him a smile of encouragement and he goes to work. Diane lets out an earsplitting scream as Kyle approaches her with the gag. He muffles her quickly and a moment later we are on our way across the lawn to his house.

The house is spotless. I don't know what I expected a serial killer's house to look like but it isn't this. The furniture is new and in pristine condition. The beige carpet doesn't have one speck of lint. The place smells faintly of oranges.

I look around for a phone but don't see one. I want to cry.

"Are you thirsty?" Kyle asks. "Hungry?"

I start to say no but maybe the phone is in the kitchen. "I am a little thirsty," I say.

"This way." Kyle leads me into the kitchen. The appliances are all stainless steel and they sparkle. The counter is a glistening, deep green granite. He pulls open the refrigerator and reveals a sparsely filled but glowing, clean interior. "Orange juice? It's freshly squeezed."

"That would be great."

He fills a crystal glass and hands it to me. I'm afraid the juice will make me throw up. I sip it slowly. "You have a beautiful home," I say.

"It was my mother's," he says. "I inherited it when she died."

"What happened to her?"

"She was murdered." His tone is clipped. He moves away and says, "My paintings are upstairs."

I've seen no phone. I follow him up the polished steps and into the first room on the right of the hall. Three easels hold paintings of what look like mythological figures. The walls are filled with more of the same. A drawing table in the center of the room holds the charcoal drawings. Two are of mythology scenes. The other looks like me.

"Did you do all of these?" I ask.

"Yes."

"They're amazing."

"Really? You're not just saying that?"

"They're incredible, Kyle." I wander past each of the paintings. They truly are brilliant. "You're into mythology?"

"Yes."

"Greek?"

"You can tell?"

"Sure." I point to one scene near me. "This is Zeus with Cronus on Mount Olympus."

"That's right! Zeus has just given Cronus the cup with the special drink to make him vomit up his children."

"The detail is truly amazing."

"The charcoals aren't quite as good." He picks up the one that looks like me. "I did this one so that I could look at you each day."

"I'm honored," I manage to say.

"I'd love to have you sit for a painting some time."

"I don't think I'm worthy of a painting."

"Oh, that's where you're wrong, Skye. Your portrait should be hanging right beside the Mona Lisa."

I would laugh at this if it wasn't so terrifying. A serial kill has a thing for me. And I'm alone in his house with him.

I don't want to encourage his adoration and I sure don't want to piss him off. I choose to let that last comment slide and I change the subject. "Could I use your bathroom, please?"

"Oh, sure. Of course." He leads me across the hall and points inside a glistening bathroom. "Right there."

"Thanks."

I smile as I ease past him and close the door. A window sits above the bathtub. It has that opaque glass so no one can see in, which means I also can't see out. Not that it would help me, anyway. What's below it doesn't matter. The window is a small rectangle, not big enough for me to fit through.

I flush the toilet, then carefully ease open the medicine cabinet. I'm looking for anything I could slip into a drink that would knock Kyle out. Or make him sick. Or kill him. The only things I find are a bottle of Tylenol and a roll of Tums. No razor blades. He uses an electric shaver.

The faucet is gold and doesn't even have a smudge of a fingerprint. I turn on the water and open the cabinet below. Extra toilet paper, soap, cleaning products. Unless I want to spray him in the face with Scrubbing Bubbles, then nothing here will help me.

I turn off the water and pull the door open. Kyle is waiting in the hall. He's holding a pair of black sweatpants and a faded Patriots' sweatshirt. He grins at me and says, "I guess we should be getting back. I know you're anxious to get back to our guest."

I follow him down to the living room. Nothing around me is big or solid enough to hit him with. I'd have to be sure to knock him unconscious; otherwise, I'd be in a whole lot more trouble than I already am.

I realize that I'm still carrying around the glass of orange juice. "I should go wash this first," I say. "I don't want to accidentally drop it or something."

Kyle frowns at the glass. "I wouldn't care if you shattered the thing."

"It looks expensive."

"Yeah. It was my mother's."

"You didn't get along well with your mother, did you?"

Kyle's eyes dart away from mine. "She did horrible things."

His voice is almost a whisper. "I'm sorry," I say.

"I've never told anyone. But I knew you'd understand."

"Of course I do."

I'm not sure how it happens but we wind up on the couch and he tells me about life with his mother. She brutalized him, emotionally and physically. Some of the things he tells me bring tears to my eyes. Other things make my stomach twist. I forget that I am talking to a killer. He is like a lost little boy seeking approval.

I am holding his hand. I'm not sure how that happened, either. "I am so sorry," I tell him.

"It's okay. She's gone now."

"You killed her?"

He looks at me in surprise. "No. I should have. But I didn't."

"You said she was murdered."

"Yes. By a man she met on the Internet. She brought him home with her and he killed her in her bedroom. I found her when I got home from work."

"Oh Kyle, that's horrible."

"She deserved it." He gives a little shrug. "Her death freed me."

A few minutes later, we are back in the garage. I didn't manage to find a phone or anything that would help me subdue Kyle. The stun gun is in his pocket. My only hope is to find a way to use it on him.

Diane's wrists are raw and bloody. She moans through the gag. Kyle snips the tie around her ankles and tells her to cooperate while he puts the pants on her. Then he tells her that he is going to free her hands and that she'd better not do anything stupid. He presses his knife blade against her neck and murmurs a last warning. Then she is free and he tells her to put the sweatshirt on.

"What are you going to do to her first?" Kyle asks me.

Boyish excitement fills his voice. He bounces on the balls of his feet. I look at Diane, at the tears streaming from her eyes. She crumbles to the floor, looking as if she has accepted defeat. Punching her had felt fantastic. But I don't want to do it again. I don't want to do anything to her.

Kyle twists the knife in his hand. "Do you want this?" he asks.

"I..." He is willing to hand me his knife. I could take it and stab him. Kill him. Why aren't I doing it?

All those murderous fantasies I'd been having roll through my mind. I'd visualized stabbing my clients. What the hell had been wrong with me?

Kyle's eyes are appraising me. I realize that my hands are shaking. "I've never stabbed anyone before," I say.

"I got sick the first time," Kyle says.

"You did?"

He's blushing. "Yes."

"Why did you continue?"

"It's my mission. I need to make sure these women never hurt another boy or man the way my mother hurt me."

"You're right," I say. "No one should endure what you were forced to."

"Or you. I can help make your father pay for what he did. If you want."

My father. I can see him in his garage with his birdhouses. The only time I'd ever seen him angry was when a playground bully had pushed me off the jungle gym. He'd had to take me to the emergency room, where I'd gotten three stitches on my forehead. Afterward, we'd driven straight to the bully's house, where my father had confronted his father. The bully's father made him come out and apologize. He brought me a stuffed bear the next day.

"Skye?"

I blink away the memory. "Sorry. I guess it's still hard for me to think about those times with my father."

"I understand." He gives me that shy smile. "I'll tie her to the bars for you now. You can take it slow. We have all the time you need."

Diane starts to edge away. Kyle grabs her by the hair and demands she remain still. I swallow the bile in my throat as he use more zip ties to strap her wrists.

After checking to be sure the ties are secure, Kyle holds the knife out to me. I take it with trembling hands. I should stop thinking. Just plunge it deep into his chest.

How much strength does it take to do that? What if I don't get it in deep enough? What if he gets it from me and stabs me instead?

What if I throw up all over his feet?

"Don't worry about the clothes," Kyle says. "Those are old. I'll burn them when you're done."

"I think I'd like to ease into this slowly. Maybe start with something that's not bloody."

"Okay. Like what?"

"I saw that stun gun you used on her. I kind of like the idea of making her sizzle."

Diane gurgles beneath the gag. Her eyes are wide with panic. I do my best to ignore her.

"It is kind of fun," Kyle says. He takes the stun gun from his pocket and shows me how to use it.

"Perfect," I say.

I take the gun from him. My heart is racing. Diane kicks at me. I step back and Kyle says, "She's a real feisty bitch. I'll tie her feet for you."

He turns to grab another zip tie from the cabinet behind him. His back is to me. The stun gun is in my hand. I hold my breath and press it against his back. Seconds later, he collapses on the floor.

Diane screams behind her gag. I yell for her to shut up. I grab the zip ties and strap Kyle's ankles and wrists together. My heart is slamming against my chest and I feel like I'm about to collapse myself. I have no idea how long he'll be out and I need to hurry.

I fish his keys from his pocket. My phone is in his van. Then I turn and head toward Diane with the knife.

She frantically jerks against her restraints. Her eyes are filled with horror. I realize that I am holding the knife toward her and she must think I am really going to kill her. "Get a grip!" I shout. I slice the ties and free her. Then I hand her the knife and say, "Drag him into the cage and lock it. I'm going out to his van for my phone. Can you drag him by yourself?"

"Yes, go!" Diane says.

I run out to the van. He has a tangle of keys and it takes me a moment to figure out which one opens the van. I finally get in, retrieve my phone, and punch in 911. The operator keeps telling me to slow down because she can't understand me. I inhale deeply and try again. She gets it this time and tells me the police are on their way. "Stay on the line with me," she says.

I head back inside the garage to make sure Diane is okay. The phone is pressed against my ear when I scream.

Diane is standing over Kyle's body. The knife in her hand is dripping blood.

36

Two months have passed since that day in Kyle's garage. Diane was not prosecuted for his murder. The prosecutor let it go as self-defense. No one mentioned that Kyle was out cold at the time.

He'd killed seven women. A shy sanitation worker who collected trash for a living and painted beautiful mythological scenes. No one had suspected him.

Diane has since become the model ex. She immediately dropped her court case against us. Elyse went back to the community college and works a part-time job.

I never went back to work at The Cutting Edge. I no longer wanted to kill my clients but I also didn't want to look at them each day. Sometimes, when I let myself think back to those murderous, bloody fantasies, I shudder at what I might have become. I was beginning to hate being around people. I was losing respect for humanity. I was losing myself.

My mother and I recently opened a business together. The place is called *It's A Dog's World*. We sell homemade, healthy dog treats and just about everything you can imagine that a dog would want or need. We also have a large fenced-in area behind the building, as well as a back room that is dog-friendly.

We bring our dogs to work each day. My mother plays New Age music and talks to people about how to communicate with their dogs. My dad has started making custom doghouses for our clients. On Saturdays, Scott joins us. It's dress-up day for the dogs. Our customers pick out the costumes and Scott takes the photo of them with their dogs. Our back wall is filled with pictures that make me laugh.

My name is Lilly Skye Destiny Summers and a serial killer saved my life.

Made in the USA
Lexington, KY
20 July 2010